D1564702

TAKE ME TO YOUR

READER

AN OTHERWORLD ANTHOLOGY

Amy A. Bartol
Tammy Blackwell
Amanda Havard
Heather Hildenbrand
Tiffany King
C.A.Kunz
Sarah M. Ross
Raine Thomas

TAKE ME TO YOUR READER
AN OTHERWORLD ANTHOLGY

Dedication

This collection is dedicated to Janet Wallace and the entire staff of utopYA. We are honored to be part of such a wonderful event.

Contents

The Divided

By Amy A. Bartol

For information on other titles
Visit the author's website:
http://www.amyabartol.com/index.html

Chapter 1 – I'M NOT CRAZY

I open the door to the backseat of the Escalade and throw my duffle bag in. When I slam it shut, the sound echoes loudly off the cement walls of the parking garage. It's a tomb in this part of my building at three a.m. The dull yellow light near the stairwell casts a long, garish shadow over the black SUV. Under normal circumstances, I never like being in here alone; but now, after what has happened, it scares me half to death.

Quickly, I move to the driver's door and open it, climbing inside. I lock the doors and start the engine. My long, dark hair spills down my back and over my shoulders, getting trapped by the seatbelt. I gather it up in a bun and secure it with a hair band from my purse before I back the car out of the space and leave the garage.

I don't feel safe again until I'm on Lake Shore Drive heading north on my way out of Chicago.

The silence in the Escalade is a definite change from the constant barrage of concerned family, friends, and acquaintances I've had to endure for the past couple of months. I know I really shouldn't blame them for their concern. I've been a bit of a mess lately. And I shouldn't be angry with them either for saying the wrong things. There are no right words to say when someone you love beyond measure is taken from you. Words become petty— small and meaningless. There is no solace in words.

The need to get away from here has been a constant ache in my chest that I've had to suppress for weeks now. I'm not supposed to leave Chicago; I'm supposed to be establishing a new normal—a routine that doesn't allow me to obsess over my fantasies. But, I've just found something in the paperwork the lawyers sent over that needs to be checked out. I know I should tell someone where I'm going, but it's really early and it seems a little rude to wake someone with a phone call now. That's not exactly true. If I'm being honest with myself, I'm not calling anyone because I'm afraid that whomever I call will try to talk me out of leaving, or stop me...and I have to go.

My escape from the city is uneventful. I watch the sunrise over the expressway, and then continue north until I trade Illinois for Wisconsin, and then Wisconsin for Michigan. As I drive behind a massive logging truck on M2, my phone rings. I eye it thoughtfully, wondering whether or not to answer it. The ringing stops and I relax. The respite is only temporary before it rings again. I sigh heavily before answering it. "Hi, Stan."

"Where are you, Vi?" Stan's stern tone is anything but welcome at the moment.

"I'm not sure. I'm a little lost—"

"You're damn right you're lost! That's why you were supposed to be in Dr. Gobel's office at nine this morning."

"Umm...yeah...that's probably not going to happen today," I say sheepishly. I glance out the window at the panorama of Lake Michigan's northern most shoreline as I drive.

"It is going to happen today! I've spoken to his secretary and she rearranged his schedule to accommodate you. Tell me where you are and I'll come get you—and don't tell me that you're at your apartment because I'm here now."

"How did you get in?" I ask.

"Your parents gave me their keys. They asked me to look after you before they went back to Miami. You were there when we made the plan; we talked about it in your team session only a few days ago."

"I remember," I mutter. "You're my advocate."

"So tell me again why you insist on living in this apartment? Matt's penthouse is so much better than this felony flat you're living in."

"My apartment is not that bad. It's an efficiency."

"Most of your neighbors are probably on parole."

"It's what I can afford on my teacher's salary," I say, equally annoyed with him.

"You can afford a lot more than this now and you know it. And you're not teaching right now anyway."

"It's what I'll be able to afford when I go back," I amend.

"It's like you're punishing yourself with this apartment, Violet."

"I'm not punishing myself," I say with my throat becoming tight.

"You could've fooled me. Now, where are you?" he asks, his voice full of irritation.

"Dr. Gobel thinks I'm crazy," I murmur.

"Dr. Gobel doesn't think you're crazy."

"You think I'm crazy."

There's silence on the other end for a moment before Stan says softly, "I think you're sad. I think you're so sad that you'll do anything to escape your sorrow. Are you taking the anti-depressants Dr. Gobel prescribed?"

"Yes."

"When did you take the last one?"

"Yesterday."

"You should've taken one this morning."

"I will."

"Do it now. I'll wait."

"I can take it later."

"Now, Vi!"

"Fine," I growl.

I pull off the road onto the shoulder and put Mattie's Escalade in park. I rummage around for a few seconds in my purse until I locate the orange-brown pill bottle with my name on it. Shaking a tablet into my hand, I pop it in my mouth and wash it down with lukewarm water from the bottle in the cup holder.

"Okay, I'm medicated," I say sarcastically into the phone.

"This is not a joke, Violet. It has only been a few weeks since you left the hospital. You agreed to outpatient counseling. I said I'd be responsible for you. Now, where are you? I'm coming to get you. You shouldn't be alone."

"I'm not alone. Mattie is with me."

There is silence on the other end of the phone for a moment. "Violet, Matt is dead," Stan says softly.

"I know. I was there when it happened," I answer with a raspy voice. My eyes fill up with tears; I take a deep breath, trying to blink them away. "It should've been me." It actually feels good to say aloud what I've known for months. I glance at Mattie's silver urn strapped in the passenger's seat beside me.

Stan nearly shouts into the phone, "It shouldn't have been you! He didn't want it to be you! That's why he did what he did, so it wasn't you! Now you're trying to ruin his sacrifice by killing yourself."

"His sacrifice! He jumped in front of a gun! Those bullets were meant for me, Stan! Dylan Harrison wasn't aiming at Mattie. He was aiming at me."

"Dylan Harrison was so strung out on heroin and bath salts that he thought he was aiming at the heretic who would destroy his master's race! I've read the police report on him. He was completely deranged. He could've been aiming at anyone that night. You and Matt just happened to be in the wrong place at the wrong time. It was bad luck, or bad timing, but it wasn't your fault."

I get angry with Stan for what feels like the first time in my life. "You should hate me! Your best friend would be alive right now if it weren't for me! I'm the one who wanted to walk home from the restaurant."

"Is that why you tried to kill yourself, Vi? Because you decided to walk home one night and a tweaking psychopath shot your fiancé?"

"No," I say with a tight voice.

"Then why'd you do it? Why'd you take all those pills?"

"I told you why. I needed them so I could hear Mattie better. He was trying to tell me something."

"You still believe Matt is talking to you?"

"He is talking to me."

"Is he telling you to kill yourself?"

"NO!" I scowl. "You know him! He'd never do that."

"Then what's he saying?"

I rub my forehead in frustration. "I told you. He...he needs me to find him. When I close my eyes at night, right before I drift off to sleep, I feel him there. It's like I'm underwater with him—I just can't hear him. I thought if I took some pills I could go deeper and find out where he is."

I remember the night I took all the sleeping tablets I was prescribed. My hand shook as I contemplated them piled within it; they were like ice in my palm. I knew it was dangerous, what I was doing, but there was no other way. I put them in my mouth, tasting the acrid medicine as it began to dissolve on my tongue. Initially, I panicked and spit them all back out, drinking giant gulps of water to wash away the evidence. But, after my fear began to dissipate, I saw my life stretch out before me—the hours, days, weeks, months without Mattie. Only loneliness awaited me: the constant, ever-present ache of loss. I could end that. I could face my fears and find him, or I could live the rest of my life in pain.

I opened my palm again, this time I didn't hesitate. As soon as I put the tablets back in my mouth, I washed them down with the rest of the water in the glass. Then, I picked up the phone and called Stan and told him what I was doing. He had shouted at me to stick my finger down my throat, but instead I had hung up on him to lie back on my bed.

As I began to drift off to sleep, I was finally able to find him after days of only murky images of him in the night. He was in a lake, deep underwater, his pale skin almost blue, as if he was bathed in moonlight. The little light shining from above the water made diamond patterns on him. His thick, black hair waved in the current, matching the rhythm of the leafy green seaweed growing all around. His hand extended for me to take. When I reached for it, he slipped through my fingertips and was violently pulled back from me until I lost him to the depth of the water. I would've followed him down, but instead, I awoke to paramedics flashing

7

light in my eyes as the siren of the ambulance transported me to Cook County Hospital.

My heart squeezes now at the memory of being taken from Mattie again. "Violet," Stan says my name like he's talking to a naughty child, "you didn't just take a few pills. You took the whole bottle. We've been over this! I've humored you as much as I can. Now I'm tired of your bullshit! I'm not going to let you do this to yourself—to me. I'm getting you help. I'm coming to get you. Where. Are. You?"

His threat is very real. My parents agreed to leave him in charge of me when they went back to Florida. He can make it so that I have to go back to the hospital. I wet my lips before I say, "Listen, Stan, I know you're going through a lot—"

"You don't know what I'm going through! Matt, my partner, the one who ran most of the operations of our company, was shot and killed a couple of months ago. I've been forced to oversee everything—make every decision—and I'm shit at it, Vi! Matt was Source Products. He was this company. Now I have a silent partner, you, who's losing her damn mind and who believes my best friend has outlived his body and is waiting in some watery grave for her to find him. SO, NO, VI! YOU DON'T HAVE A CLUE WHAT I'M GOING THROUGH!"

I cringe, and then say quietly, "I found something last night when I was going through some of the papers the lawyers sent over. Matt owned property in Michigan—in the Upper Peninsula, Stan. Did you know that?"

"No," he says irritably. "So what? He was in the thirty under thirty wealthiest men in America. He had a lot of private holdings."

"This one is different. It's a lake. He owns an entire lake."

8

"Owned, Vi, owned. Matt is dead. You own it now. And again, so what?"

"As far as I can tell, it's the first thing he ever bought."

"That makes sense. It's a bad investment."

"There's a house. I have the key."

"Where?"

"It's near a little town called..." I pause.

"Vi?" he asks. "Where was that? You cut out!"

"I'm losing the signal," I lie. "I'll call you when I get there. Promise."

"Violet!" Stan's angry voice shouts, but I hang up. I wince and silence my phone.

I look at Mattie's urn next to me and say, "Stan's gonna be bitter, but we can't have him sending the police to take me into custody so he and Dr. Gobel can decide if I'm sane."

Intending to merge back onto the road, I scan the rearview mirror, catching a glimpse of my reflection. It shocks me a little because I hardly recognize myself. I look crazy. My long brown hair is piled on top of my head in a messy bun. The dark circles under my eyes make them seem even bluer, haunted. My skin is so pale it nearly glows; I haven't been out in the sun in weeks. It's nearly the summer solstice and my flesh indicates that it's the middle of winter, which wouldn't be so bad if I hadn't lost more weight than I care to admit. My white, v-neck t-shirt hangs on me and my cut-off boyfriend shorts are baggier than normal...and it probably doesn't help that I'm still wearing my slippers. I look like a strung-out teenager, not the once-confident, responsible, twenty-four-year old I used to be. I shiver.

I take off my slippers and toss them in the back seat. I reach back and find my sandals on the top of my duffle bag and slip them

on. Using the brush from my purse, I take down the bun and pull
my hair into a sleek ponytail instead. I locate lipstick and apply it.
"You're not crazy," I tell my reflection. "You're going to find him.
And anyway, crazy people don't wear lipstick...at least not on their
lips." I scrounge around in my purse again for my dark sunglasses.
I put them on to hide the circles under my eyes, and then I pull
Mattie's truck back onto the road.

Chapter 2 – SOURCE ONE ALPHA

After a few more hours of driving, I pick up the map from the seat next to me and try to read it. I'd traded M2 for some serious backasswards roads awhile ago and have been fairly lost ever since. I pull the truck over to the shoulder while I study the map again, and then search around through the window, finding nothing but extremely tall pine trees. Mattie's company, Source Products, designed the custom GPS in this car, but I've never figured out how to use it. Since Mattie was the rocket scientist, I left him in charge of programming it whenever we left the city.

I growl in frustration. "There are no road signs! Why are there no signs? How do Yoopers find anything? Do they navigate by sense of smell?" I hold up my phone, hoping to get a half a bar so I can use my GPS app. It may as well be a brick because there's no reliable service here in this part of the Upper Peninsula. It's probably my bad karma for cutting Stan off earlier.

"We're soooo furrreaking lost!" I say conversationally to Mattie's urn. "I have no idea where your house is, do you? I can't even find the lake on this map! It's like it doesn't exist! Dammit!" I rest my forehead against the steering wheel. "You should be driving, not me. Do you want to help me out here?" My throat gets tight and I hold back tears.

All at once, silver lights brighten the car's console and the windscreen of the car becomes nearly opaque. Mattie's face appears on the windshield as his voice pipes through the speakers in surround sound. "Engaging autopilot. Destination?"

My heartbeat flutters in shock at the sound of his sexy voice. "Oh my God, Mattie?" It should've come out as a shout, but it comes out in a whisper.

"I am unfamiliar with 'Omygodmaddey.' Please input coordinates for 'Omygodmaddey.'"

Understanding slowly dawns on me and I whisper, "You're not Mattie! You sound just like Mattie!" My stomach tightens painfully.

"I am Source One Alpha," the deep voice coming from the speakers states. "I'm endowed with the voice frequencies of my creator, Matteyo Dillinger."

"Mattie designed you?"

"That is correct."

"What are you, a computer?" I ask incredulously.

"Negative. I am Source One Alpha."

"What's Source One Alpha? "

"In technical terms or laymen's?" he asks.

"Definitely laymen's."

"I am A.I."

"A.I.?"

The voice sighs heavily, like it's human and not a machine. "He said you were not technologically savvy. He wasn't lying. "

"Who said that? Mattie said that? You talked to him?"

"Yes. We spoke often. He is my creator. A.I. is an acronym for artificial intelligence."

"So, you're a smart computer?"

12

The image of Matt on the windshield frowns. The driver's side door opens on its own. "Call me a computer again and you can walk. Matteyo refers to me as So-wah. On the surface I'm cybernetics, but let's just say I am."

"You are? You mean you exist?"

"I do."

My heartbeat triples and I consider unbuckling my seatbelt and running from the vehicle, but I can't make myself leave, not with Mattie's face staring back at me. I'll endure anything just to hear Source One Alpha talk to me again.

"Umm, I'm sorry. I didn't mean to insult you." I panic a little when the driver-side door closes by itself.

"Take a sip of your water. Your heart rate is well beyond an acceptable level," SOA says.

I do as it suggests, anxious not to offend it again. "So, why don't I know about you? I must've driven in this car a hundred times and you never once spoke to me."

"I was classified."

"Mattie, uh, Matteyo didn't want me to know about you?"

"Correct."

"Why?"

"He wasn't sure if he could trust you."

"Trust me? Trust me with what?"

"It's classified."

"Declassify it."

"No."

I exhale in confusion. "Then, why are you talking to me now?"

"Matteyo gave me instructions. If you're ever in dire need of my assistance, I'm to help you."

"Right. Of course," I say with a mixture of shock and frustration.

"How can I assist you?"

My hand trembles as I rub my forehead, trying to ease my growing headache. I pause and ask, "I'm lost. Can you take me to Matteyo?"

"His remains are in the vehicle with you."

I suddenly feel chilled. "How did you know that?"

"I scanned the contents of the car."

"How did you do that?" I whisper.

"In technical terms or laymen's?"

"Laymen's! Always laymen's!"

"I scanned the contents of the vehicle on a molecular level. It's a mathematical certainty that the urn on the passenger seat contains the remains of Matteyo Dillinger."

"Okay." I rub my hands over my arms trying to dispel the goose bumps. "Have you ever been in this area with Matteyo before?"

"Yes."

"Do you remember where you were?" I ask anxiously.

"I don't forget anything."

I roll my eyes. "Okay. Where were you the last time you were in this area?"

"Matteyo's residence."

"Is it on a lake?"

"The residence is approximately fifty-two yards from a body of water."

My mouth becomes dry. I take another sip of water before I ask, "Can you take me there—on like, autopilot or whatever?"

"Yes."

Elation washes over me and I wait for the car to move. When it continues to idle, I roll my eyes again. "Will you please take me there now?"

"We will not make it to the destination without stopping for fuel for this substandard vehicle."

An ironic smile twists my lips. "How is this substandard? It's an Escalade."

"It operates on fossil fuel. It's a P.O.S.," SOA replies with attitude in his tone.

Despite everything, I smile. "We should get gas then," I agree. "Do you want me to drive?"

"No," SOA states as the windshield brightens to full-transparency.

"You say that like there's something wrong with my driving."

"You speed, you fail to maintain a proper distance from the vehicle in front of you, you demonstrate improper lane changes, you talk on the phone while you drive, and you drift."

I frown. "I don't drift."

"You drift. I will drive."

As the truck pulls back onto the road on its own, I clutch the steering wheel in fear. The wheel begins to retract from me. "Do not touch the steering wheel while I'm driving." SOA orders.

I flinch and drop my hands from it. I bite my thumbnail anxiously for a few minutes until it becomes clear that the truck isn't going to plunge off the road. When I begin to relax a little, my phone rings. I pick it up, see that I have one bar of connectivity, and glance at the display. It reads: "Private." I move my thumb to answer it.

"Do not answer that call," SOA orders. The windshield darkens again so that I can see his face on it.

My eyes widen. "Why not?"

"The caller is attempting to trace the call and locate your position. You need to destroy your SIM card."

"My what—who's trying to locate my position? How do you know that?"

"They are triangulating your position now. Destroying your SIM card is your only option to avoid detection. You will find it in the back of your phone. "

I scramble to open the back of my phone when my window opens. "Throw your phone out the window. At this velocity, the impact will destroy it."

I don't know if it's because it's Mattie's voice telling me to do it or his image on the windshield, but I immediately toss my phone out the window. As I look out the back, I see the phone bounce on the pavement and break into piece. The truck brakes and stops in the middle of the road. Then, SOA reverses the Escalade and backs over my phone for good measure.

The truck pulls away again and I ask, "Do you mind telling me what the total hell just happened?"

"They are looking for you."

"They? Who're they? Stan?"

"Not Stanley Parker. Maybelle Younger and her associates."

"Maybelle? You mean Mattie's ex-girlfriend May?"

"The very same."

"Why does Mattie's stalker want to track me? He's the one she's always wanted. She's obsessed with him."

"She is attempting to locate the remains of Matteyo Dillinger."

"What!" I breathe in disbelief. "Why?"

"I do not have that information."

"Then how do you know this?" I ask incredulously.

16

"She is in the penthouse apartment now. She is destroying everything in her search for his ashes."

"She's in his apartment now?" I ask in disbelief.

"Correction, she is in Matteyo's former apartment, which now belongs to you. I have security access to the Chicago residence," SOA states. His image disappears from the windshield to be replaced by a security camera feed of the penthouse. Several very fit men in dark suits are breaking up the furniture, turning over tables, and cutting fabric from the elegant chairs. I locate May in the middle of the room with her ear to her phone as another dark-suited man uses a laptop next to her.

I watch as May paces back and forth, her long legs avoiding the chaos all around her. She tosses her perfect blond hair, appearing to grind her teeth in frustration. After several more moments, she throws her phone across the room and puts her hands on her hips.

"Why are they looking for Mattie?" I wonder aloud as I watch them topple bookcases.

"That information is classified. I have alerted the police. They will not remain there long."

"It's classified? You know what this is about?" I ask, forgetting to be afraid for a second. "You'd better start talking right now! I need to know what the hell is going on here!"

"You are in danger. Maybelle Younger intends to recover the remains of Matteyo Dillinger. It will only be a matter of time before she locates you."

"Oh my God! Why is Mattie's ex-girlfriend such a total psycho? What can she possibly want with his ashes?"

"The logical explanation is that she would like him back."

Goose bumps break out on my arms again. "Is he contacting her, too? Does she know something?"

"Maybelle knows many things. But, it's my understanding from my conversations with Matteyo that he would prefer not to converse with Maybelle on any occasion for any reason. I believe that would extend into his death."

The windshield lightens and the security camera feed from Mattie's apartment disappears. "She came to his funeral, you know?" I murmur.

"I was unaware of that information."

"I don't remember much about that day...it's all sort of a blur, but I remember her. She was unforgettable."

"You were still prescribed pain medication at that time. You had just left the hospital."

My heart erupts again to pound in my chest. "How do you know all that?"

I have security access to all of Matteyo's former residences and his organization, Source Products. People spoke of little else. I understand that one of the bullets that killed Matteyo also penetrated you as well. You were in intensive care for several days after the shooting."

I feel sick. I open the window wide to get air.

"Have I upset you?"

"I'm fine," I lie. After a few moments, my heartbeat slows and I close my window.

"What do you remember of Maybelle Younger on the occasion of Matteyo Dillinger's funeral?" SOA asks.

"She was being even crazier than usual, which is really hard to top because every time I see her she acts deranged."

"In what way?"

18

I sigh. "She offered to buy Mattie's ashes from me."

"And you found that crazy?"

"Uhh, yeah. Insane," I agree with a nod.

"And how did she take your refusal?" SOA asks.

"Not well. Stan had to practically drag her out of the wake. She was screaming at me, telling me how much I didn't deserve him."

The truck slows and pulls off the road into a small, rundown convenience store gas station. SOA puts the Escalade in park near a gas pump and turns off the engine. "We need fuel in order to make it to our destination," SOA states.

Still preoccupied with my memories of Mattie's funeral, I just sit there staring at the convenience store ahead of me. "This is the only fueling station around for several miles," he adds.

"Okay," I murmur absently. I pull on the handle of the truck to open the door but it doesn't budge. My brow furrows in confusion. "Umm, we need gas, right?"

"Yes," SOA states.

"Okay. Open the door and I'll get some and then you can tell me everything you know about May on the way to Mattie's house." I try to open the door again. It doesn't move.

"I am uncomfortable with this fueling station."

"Urr...what? Why?"

"There are five large males in this establishment."

"Uhh...okay...is that bad?"

"Two of them are attempting to conceal their presence from us."

"Oh," I say, feeling nervous about this new tidbit of information. "What if I just jump out, use the pump, and pay with a credit card? I won't even have to go into the store."

"That is not a good option. Maybelle Younger will track your credit cards. You have one hundred seventy-two dollars and eleven cents in your purse. Pay in cash."

"You scanned my purse?"

"I did."

"Maybe we should go somewhere else?"

"We do not have enough fuel to make it to the next station."

I exhale a long breath. "Ohh-kay, it looks like we're out of options then. So...I'll get gas and go in..." I pull on the handle again and find that it's still locked. "So-wah, are you worried about me?"

To my surprise, SOA answers, "I am."

I almost smile. "I do have mace..." the door still doesn't unlock. I sigh, "Unless there is another option—"

The door unlocks with a click. "Be careful."

Nervous now, I open the door and step out of the truck. It smells different here than a gas station in the city. There's hardly any exhaust fumes, just the sweet scent of pollen on the wind. As I shut the door, I notice that the truck's windows have all darkened; no one can see inside. I take the nozzle off the gas pump and insert it in the tank before choosing the ultra grade. I wait several moments for the pump to engage, but it doesn't reset. I look toward the convenience store. After a few moments of staring at the outline of the clerk behind the counter, he moves to push a button. The pump resets and I fill the tank.

When I'm done, I walk slowly toward the store, wiping my sweaty palms on the front of my denim shorts. I pull the door open; a bell above it clangs loudly. A twentysomething man, leaning against a magazine rack, idly flips through a Guns magazine. He rubs the bristles on his chin as he eyes me critically. The conversation that was transpiring between the clerk and the rough-looking patron leaning against the counter abruptly ends with the bell. I ignore them all and move to the aisle that's filled with cheap bottles of wine and liquor.

I pluck two bottles of red and a bottle of white from the shelf and then turn back toward the counter. They're all watching me. I hesitate for a second, staring back at them. The clerk has a skeptical look in his eyes. Without glancing away, I defiantly take a bottle of inexpensive vodka from the shelf, adding it to the others in my arms. The bottles clink together in protest. When I reach the counter, I push them onto it.

"I had eighty dollars on pump one," I state clearly, before selecting a pack of gum from the stack beside the cash register and laying it next to the bottles.

The clerk stares at me for a moment; his eyebrow arches in challenge. "You sure you're old enough to be buying alcohol. Lemme see some I.D." I relax. He's not some backwoods hick ready to abduct me. He's actually sort of cute in an outdoorsy, I-kill-my-own-food kind of way. His eyes show no wrinkles around them, so he might be my age, but his beard makes him seem older.

I pull my wallet from my purse and hand him my I.D. He studies it for a second before he takes off his camouflage baseball cap and scratches his short, dark hair. His strong arms are covered in heavy sleeve tattoos—this can't be his only job because no one gets arms like that by hanging out in a gas station all day. "What brings you to the U.P. from Chicago, Violet O'Shea? Business or pleasure?"

"Uhh...pleasure—vacation," I lie and eye the bottles of alcohol on the counter. "A friend of mine lent me his house for a few days. I'm just going to lay by the lake—read a little—veg. "

21

He pauses in his assessment of the bar code on a bottle. The man next to me straightens a little—stiffens. "Your friend gotta name?"

"Yes." I nod, pretending to play coy, but all of a sudden I'm back to being uncomfortable.

When I'm not forthcoming with that name, the clerk says, "Well, looks like you're either having a party or a funeral, Violet." He smiles at the bottles in front of him.

"Something like that," I reply with a wary smile. "How much do I owe you?"

He puts his hat back on his head and begins to scan the items into the register. "Where are you staying? What lake? Is it around here?" the clerk asks casually, his blue eyes glancing at me.

"Why?" I ask in my best don't-eff-with-me tone. "You thinking of stopping by?"

The clerk frowns. "Ned and I could check on you. It can get scary up here when you're all alone, eh, Ned?" he asks his friend next to me with a lift of his chin.

"Eh, Clyde." Ned nods sharply. "Scary."

"Who says I'm alone, Clyde?" I ask and glance out the window. I see two men in white wifebeaters and camouflage cargo shorts by Mattie's truck taking an interest in it. It's nearly impossible for them to see anything inside of it because the windows are almost opaque. Suddenly, the truck's alarm goes off, scaring the bejesus out of the one nearest the vehicle, causing the other one to double over with laughter.

Clyde growls, "Travis, go tell those two idiots to leave the truck alone!"

The man by the rack closes his magazine, stuffs it back on the shelf, and shuffles toward the door. Once outside, he says

22

something to the two by Mattie's truck before they all move away from it to light their cigarettes at a safer distance from the gas pumps. The truck's alarm goes silent a few moments later.

My focus returns to Clyde as he asks, "You might want to add some sunscreen to this. You look like you burn easily, especially if you're out at Nee-Ba-Naw-Baigs Lake." He watches me, like he's assessing my reaction.

I glance outside at the overcast sky. "It looks like it could rain soon," I reply.

His frown turns darker, "Still, you can never be too cautious up here, especially on that lake."

I shrug, "Okay, let's err on the side of caution then."

He doesn't smile as he adds the sunscreen to the total. The register dings and Clyde mutters, "One twenty sixty-six."

I pay him after he puts my bottles in a brown paper sack. He hands it to me, but doesn't let go. "You take care now, Violet," he says, his blue eyes bore into mine. The bottles within the bag bang together. When I pull a little harder on it, he lets go.

"Thanks," I manage to say before I turn and walk to the door. Outside, I pause as Travis and his wifebeater-clad friends walk toward me. I shift the bag to one arm; my other hand goes to my purse to scout for my mace.

The engine of the truck roars to life and the passenger-side window opens a crack. SOA's voice shouts loudly, "You coming, sweetheart?"

The men in front of me stop. My voice shakes, "Yeah, babe. I got you some gum." I walk past Travis who watches me like I'm his next meal. When I make it to the truck, the door automatically unlocks and I climb inside, placing the bag on the passenger seat next to me. I pull out the vodka and take a large swig. I gasp; the liquid burns a trail to my belly.

"You shouldn't consume alcohol while taking your medication," SOA scolds. I try not to think about how truly bizarre it is to be reprimanded by a navigation system.

I let out a shaky breath. "I'll stop taking my medication then." The engine revs on its own and the truck backs up from the gas pumps on autopilot. As it pulls away from the gas station, I ask, "So-wah, are we going to Nee-Ba-Naw-Baigs Lake?"

"Some locals refer to Matteyo Dillinger's lake by that name."

"Why? Does it mean something?" I'm afraid of the answer.

"Nee-ba-naw-baigs is Ojibwe; it means water spirits. Some of the locals believe the lake is haunted."

"Why would they think that?" I ask.

"That information is classified."

Chapter 3 - BLACK WATER

In less than twenty minutes, SOA pulls off the road and onto a long dirt path partially hidden by dense trees. If I were driving, I would've never seen it. Bouncing and jarring over huge, muddy potholes, the ride is treacherous. I hold tight to the door handle as we traverse a shallow stream and avoid a downed tree. We pass by a small log cabin in the woods. Branches screech against the side of the truck as we go deeper in; the trees get closer together.

I'm almost afraid to see what's around the next bend, but soon the trees part and we come to a clearing. When a house comes into view, my mouth gapes in awe. Cobblestone chimneys rise under towering blue pine trees; they cut across the multiple rooflines of cedar, moss-covered shingles. Ivy crawls over the enormous, gray stone walls of the house, outlining a score of windows. It's a curious mixture of heavy stone and light glass with mountainous, gray cliffs rising in the background, making for a stunning vista. Seeing those cliffs, I have no doubt where the stone that comprises the house had been quarried.

SOA stops the truck in front of the slate gray steps that lead to the turret-like entryway. I stare at the two enormous double doors.

"This is it?" I ask SOA, already knowing the answer.

"It is."

"Okay," I exhale the word, "wish me luck."

"Why?"

"Never mind," I mutter.

I unbuckle the seatbelt from around Mattie's urn next to me. Lifting it in my arms, I hold it close. I feel the heavy coldness of the smooth metal through my t-shirt; it chills my skin. Slowly, I emerge from the car and face the house. It's beautiful and watchful; it studies me. A shiver of fear runs through me as I walk up the stone steps to the imposing carved doors. The wood is textured to resemble the scaly skin of an alligator, while large, cast-iron doorknockers in the shape of trident-wielding Poseidons stare back at me menacingly.

Fumbling for the black key in my pocket, I push it into the lock. The eyes of Poseidon light up with green fire. In a flash, a green beam infuses me, scanning my entire body. A second later, it extinguishes and one of the doors opens for me to enter.

"Holy. Freaking. Crap!" I breathe and try to recover.

"You may come in," Mattie says from inside the house.

"Mattie!" I squeak his name, stumbling past the threshold beneath the sparkling crystal chandelier in the foyer. I rush into the main room of the house that has a breathtaking view of the lake through an almost seamless wall of windows. I turn in circles looking for him, but he's nowhere.

I'm alive for the first time in months only to die again within seconds when he says, "I am not Matteyo Dillinger. I am Source One Alpha." His tone is curious, like he cannot figure out why I keep making the same mistake.

I nearly choke as my throat squeezes tight. I try to ignore it and ask, "How did you leave the car, So-wah?"

The windows in the house begin to darken, shutting out the increasingly overcast sky outside. What I thought to be mounted track lighting on the elegant, barrel-vaulted ceiling above turns out to be high-powered laser-like lights that manifest and stitch together a holographic image of Mattie...or in this instance, SOA. His image walks on air toward me as he says, "I maintain security for all of Matteyo's former residences—your residences."

I can hardly breathe with him in front of me; it's like looking at a smoky version of my fiancé. His black hair is short in the back with longer bangs in the front, accentuating his masculine jawline. He looks at me with eyes the color of which I've never seen on anyone else; they're midnight blue. His height is exactly that of Mattie's. The top of my head barely reaches his chin.

I try to touch his strong chest. My fingertips slip through air, and are bathed in SOA's projected light. To cover my disappointment, I mutter, "You're doing a masterful job of keeping people out of the penthouse. Maybelle & Co. just trashed it."

SOA smiles at my sarcasm. "I wasn't trying to keep her out. I'm keeping track of her. If I know where she is, I can protect you. Your possessions can be replaced. You cannot."

"You think she'll try to hurt me?" I ask.

"The probability is not in your favor. You have what she desires most."

I clutch Mattie's urn tighter. "She's not getting any part of him," I promise with a shake of my head.

"I will protect you, Violet."

I turn away from SOA and drag my eyes to the view of the lake outside. My stomach clenches. I forget everything as I walk toward the window with Mattie's urn pressed to my chest. The glass slides open revealing itself to be a door. I glance over my shoulder at SOA.

"It's automatic," he states by way of an explanation. "It senses your intention."

Unnerved by the automation embedded in the house, I step outside onto the stone porch. Black clouds hang above the lake, rolling off the peak of a cliff face that shelters the lake on three sides. Mist, like smoke, rises from the black, glassy surface of the water.

My heart pounds in my chest. I have a sense of déjà vu—although I've never been here, I feel as if I have. I leave the porch and hurry down the rough stone path to a wooden dock that extends out over the water. The dark planks creak in protest as I walk to the end of it. I scan the perimeter of the lake for other houses, but there aren't any; neither are there boats or swimmers. There's nothing and no one around for miles; it's all just huge pine trees, wilderness, cliffs, and wildlife. I set down Mattie's urn on a plank, hiding it between two posts, away from the water. After I straighten, I can't help it, I scream his name. "MATTIE?"

My voice echoes off the gray and brown striations of rock from the imposing cliffs. Blackbirds take flight, flying away from my blunderbuss. "MATTIE, I'M HERE!" I cry.

Hurriedly, I strip off my white t-shirt and denim shorts and toss them over Mattie's urn. In my bra and underwear, I plunge into the water. White bubbles stir furiously around me. The water is cold, deep, and ancient-glacier-made. My pale skin looks green beneath the surface. I come up for air, swim away from the dock, and then dive under again. It's so dark; I swim underwater with my eyes open, searching. I come up for air panting. "MATTIE?" I yell again in growing desperation. I dive under again and scream his name. Bubbles rise from me.

I surface again and this time I'm crying. I take several gasping breaths while treading water. A part of me knows I'm crazy—is sure of it. No sane person does this. But, another part of me is sure that he's here. Bone-deep certain. I submerge and swim downward. My ears hurt from the pressure and my lungs, they burn.

Swimming through tall seaweed, it pulls at my hair and waves in my face. As I move around it, a ghostly silver shape looms in front of me. It's massive, jutting up from the dark depths of the water like a submerged skyscraper. Silt and sediment covers it, but as I near, light from above shines through, showing it to be metallic. I reach out and touch the object, brushing away some of the algae. It's a plane except it's like no plane I've ever seen.

My heartbeat triples; I exhale everything I have in my lungs and run out of air. Frantically, I scramble to get back to the surface. I break through and inhale a gasping breath, "Gahhhhaaahh." Trembling, I force choking gasps of air into my lungs. How did someone crash a plane here, I wonder? I take another deep breath and my ability to reason becomes a little clearer. The scale of that thing in the water is way too big to be a plane; it's something else.

My thoughts are interrupted when something floats to the surface near me. The exposed, white underbelly of a dead fish bobs like a cork. I splash at it to move it away from me. My hand bumps into another dead fish as it emerges from the deep. I kick my feet and wave my arms in the water, backing away from the corpses, only to feel several more brush up against my back. I spin in a circle and discover that I'm surrounded; a growing circle of lifeless fish drift on the ripples I've created. I panic, biting my lip and whimpering loudly.

Something frigid touches my ankle. It encircles my leg and tugs gently. I inhale a deep breath, preparing to scream when I'm

29

pulled abruptly beneath the surface of the water. With my eyes wide open, I gaze upon Mattie's face as he stares back at me. His dark hair waves in the current. He looks nearly perfect, if not exactly normal. His bare skin is so pale it looks blue, but the awful gunshot wounds that had torn holes in his broad chest are no longer visible. He's the same: rugged and handsome to a fault.

Reaching out, his fingers cup my cheek; they're like ice. His thumb rubs over my skin. Instantly, I no longer feel like I have to hold my breath; it's as if I've lost the need for air. Tentatively, my fingers move to touch him, but recoil at how cold he is. His other hand comes up to cover mine, drawing it back to his cheek. He closes his eyes for a moment, as if savoring my touch. He turns his lips to kiss my palm; my skin looks green in contrast to his. When he opens his eyes again, his thumb begins to trail from my face down my throat as he studies me. He traces my clavicle and moves further down, slowly over my breast, to my abdomen. He pauses.

My scar is still pink and ugly where one of the bullets had exited his back and penetrated me. As his thumb rubs over my bumpy skin, his eyes meet mine again. The pain I see in them is my undoing. My face changes from shock to grief. His arm wraps around me and he pulls me to him. I grip his powerful back as my lips brush his cold neck.

Thrashing in the water near us makes him let go of me abruptly. Suddenly, I feel the need for oxygen. Mattie puts his finger to his lips and shakes his head. He begins to fade away. Desperate to stay with him, my arms try to clutch his chest but they only slip through him now as he dissolves in front of my eyes.

The thrashing grows louder right before strong arms grab me around my chest, dragging me back to the surface. Choking, I inhale water and air. I'm forced to look up at the gray sky as I'm towed through black water. I cough and gasp, and then struggle against the person pulling me away from Mattie, but I'm weaker than I know and I can't twist free from the arm that has a vice-like grip on me. As we reach the dock, I'm shoved to the ladder. I thread my arm in it, turning to see who just dragged me away from my love.

Clyde breathes heavily next to me. He's still in the same t-shirt that he had on at the convenience store earlier today...and he looks far from happy.

"You always swim alone?" Clyde demands. His eyebrows come together in a frown over his blue eyes as he pants and wipes dripping water away from them.

"What are you doing here?" I scowl.

"Saving your ass apparently!"

"Saving my—from what?"

"You were drowning!"

"I wasn't drowning!"

"You weren't swimming! You were underwater forever! What were you doing out there, fishing with dynamite?"

"Fishing with..." I look to the middle of the lake; the dead fish are still floating where I'd been. "I was..." I remember Mattie's finger to his lips, "taking a dip." I turn toward the ladder and have trouble grasping the rung to pull myself up. My joints are stiff. I'm shaking, frozen to the bone; goose bumps cover my flesh.

"You're an ice cube!" Clyde says. He takes my hands in his warm ones, rubbing and blowing on them. "Here, we have to get you out of the water." He nudges me to turn away from him, and then he puts one arm around my waist from behind, guiding me up the ladder.

Standing on the dock, I hug my arms to me as I face Clyde shivering. "Why are yyyou hhhere?"

He strips his wet t-shirt off; the tattoos that start on his arms cover his chest as well. Dark, scrolling marks forming beautiful symbols accentuate his muscular build. Wringing his shirt out, it drips water on his soggy shoes; he didn't stop to take them off either before he jumped in the water to save me.

Clyde frowns, "I live here!" He points in the direction of the house. "You passed by my cabin on your way up to the main house. I maintain the property. What are you doing here? Where's Matt?"

"I..." I swallow hard, trying to get the words out, "he... died...I ooown the ppproperty now."

Shock registers on his face. "He what?"

"He dddied," I whisper the words.

"Bullshit!" Clyde scowls, "You're lying! I'd know if he was dead!"

"You'd know...hhhow?"

The screaming of birds distracts me. I gaze over Clyde's shoulder, seeing a flock of blackbirds swarming around the spot where I'd been in the water, diving at the circle of dead fish. His eyes follow mine.

I don't know how long we stand there watching them feast on floating carnage before I feel a tug on my arm. "C'mon. You have to get inside. Your lips are blue." He nudges me gently on my arm again and I allow him to lead me to the house.

When we reach the stone terrace, Clyde asks, "Are you hungry?"

I bite my quivering bottom lip, and then I say. "I'm fffine."

"You're not fine; you're freezing and I can't get answers from you until you warm up." He nods toward the house. "Go inside. I'll go get us some dinner and be back soon." He waves his hand in front of the glass and it opens for me to enter. He nudges me inside; the glass closes behind me. Clyde walks away from the porch, heading around it toward the front.

Chapter 4 - DUSK TO DARK

After Clyde walks away, SOA manifests next to me. "You are dangerously close to hypothermia," he states.

"And I'm ccccold, tttoo," I say with my teeth chattering. Water drips from me onto the beautiful hardwood floor. Waiting just long enough to make sure Clyde is gone, I stumble back to the glass door. I have to get back to Mattie. I pause in front of it, but it doesn't open. Waving my hands, nothing happens.

I glance over my shoulder at the smoky image of SOA. "So-wah, the dddoor won't ooopen."

His mannerisms are like Mattie when he says, "I know—I'm controlling it. You cannot go outside."

"WWWHAT?" I shout with my hands balling into fists.

"Matteyo programmed me to protect you when he cannot. His directives have been activated. There is a high probability that you would become hypothermic should you go back outside now. You cannot leave until your core temperature improves."

My mouth drops open before I snap it shut. I stomp toward the front door and when I reach it, I find it locked as well. "BBBut I hhhhave to get out now! I nnneed to go to hhhim!" I rattle the handle, but it won't open.

"You need to go to who?" SOA asks.

"Mmmattie! He's in the lake."

34

"Matteyo Dillinger is in the lake?" SOA asks.

"Yes! He's in ttthere. I sssaw him. He hhheld mmme in his arms." I go to the back door again. It still doesn't open. I turn toward SOA in frustration, folding my arms over my chest as I tap my foot.

"His presence is irrelevant. The protection directive supersedes anything else. I have raised the temperature in the house several degrees, but if you would like to get outside sooner, I suggest you take a hot shower. There is a bathroom attached to the master suite. It's through there." SOA points in the direction of a doorway to my right.

I blanche. "You're kkkidding, rrright?"

"I am serious." SOA says, his smoky image crossing his arms to mirror mine.

"Wwwhat's going on hhhere, So-wah? Why is Mmmattie in the lakkke?" I ask.

"I have no knowledge of Matteyo Dillinger being in the lake other than what you've told me."

"Tttell me abouttt the silvvvver thing out ttthere in ttthe waterrr."

"That is classified."

I turn to look out at the lake before I growl in frustration. I give in and move to locate the master suite on the main floor. It's huge and has a stone fireplace similar to the one in the main room that roars to life as I pass it. An elegant, but simple bed on a raised dais comprises a portion of the far wall. The ceiling above it is glass and I wonder how many nights Mattie laid there awake gazing at the stars.

I continue to the master bathroom; it has a huge glass-enclosed walk-in shower that is already on. Steam rolls from it when I open the door. After I undress and enter, it takes several minutes for me to stop shaking. When I do, I turn off the shower and find a towel, wrapping it around me. I drag my fingers through my hair to untangle it. Moving to the bedroom, I find Mattie's closet; it's nearly as big as my entire apartment. I rummage through the drawers, choosing a white t-shirt, cream-colored cable knit sweater, and a pair of black cargo shorts with a drawstring waist that fit me like capris.

As I pull on his oversized sweater, Mattie's scent assails me. Holding the crewneck collar to my nose, I walk out into the bedroom again and study the view of the lake. I found him! I think as I hug myself. A part of me is elated and an equal part of me is terrified. My mind races with questions. What the hell is happening? Why is this happening? Why is he here? What if this is it? What if this is as close as I can ever get to him again?

A desperate longing twists inside of me. If he can't join me here, maybe I can join him in there...or maybe...maybe I'm completely crazy. Maybe I'm just seeing what I want to see—like Dr. Gobel had said. Maybe I've lost my damn mind.

Pounding on the glass outside startles me from my thoughts. I rush back into the main room, nearly tripping over a lounge chair to see Clyde on the back porch. Standing by the glass door, Clyde tries to hide a smile at my clumsiness. He has changed into a black t-shirt and jeans. With his tattoos, he looks like he should have a guitar strapped to him, ready to take the stage in front of a hoard of adoring women.

Feeling my cheeks turning red, I pull the white blanket off the chair and wrap it around my shoulders. Cautiously, I approach the door. Clyde spreads an arm wide, indicating the table on the porch.

In the growing dusk, the lantern in the center of it casts flickering light on two elegant table settings.

My eyes search for SOA, but he's not visible. As I near the glass door, it slides open. Cool air of approaching darkness touches my face along with the aroma of food. "Pizza," I say with a sigh, feeling hungrier than I have in days. My stomach growls and I realize I need to eat.

"And salad and bread sticks," Clyde adds. He holds up a bottle of red wine. "And you had the wine."

"Hey, that was in the truck!" I state.

"Yeah, so was this," he says, picking up my purse that has obviously been gone through.

He sets them back down on a chair, and then pulls out a seat for me facing the lake. "Sit," he says, more like an order than an invitation. Knowing that I can't very well go search for Mattie again with Clyde lurking around, I sit down and allow him to push in my chair. He takes a seat next to me. Twisting the cap off the wine, he pours some in a beautiful wine glass before handing it to me.

"Pizza?" he asks with a tilt of his eyebrow.

"Please," I murmur.

He loads a gigantic piece on my plate with a generous amount of salad and a breadstick. He sets the plate in front of me. "Dig in." Lifting his glass, he waits for me to do the same.

"Cheers," I say, extending my glass to his.

We eat together quietly and my eyes stray to the lake often. Clyde refills my wine glass whenever it's half-full. I have no idea how much I've truly had to drink, but I'm beginning to feel the effects of the alcohol. When I set my napkin back on the table,

Clyde abruptly pulls my chair to face him and asks, "Who are
you?"

Startled, I answer honestly. "I'm Violet O'Shea."

He pulls my plastic school ID card from his pocket. "Art
teacher, Chicago Public Schools."

I nod my head. "That's right." I take the card from him.

He reaches in his pocket again, pulling out my prescription
bottle of antidepressants from Dr. Gobel. He sets them on the table
like an accusation. "What are you doing here, Violet?"

I immediately take the medication from the table and shove it
in my pocket with my ID. My chin drops and I mumble, "I told
you. I own this house now."

"Yeah, you told me. Matt's dead, right?" Clyde says
sarcastically. "How'd he die, eh?"

"Someone shot him," I murmur.

He nods skeptically. "These gunshot wounds killed him, and
then what? Matt just left you this house?"

"Everything...he left me everything."

"Why would he do that?" Clyde scowls.

"I was his fiancé," I say candidly.

Clyde's eyes widen. "His fiancé? But you're..." He looks me
over from head to toe.

I touch my hand to my hair, knowing it looks a bit wild. It
spills over my arms in brown waves. "I'm what?"

"Human," Clyde says softly, watching my reaction.

I blink before I look down at myself, and then back at him.
"Uh, yeah, I'm not a Barbie like he used to date. I'm normal, just
like you."

His lips stretch in a grim line. "Yeah...just like me."

He jumps up then in agitation; his chair skids away from him. Striding to the glass door of the house, it opens instantly for him. He enters yelling, "SO-WAH!" SOA materializes in front of him and Clyde rants, "WHAT THE FFFFUUU—"

"Careful," SOA cuts him off in warning, "don't lose your head."

I rise from my seat and go to the doorway. Clyde growls at SOA. "Matteyo can't be dead! I'm still marked!" Clyde holds up his wrist, displaying his tattoos. "Where is he?" Clyde demands.

"That is classified," Source One Alpha states.

"Who else knows Matt has divided?" Clyde demands.

"Maybelle Younger and—"

"MAY KNOWS!" he shouts, his hands balling into fists. "Ffffffaaaaaa! We're screwed! It's only a matter of time before she comes here! We gotta go!" Clyde starts ranting again, but in a language I've never heard before. I watch him for a few moments and hear SOA answer him with the same gibberish.

Paling, I feel disoriented. I turn away from them to stare at the water. Darkness is descending and a storm will be rolling in soon; lightning flashes in the sky beyond the cliffs. The wind is still calm yet, but the temperature is dropping.

I shiver and pull the blanket closer. The phosphorescent glow of fireflies illuminate randomly across the patio. But, over the lake where I'd been earlier, it's a different story. The fireflies have collected like a neon sign, blinking as one as if to say: here, here, here.

Clyde approaches me from behind and grabs my elbow. He snarls, "We have to go. Now!"

"What? Why?" I argue, trying to wrest my elbow away from him, but his grip is too strong.

"So-wah was listening in on May when she was trashing
Matt's apartment; he has filled me in on what's been going on in
Chicago for the past few months. Matt's an idiot—I don't care if he
is the most powerful being on the planet; he's still an idiot! What
was he thinking? By making you his fiancé he has made you a
target! The shooting wasn't random. They tried to assassinate you
when they found out that Matt intended to marry you."

"What are you talking about?" I ask. Adrenaline enters my
bloodstream like a chemical reaction. "What kind of person does
something like that?"

Clyde lets go of my elbow and uses his fingers to tick off
suspects. "May Younger, her family, the Gramercies—take your
pick. They're not about to let Matteyo marry a human. He's the
Sweven. He can make you his slave, but you can't be his wife!"

"His slave?" My mind reels at the implication of that word.
"Who are you freaky people?"

He groans and threads his fingers behind his head before
looking up at the sky. "You think we're people? We're Willas!
How can you be Matt's fiancé? Why didn't he tell you anything?"
He grasps my elbow again and pulls me toward the house, picking
up my purse in his other hand. "Do you have anything else you
need? We're leaving now."

"I'm not going anywhere!" I fight against him in earnest.
Dragging me inside like I weigh nothing, he grabs my wallet out of
my purse. He shoves it in his back pocket before tossing my purse
aside. Then he changes tactics; bending down, he hoists me over
his shoulder. When I struggle to break free, his hand comes up and
swats my butt. "Stop! If they find you, you're dead."

He moves toward the front door. In moments, we're outside by
Mattie's SUV. He sets me down on my feet and opens the

passenger door for me. "WAIT!" I shout, resisting his hand on my back as he urges me to get in. "You said something before about Mattie being divided! What did you mean by that?"

Clyde pauses. He takes my wallet from his pocket and throws it on the seat before he says, "Matt's energy was divided from his body. He was shot, right?"

I nod.

He shakes his head. "It would've probably stopped his heart for a few days, but his body would've healed itself. His energy would've remained until his body was fixed. Something happened to divide him from his body."

"He would've healed? How's that possible?" I ask, as fear raises bumps on my flesh.

"We're not like you, Violet. We have several more chromosomes than you and our genes that control the integrity of those chromosomes are—we don't have time for me to explain this!" He moves to pick me up again.

I try to distract him. "You're not like me?" I reach out and touch his warm arm, tracing the serpentine symbols that twist over his wrist. "What are you like?"

When my eyes meet his blue ones again, he says, "I'm like all the other Willawayetians. Matt is one of us—the strongest—the Sweven."

Whatever color I had in my cheeks has to be gone. "So...you're, what? An—"

"Alien," he says before I can get the word out. "But I'm sure I've been here longer than you, so technically you're the noob."

My hands begin to tremble, but I smirk in disbelief, "How long have you been here?"

He shrugs. "A few hundred years."

My mouth feels dry as I say sarcastically, "Only a few hundred?"

He gives me the first smile since the convenience store. "Yeah, but I'm very young."

My fingers recoil from him. I take a step back. "Matt is an alien?"

Clyde's smile slips away. "He's the Sweven—the vision in our dreams and our ruler in this district."

"This district?" I squeak.

"Earth," he replies.

"Why are you here?"

"Why are you here? Why is anybody here?" Clyde asks with exasperation. When I just stare at him he growls and says, "Think of Earth as a fiefdom. Matt is the overlord of this planet. He holds it for our race."

"Matt is the ruler?" I choke on the word.

"He is," he replies grimly. "There are other Willas in other realms who are equal to him in power. But make no mistake, he is feared everywhere. He's the ruler of this district."

"When you say ruler—"

His eyes narrow and he moves to try to pick me up again. I hold up both my hands and rest them against his chest. "Wait!" He stops, looking at my hands on him. "How can you tell that Mattie is still your leader—even when he's...urr, divided?"

"My markings would've disappeared if he'd been destroyed."

"You'd lose your tattoos?" I ask. "How? Why?"

"That's not important now! How did Matt become separated from his body?"

"I told you! Someone with a gun—"

Clyde sighs in frustration. "I mean after he was shot. What happened afterward?"

"One of the bullets tore through Mattie and into me. We fell together on the sidewalk; he was lying next to me." I glance up at Clyde's eyes and my throat tightens painfully, making me whisper, "There was so much blood."

"Then what happened?" he urges me.

Removing my hands from him, I rub my forehead, trying to think. I swallow hard against the lump in my throat. "Then he said he loved me—that everything would be okay." My voice gets thin again. "He reached for my hand—he was the one dying and he was trying to comfort me. He's like that—always in charge, you know?" I ask.

Clyde nods, "I know."

"The paramedics—they wouldn't let me stay with him! I begged them, but they wouldn't listen to me. They strapped me to a gurney—I don't remember much after that. When I woke up, I was in a hospital room—Stan was there."

"Stanley Parker?"

"That's right, do you know him?

He snorts and says, "Yeah, I know him—Matt's one-hundredth college roommate, complete slacker, along for the ride."

I ignore his comments. "He told me Mattie was dead. He said Mattie's body was a mess. Mattie didn't have any family and I was sedated, so Stan made the decision to have Mattie cremated. He made all the funeral arrangements."

"He had Matt burned! Of all the stupid—" Clyde exhales a deep breath in an attempt to gain composure. "You're sure? Does he still have him? Where are Matt's ashes now?"

"Safe," I lie. The urn is on the dock by the lake, hidden under my t-shirt, but I'm not telling him that.

Clyde grasps both my upper arms and lifts me off my feet to his eye level. With his jaw clenched tight, he says, "Where are Matt's ashes? We need them, Violet. Without them, I have nothing to bargain with May or the Gramercies for your life."

Whatever fear I was feeling at his anger and strength is pushed back at the mention of May's name. "She's never getting him!" I promise with a scowl.

"You might feel differently when she's ripping your teeth out one by one," Clyde counters.

"I'll take my chances," I growl.

"You won't be alone!" he retorts. "I'm obligated to protect you. Wherever you go, I go—and I gotta tell you, we're outnumbered and outgunned. Without his ashes, we have nothing!"

"I don't want your help! I want you to leave me alone!"

His lips stretch in a grim line. Pivoting, he dumps me on the passenger seat of Mattie's truck before he slams the door shut. He's at the driver's side door in only a fraction of a second, climbing in and starting the ignition. "I don't care what you want. You'd better start listening to me; I'm the only friend you've got."

"My friends don't abduct me, Clyde," I retort, going for the door handle to escape.

His hand glows with green fire as he lifts it up. My door is frozen shut. I try to lift the lock, but it won't budge.

I glance back at Clyde, breathing heavily.

"They do if you're marked for death."

The rain begins to fall outside. It spatters the windshield in soft drops that cut the beams of the headlights. As I look out at it, a hulking shape ape-drops from a tree in front of us...and then another and another and another. A shadowy figure sidles down the dog-eared ivy from the rooftop of the house. Fear like I've never known before makes me feel as if I'm swallowing marbles.

Clyde groans next to me. Urgently, he looks in the backseat and finds the brown bag he gave me at the store. Plucking the tube of sunblock from it, he twists off the cap. He lifts my hand in his and squeezes a huge dollop onto my palm. "Smear this on your skin," he says.

"Who are they?" I ask.

"They're Gramercies," he says. "Put it on!" He shoves my hand toward me.

In shock, I rub my palms together, and then apply the lotion to my legs.

"Get your arms and face, too," he urges. "Hurry!"

Absently, I rub my arms, and then with what is left, I apply it to my face. While still rubbing my skin, Clyde holds up the vodka and takes a giant gulp of it.

"Did you put that on your lips?" he asks.

"No," I shake my head.

"Good. Don't." He lowers the vodka and hides it behind the steering wheel as he pours a little in his hand, rubbing it on his neck like cologne.

"Are ya gonna share that?" I grasp the neck of the bottle, touching his hand.

He flinches and yanks his arm with the bottle back from me. Smoke and red welts rise from where I touched him. "Ahhh!" he hisses. "Do me a favor and try not to touch me with that crap. And if you want to live, play along!"

The doors of the truck all unlock, seemingly on their own, and fly open. The shapes move so fast they blur, and then stop just

45

outside the pools of light from the truck. This must be madness, I think. I've gone mad.

Chapter 5 – ASHES TO FIRE

"Just so you know, we're probably dead, unless you want to tell me where Matt's ashes are," Clyde mutters grimly. I shake my head no. "We're screwed," he says under his breath, before he stumbles drunkenly from the truck to face the men outside.

Thunder rumbles in the distance as rain makes dark marks on Clyde's t-shirt. He raises the vodka bottle to his lips and takes a huge sip. Pulling it away from his lips, he wipes his mouth on his sleeve, swaying a little. After squinting into the darkness, he grins broadly. "Heeeyyyyy! It's the Gramercies!" he laughs drunkenly, gesturing in their direction with his arm. "Gramercies...do you guys ever just laugh at the irony of your name? You know, since you're all such ruthless, unmerciful bastards?" He takes another swig of vodka.

Five men prowl forward from the shadows and into the pools of light from the headlights. One has on a long, black leather coat with a soft cowl-like hoodie over his short blond hair "You're funny, Clyde, for a member of the Parish family," comes his deep, rumbling voice. He scratches his beard; he's a beast of a male who looks like he lives at the gym. "It's tragic how your uncle sold you into servitude—he probably wasn't aware of just how entertaining you can be."

Clyde receives the comment with a grin. "It's sad, eh, Milligan, to be so misunderstood? He's a serious Willa. No sense of humor." He squints at the males next to Milligan. "Did you bring the whole gang with you? It's Joplin, Tellico, Ellis— FLOYD!" He points at the enormous one who looks like he regularly chews on nails. "I see the arm grew back, Floyd! You can't still be mad about that—you dared me to rip it off—"

Milligan puts up his hand as Floyd takes an aggressive step toward Clyde. Floyd stops, but he watches Clyde with a vicious snarl on his lips. Rain drips off Milligan's woolen hood. "This isn't a social call. We're looking for something. Maybe you can help us out with it?"

"Maybe I can, but can you answer me a question first?"

"What's that, Clyde?" Milligan asks with a sinister smile.

"Why do you guys always have such shit timing? Can't you see I'm on a date here?" Clyde gestures to me in the truck.

"She must not know who you are," he smirks. "Or does she like slaves?"

"Sweetheart," Clyde calls, reaching out his hand and gesturing for me to join him. "Come here."

I feel my heart speed up and beat out of sync. My eyes follow the length of Clyde's outstretched arm to his eyes. He squints at me silently, his blue eyes communicating the weight of his request. I square my shoulders and emerge from the truck. Rain wets my hair as I try to plaster a sensual kind of smile on my lips.

I walk to his side. Clyde gathers me to him when I'm within reach; his hand cups my butt as he draws me to his strong chest. The caress causes my skin to alight with a new awareness of him. His other hand threads in my hair, holding my head still so I can't pull away as his lips move to mine. He kisses me deeply, and I

48

groan in surprise, not only because I didn't expect him to kiss me, but also because the heat of it sends shivers through me.

Slowly, Clyde ends our kiss, pulling back and biting his bottom lip for a moment as he gazes into my eyes, like he felt something, too. "She doesn't know what I am. She only knows that she likes it. Isn't that right, Brie?" Clyde calls me by the wrong name with a wicked smile. He pretends to look me over with lover's eyes.

I twirl a piece of my hair around my finger as I smile softly. "That's right, baby."

Clyde acts like he can't look away from me as he says to Milligan, "I know you're not here to see me—an untouchable. I haven't seen Matt around lately. He doesn't check in with me."

"We're not looking for Matteyo. We're looking for his human."

"His human?" Clyde's eyebrow rises in question as he glances at Milligan. "Matt has a human?"

Milligan sounds amused. "He does. Or did. He doesn't have much of anything now." Deep rumbling laughter comes from the Gramercies behind Milligan. I stiffen and Clyde pulls me tighter to his chest in warning, rubbing my back.

"I haven't seen Matt in over a year. He doesn't check in with me. Tell him to call me when you find him, there's a bunch of shit I need from him." Clyde's arm shifts to my shoulder as he turns and walks us back toward the house.

"Where are you going? We're not done here, Clyde."

Clyde doesn't stop, but moves toward the front door of the house. "Fine, just let me get rid of Brie so we can talk more openly. I don't want to have to censor her because you've said too much."

Headlights from the dark part of the driveway turn on, illuminating us all. I look over my shoulder at the feminine form emerging from the vehicle. I recognize May instantly. The hood of her scarlet coat covers her long blond hair and most of her face, but I'd know her anywhere because of her bearing. She walks with the poise of one who expects the world to bow at her feet.

"That's her," May growls behind us. "Matt's little toy woman."

Clyde pauses; I glance at him, seeing his eyes close in frustration. When he opens them, he turns us back around to face May and the Gramercies. May stops beneath the soggy pine trees near Milligan. She swipes the hood away from her face, exposing her ivory skin. Thick, red lipstick stands out starkly on her sculptured lips as she smiles at me.

"Where are they?" She asks me.

My eyebrows rise. "Where are who?" I murmur.

"Matt's ashes?"

I shrug. "They're at my apartment," I lie.

A skeptical look crosses May's lovely face. "We've been to your hovel; they're not there." She holds up the papers from the lawyers—the ones with the details of this lake property. She throws the papers at me; the white leaves curl and scatter, floating to the muddy ground between us.

I would turn and walk away from her, but Clyde has me pinned to his side like a kept animal. Clyde leans drunkenly on me as he says, "We don't have Matt. He's gone. Bye-bye! I'm sure he'll find you when he grows a new body and reunites with himself, it should only take a couple hundred years. He probably knows you tried to kill him; I'm sure you'll be the first one he looks for."

May's beautiful face looks wasp-stung as she jerks her cherry-red fingernail at me. "I tried to have her killed! She's going to ruin

50

everything! She has enslaved Matteyo. I was only trying to free him!"

"Free him!" Clyde laughs, "Your drug addict blew him full of holes! You divided him! You think he's not going to be upset about that?"

"All I need are his remains. I'll have the proverbial genie in a bottle. He'll be beholden to me when I let him out and reunite him. I just have to locate where he has collected—"

Clyde doubles over, dragging me with him as he laughs himself silly. He straightens and looks at May. "You think so?" Clyde shakes his head. "I think you're delusional. I think he'll just be really pissed off when his soul merges with his body again. He's the Sweven; he's beholden to no one." He speaks to the conclave of wet monsters next to her. "May is just going to get you killed. You know that, right?"

May's voice is thin when she says, "You're the one who is as good as dead, Clyde. I've already spoken to the Dexfields. They'll pay me any price I ask just for the honor of cutting your head off! So don't speak your heresy to me!"

"Heresy? You think you're the authority now?"

"I'm acting on Matteyo's behalf as his intended geltry."

Clyde laughs with derision. "You're not his geltry! She's his intended geltry!" Clyde indicates me with a nod. "You're the hag he threw away. How long has it been, a couple centuries? Get over it! The only thing you are to him is a stalker."

"I have the bloodlines—"

"My family had the bloodlines, too. Look what happened to us. That's the thing about blood, May, it's worthless without power."

"You're a heretic!"

51

"It's not heresy I'm speaking, May. It's fire." Clyde's grin is deranged, like a cornered dog's. He takes another huge swig of vodka before he pulls the bottle from his lips. He spews the alcohol in a shower at May and Milligan. At the same time, green orbs of light the size of his palms manifest in his hands like magic. Touching the light to the alcohol fountain spraying from his mouth, it ignites the mist. He resembles a dragon breathing green fire.

May and Milligan become torches engulfed in the flames. Hair and skin burn with the acrid smell of a crematorium. Joplin whips his coat off, throwing it over May's screaming head to extinguish the fire, but Milligan continues to burn with unearthly shrieks. Clyde tosses the rest of the bottle of vodka at him and he becomes unrecognizable within the inferno.

Clyde lets go of me and pushes me in the direction of the house. "RUN!" he yells.

My footsteps make crunching sounds as I crush pine needles in my attempt to make it to the front door. Before I get there, I'm lifted off my feet and held fast against a hard body. My heart convulses in fear when I glance at Floyd with his Neanderthal face mere inches from mine. His breath hisses like a viper in my ear as he spins me around.

Tellico and Ellis attack Clyde with brightly colored orbs of orange and lavender light. It issues from each one, like a battle of lost souls in the night. They stretch and coil and crouch, their light bleeding like terrible banners when they throw them. Trees splinter and catch fire as Clyde evades each comet. He returns their colorful barrage with a green light of his own; but with every return volley his light pales, becoming less emerald and more lime.

I struggle in Floyd's arms, but it's a simple thing for him to hold me. He's over a foot taller than me with a hundred times my strength. As I watch the fight between these strange creatures, I realize that with each shot they take, their lights get dimmer and dimmer, until finally, they're just throwing sparks at each other. Clyde slumps behind a fallen tree, panting and waning in the rain. Thunder rumbles in deep, piercing claps.

Joplin steadies May with an arm around her shoulder. She looks gruesome; half of her face has been burnt to peeling flakes of charred, blackened skin like corroded metal upon rust-colored flesh. She leans heavily on him, as she says, "Floyd," her voice the pitch of a rusty gate, "make her tell you where she's hidden the urn!"

Floyd gives me a wicked grin. "What do you taste like, little human?" He asks me. His tongue snakes out of his mouth and he presses it to my cheek, licking me. I hear sizzling sounds; smoke and flames rise from his mouth, his tongue melting within it like he consumed battery acid. Screaming in pain, he drops me as he clutches his hands to his mouth in agony.

Set free, I run for the house. Poseidon's eyes mounted to the door brighten when I near it, scanning me with green light. It opens immediately. Pounding feet behind me makes me look back at Floyd. Blood and saliva drip from the corners of his mouth, but it's his eyes that scare me most; they're murderous.

I enter the foyer and SOA manifests near me. "Get behind me," SOA orders. I obey. When Floyd crosses the foyer, high-powered red beams of light from the tracks on the ceiling shine down on him, cutting his torso in half. The pieces of him slip to the floor to flop around like caught fish on a ship's deck. I scream in terror and back away from the bloody horror in shock.

53

Just when Floyd stops twitching, Clyde is shoved into the foyer to shield Ellis and Tellico behind him. With his hands behind his head, Clyde slowly comes toward me into the main room. His expression is grim as he stares at me with a look of apology in his eyes. Tellico raises his hand and shoots orange beams of light at the ceiling, disabling the lasers mounted there. SOA's hologram disappears from sight as sparks rain down from above.

Joplin enters moments later, helping a wheezing May into the house. She shuffles through the foyer and past the bloody mess that used to be Floyd. Pausing at the entrance of the main room, May shrugs off Joplin's hand on her arm. Gingerly she lifts her watch and opens the face of it. She plucks out what looks like microscopic dust specks and pinches them like nutmeg over her burned face.

"Have you found the urn, yet?" May demands. She adds another dash of dust to her burnt scalp where her long, silky hair was singed off. Her face is forming a film, not unlike cobwebs, over the damaged area.

Ellis shakes his head, his brown hair falls over his thick forehead. "It could be anywhere."

"Make her tell you where it is!" May growls, closing her watch face with a snap. Her hairline that was destroyed is beginning to sprout new growth. Blond, spiky wisps push through the webbing over her scalp.

Ellis leers at me before he frowns. "She's covered in zinc oxide," he replies, his brown eyes scanning me. "I can't even touch her!" He extends his hand towards me. "See?" he says in frustration. "I can't levitate her while she has that crap on her skin. It repels everything."

May lifts her hand; it glows red. She directs her palm towards the bookcase. Thick, heavy volumes fly off the shelf towards me as she swings her hand in my direction. I put my arms up to protect my face, cringing as I see them coming. When the first leather bound book is a fraction from striking me, it stops dead and drops to the floor in front of me. The other books take the same course. May hisses, "There's an entire lake in the backyard. Go wash her off! Then you can employ any means necessary to make her talk."

"Zinc oxide is insoluble in water," Ellis complains.

Joplin pitches a bottle of wine from Mattie's kitchen at Ellis; he catches it easily. Joplin gives him a brilliant smile. "Pour this on her and then drop her in the water. The acid in the wine will take it off. Make her scrub in there or she never comes out."

Ellis's thuggish face lights up; he smiles at me wickedly. "It's an expensive bottle, but she's worth it." He sets the wine on a table. Shedding his dark trench coat, he straightens the sleeves of his thin, black cashmere sweater. He extracts gloves from his coat pocket and puts them on. Retrieving the wine, he approaches me in an assessing way.

"Don't do this," Clyde growls at Ellis, but Tellico has taken off his black belt and wrapped it around Clyde's hands, restraining them behind his back.

"Shut up," Tellico sneers at him before he levitates a marble figurine of the world from the coffee table and bashes it into the back of Clyde's head. Clyde falls into a chair by the glass door. Blood trickles from his scalp onto the white fabric, staining it red.

"Here we go, Violet," Ellis says. With his meaty fist full of my sweater, Ellis drags me outside and down to the end of the dock. Using one hand, he dangles me over the water. "You're a real beauty, eh—so petite. I like 'em small," he winks at me. "There's something about ya—I see what the Sweven saw in you."

"You're disgusting, Ellis!" I try to scratch his face but he leans away from me.

"Oh-ho and lively! Ready to get wet now?" he asks. He holds the wine bottle away from him and the cork pops out of the bottle, as if it were champagne. He holds it over me, pouring wine on my face. My eyes squeeze shut as I sputter. He douses wine on my hands and sprays some on my legs. When the bottle is empty, he tosses it, making a splash in the water. He sticks his finger near my face. "Scrub hard now. I want to touch every inch of you."

He opens his gloved fist and drops me in the icy water; I begin to sink to the bottom. Struggling to pull my sweater off over my head, I free myself from it. I kick out underwater, swimming as far as I can away from the dock.

My lungs ache from holding my breath. Unable to go further without more air, I resurface and glance back at the dock. Ellis raises his hand and a burst of lavender-colored light illuminates the sky above me. When he locates me, Ellis steps off the wooden planks of the dock. His dress shoes splash on the top of the water and he strolls toward me on the surface as if it were a puddle on pavement. I make a gagging sound and turn to swim in the opposite direction, but within a few seconds, Ellis reaches down and yanks me out of the water by my neck.

He has taken off his gloves and my throat burns as he holds me out from him with his arm extended. "You can't go now, Violet. We're about to have some fun." Ellis's smile is nefarious. He licks his lips, beginning to say something else when he stops abruptly and looks down at his feet.

His expression changes instantly from one of satisfaction to one of terror. As I clutch his hands at my throat, I feel his skin grow icy. His face begins to wrinkle, his hair turns white. His ruthless brown eyes sink into his skull as his flesh retracts, losing hydration. They dry up like beads of glass. His nose collapses into his face as his lips curl up, receding from his teeth. Ashy skin flakes from his cheeks before it crumbles like sand and drops into the water beneath us.

The light from above extinguishes as Ellis's arm that holds me extended breaks off suddenly; I plunge back into the black water. The rest of Ellis caves in and splashes beneath the surface, leaving just his clothes floating near me. I scream, but all that comes out are shallow horror-filled whimpers. "Mattie?" I croak his name as I begin to cry softly, but there is no answer.

May's garbled voice yells from just outside the house, "Ellis?" The entire interior is illuminated behind her. She limps further out onto the patio, looking toward the dock. Tellico and Joplin are still inside, tearing the rooms apart looking for Mattie's ashes. Clyde remains slumped in the chair just by the door, unconscious.

My eyes shift to the dock; I can just make out the silhouette of Mattie's urn beneath the white of my t-shirt. She'll find him, I think as I struggle to keep my head above water. "She's not getting him," I murmur aloud.

As quietly as possible, I swim back to the dock. When I make it to the ladder, I ease myself out of the water.

"Ellis?" May's harsh voice drifts to me from somewhere near the other end.

I creep to the post that hides the urn. Chilled to the marrow of my bones, my hands shake as I uncover it. It's smooth to the touch like a river stone. I fumble to unscrew the lid. The planks creak on the dock as May nears me. I back to the ladder and hold the urn out over the water.

"Stop!" May makes a harrowing screeching sound when she sees me and realizes what I'm doing. She extends her hand; it begins to glow with red light. I tilt the opening of the urn toward the water threateningly. She immediately drops her hands and takes a step back. "Wait!" She gives me a glare that would turn my bones to dust if it could.

"Let Clyde go," I order with venom.

"Do you have feelings for Matt's slave? That's priceless!" May tries to smile, but her burnt skin pulls; soot cracks and falls from it. Her smile turns rancid and becomes a wince. She calls over her shoulder, "Bring Clyde here!"

Tellico and Joplin spill out onto the porch. When they see us, Tellico goes back inside for a moment. He must have flipped a switch in the house because lights turn on and glow from each post along the dock, defining our features with a soft haze.

"What did you do to Ellis?" May asks as she looks around.

"He couldn't swim," I lie. "He drowned."

The webs of new flesh on May's cheek get thicker; tiny, dust-speck spiders crawl in and out of it. May's scowl is one of unease. "You're lying! He doesn't need to swim! What did you do to him?"

"I didn't do anything to him," I answer honestly.

Fear enters May's eyes as she asks, "He's here, isn't he?"

"Who?" I counter, wanting her to say his name.

"This is where he has collected. His spirit is in the lake, isn't it?"

"What are you talking about?" I ask with a shiver.

"It doesn't matter if he's here. He still needs his remains and an energy source to reunite," she murmurs.

Tellico emerges again from the house, this time with Clyde. He and Joplin drag Clyde down to the dock. They drop him near May's feet. He curls up and groans, clutching his head.

May looks deeply concerned now. She extends her hand to me once more and motions me with her fingers. "Give me the urn, Violet, or I'll kill him," she threatens.

My knees strike together in fear. I want to run senseless into the night.

Clyde stirs. "Don't give him to them, Violet!" he groans. "They're gonna kill us anyway!"

My eyes connect with Clyde's and I know he's right. "I'm sorry," I murmur to him. "A toast then, to the dying and the dead." I tip the urn.

May's hand comes up again, her sharp nails scratch the air. An anguished sound drones from her as Mattie's ashes cascade from the cold vessel. They fall down to drown in black water. The lake takes them over and hisses like I touched a hot iron to it. A blue glow emerges on the surface. Cerulean mist rises up, swirling and billowing. It entwines as it reaches toward the sky, growing and climbing over itself like a winding beanstalk of water and light. It illuminates the night in a fiery blue aurora, connecting with the storm clouds above.

Deep rumblings of thunder fall down on us; they ripple the water below. My hand weakens in fear and the urn slips from it, hitting the lake with a splash. An instant later, an enormous shaft of white lightning spews downward from the sky. It encompasses the stalk of blue light, turning it bright white and tearing the night in two. I flinch as electricity hits the black water, branching out in a roadmap of fiery veins. I'm knocked off my feet, blown back from the exploding current.

We lay on the dock like pearls from a broken necklace. The smell of burnt fish is everywhere; it sticks in my lungs as would tar to a rooftop. Certain that I'm dead, I close my eyes to wait for everything to fade away and my pain to end.

Chapter 6 – I MIGHT BE CRAZY

I open my eyes to find it's darker again. All but one of the lights has extinguished. My cheek rests against a wooden plank. The lightning and rain have disappeared, but an unearthly crack of thunder shears the air around me, causing me to grimace and scrunch my face up tight. The dock trembles at the sound, threatening to plunge us into the lake. I gather my limbs to me, curling up in pain. My eyes open again just as a man-shaped silhouette of fire rises straight up from the water. I blink hard, and then stare at his flickering flames as he walks forward over the lake towards us.

The man of fire pauses and bends down, lifting Ellis's clothing from the water. The fire begins to change to flesh as the flames extinguish. He shrugs on Ellis's dress pants; they hang loosely over his flat stomach and hips. Strolling barefoot on the surface again, he grows nearer.

"Mattie," I murmur as my heart races. He's bare-chested; my eyes drink in his flawless skin, noticing how it pulls taut against his lean-muscled abdomen, accentuating the perfection of his physique. His black hair is made even more so, wet and slicked back from his handsome face. It's longer, too, than it had been a few months ago when I last saw him alive. Bristles of a beard cover his strong jawline, making him look different because he always maintained a close shave...and his eyes...his eyes glow blue like captured moonbeams.

When he reaches the dock, Mattie doesn't hesitate, but comes right to me. I feel him before he even touches me. He's electric and when his skin meets mine the current within him jumps to me. It's painful at first and I grimace, but then the energy subsides. He scoops me up in his arms and I relax against his warm chest. With his finger, he brushes my hair back from my eyes. "Violet," he says my name softly.

His voice is Mattie's. It causes my throat to tighten instantly. "Mattie?" I croak again, unable to say anything more.

Joplin stirs to life near us and climbs to his feet. He looks as surprised to be alive as I am and even more shocked to see Mattie. Mattie's eyes leave me for a moment and his expression changes in an instant from adoring to vengeful.

Mattie continues to hold me effortlessly with one arm while he lifts his other. In his palm, a marble-size ball of blue light forms and grows. It's looks like a perfect sphere of blown glass. As it gets bigger, I see inside the circle. White clouds swirl along with silvery shimmering bursts of energy.

Joplin sees it, too; he raises his hands out in front of him. "I was ordered to be here. It's not my fault!" The light in Mattie's hand continues to grow bigger and brighter, making Joplin more desperate. Panting, Joplin points at May. "She had you killed! It wasn't me! She wanted your girl dead, but you were hit instead!"

A snarl rips from Mattie, like something wild abides inside of him. Without a word, he winds his arm back and throws the orb at Joplin. It strikes him in the head, exploding his brains all over Tellico next to him. Joplin's body falls to the dock in a puddle of blood. Tellico sinks to his knees in supplication, but it does no good. Mattie throws another blue ball of light at him and he's nearly torn in half; pieces of him fall everywhere.

May pushes herself up from her sprawled position on the planks. She rises to her knees and bows her head to Mattie in surrender. "Matteyo, I'm the one who came to help you—" When light begins to form in Mattie's hand once more, May screeches, "You can't kill me, Matteyo! It'll be war." Fear and desperation drip from May as she wrings her hands, unsure of what he'll do.

Mattie growls in frustration before he grits his teeth. "Run, Maybelle," Mattie says with a look of pure malice, "run far away and hide until I forget about you."

May gets to her feet and does as he ordered. She runs past us, out over the water at a speed I can't even fathom. Her feet make small splashing sounds as rippling rings billow out in her path over the lake, but they quickly fade and disappear as if they were never there at all. It only takes her a few seconds to fade into the night.

"Are you hurt?" Mattie asks while his hands travel over my limbs in an assessing way.

I shake my head no, but my lips answer, "I don't know."

He buries his face in my neck, holding me like we're the only two here. "Violet," he says with his lips, nuzzling me. My body becomes alive in an instant, craving his touch. "You came for me."

"You can't be real," I murmur, my hand traces the muscular curve of his shoulder. My tears blind me.

"This is real. I'm real," Mattie assures me with a look of concern that melts my heart. "You saved me."

"How did I do that?" I ask.

"You reunited my spirit with my body when you poured my ashes into the lake."

His eyes are losing their glow, settling back to a normal hue. It reminds me that he's not the Mattie I know; he may be the same person, but he never showed me this side of himself before. He never trusted me with his secrets. "I missed you so much...but I've been missing a lie. I've been in love with a lie," I murmur. I'm trembling all over and I can't stop.

"Shhh, you're going into shock, Vi. You're safe now—everything will be okay—I'll take care of you. I'll fix everything. I promise." He kisses my temple, and strokes my hair.

I want to believe him. "You took all those bullets for me," I whisper.

His lips turn down in a grim line. "That should never have happened. I was blind. I underestimated my enemies. It won't happen again. From now on, you'll always be protected."

Clyde groans and tries to sit up, but he clutches his head and lays back down on the dock.

"Stay there, Clyde," Mattie orders with concern in his tone. "I'll be back shortly to help you. I'm just going to take Violet to the house." He moves at a speed that makes me dizzy. In an instant, we're on the porch. The glass door opens for us and he carries me over the threshold. Mattie places me gingerly on a leather chair with a matching ottoman. Taking the blanket from the arm of it, he lays it across my knees. He sinks down to my eye level and uses his finger to tuck my hair behind my ear.

"You're safe here, Vi. I won't let anyone hurt you. Do you understand?" he asks me gravely. I nod because my throat is so tight I can't speak. He places a kiss on my forehead, "Don't be afraid. I'll be right back."

I nod again. He immediately rises and is gone before I can blink. As soon as I realize that I'm alone, I put my hands to my face. It takes me a second to realize I'm crying. I pull my hands from my eyes and look around, spotting a box of tissues on the side table next to me. Reaching for it, my arm shakes so much I knock over a picture on the table. I pick it up to set it back where it had been until I notice it's a black and white picture of Mattie. I wipe my tears on my sleeve. He's standing in a field in front of an enormous zeppelin. Next to him is a bald man with spectacles and a white handlebar mustache. The caption reads, "With Ferdinand, 1910." My finger traces Mattie's young face, his three-piece suit, the chain of his watch fob that hangs from his vest pocket...the frame slips from my fingers and shatters on the floor.

Rising from the chair, I stumble toward the front door. A groan slips from me when Floyd's dismembered body in the foyer blocks my path. I look away from him as I skirt his blood and flee from the house.

I walk numbly by the open passenger door of the Escalade. When I realize my wallet is lying on the seat, I go back and pick it up. Looking in the back seat, the bottle of white wine peeks out at me from the brown bag. I take that, too. Moving away from Mattie's car, I unscrew the cap to the wine and take a deep sip. The headlights of May's Mercedes SUV blind me. I walk toward them.

When I get to May's car, I open the door and climb in. The keys are in the ignition. Starting the engine, I turn the truck around and miss Milligan's charred body by inches as I pull away from the house.

I should probably tell Mattie where I'm going, but he might try to talk me out of leaving, or stop me...and I have to go because, what do you say to someone who has lied to you about who he is? What do you say to that same person when he comes back from the dead and slaughters his enemies? Or, better yet, what do you say to an alien? Words fail me right now; I'll say the wrong thing.

The silence in the Mercedes is definitely unwelcome, so I flip on the stereo and put the accelerator to the floorboard. The car rattles as it hits rocks and branches with bone-jarring effects. I clutch the steering wheel tightly and concentrate on the obscure road. There is only one thing for which I'm fairly certain: I can't tell Stan or Dr. Gobel about this. They'll lock me up and I'll never see daylight again.

Through force of will, I make it to a paved street and turn onto it, pushing the SUV as fast as it'll go. Tears drip from my jaw onto my damp shirt; I wipe then away roughly with the back of my arm, but my eyes never leave the road. I'm having a hard time staying within the lines. I'm desperate to stop the car, but too afraid to ease my foot off the accelerator. I keep riding the snake of blacktop, following its serpentine twists and turns, looking for the tail of the beast so that I can get away.

Street lamps illuminate a town ahead, the lights from which blur and elongate as I drive past. My eyes grow heavy from fatigue. A car passing me, going the other direction, honks furiously as I drift into the opposite lane. I correct the wheel, dodging back onto the right side. Yellow snake eyes appear ahead; as they grow nearer, they morph into the neon sign of a motel. Unable to go further, I pull off the road and park in the lot near the office. It's a motor lodge; all the beige-colored doors on both levels face the wrap-around parking lot.

My forehead rests against the steering wheel as I gather the courage to exit the security of the car. After a minute of deep breathing, I lift my head, opening the car door and braving the short walk to the office. To my relief, the glass doors aren't automated. I pull one open; the scent of coffee stains the air. The lobby is like a fishbowl with picture windows on three sides. I pass a rack of brochures by a fake potted plant and stop at the front desk. The night clerk is alone watching highlights of the Tigers' game on the news. He glances at me through black-rimmed glasses. I manage to mumble my way through procuring a room.

After I pass back the signed credit card receipt to him, he gives me a plastic key within a sleeve, saying, "Room 110—through the doors—turn right—straight down."

"Thank you," I murmur.

I exit the way I came in. Turning right, I pay attention to the numbers on the doors, watching them ascend as I pass each one. I stop in front of a door with a floodlight mounted above it. Locating room 110, I fumble with the keycard. A car door opens and closes near me.

"Violet," Mattie says softly from behind. My heart flutters with desire at the sound of his voice, and then it pumps harder with fear. The basic survival urge of fight or flight nearly overwhelms me. I have no fight left in me at the moment, so there is really only one option. I stiffen and hurriedly place the card in the lock, shoving the door open. "Wait, please!"

The anxiety in his voice makes me hesitate. I glance over my shoulder; he's still bare-chested, wearing the damp, gray dress pants that belonged to Ellis.

"How did you find me?" I ask, leaning against the doorframe for support.

"I've been following you since you left." He uses his thumb to point over his shoulder at his Escalade next to the Mercedes.

"I didn't see you."

"I didn't want to scare you, so I didn't use my headlights. I was afraid you'd wreck."

"Couldn't you just use your super-alien powers to levitate my car and save me?" I ask, my voice thin and raspy, sarcasm my only weapon.

"I don't know—maybe—I couldn't risk it. You're too important to me. I'm a little weak right now."

I pale because he's serious; the information unsettles me even more. "Are you okay?" I ask, worriedly.

He scoffs for a moment, highlighting the ridiculousness of my question, but answers, "I'm physically fine, just weaker than normal."

"Is Clyde okay?" I begin to panic. I left without finding out.

Mattie's eyebrows rise in surprise before he says reassuringly, "He'll be okay. He heals quickly. So-wah contacted Ned. He'll take care of him. Are you okay?" Mattie asks.

I shake my head. "I don't think so. No." My chin trembles for a moment before I clench my teeth and swallow past the lump in my throat. "I'm pretty sure I'm not okay. I don't think I can talk about it right now, Matteyo."

I make a move to enter the room, but pause and cringe in a bracing way when Mattie extends his hand to me and says, "Wait."

He reads my fear and lowers his hand, balling both of them in fists. The starkness of his gaze roots me where I am as he comes closer. His shoulders round protectively towards me as his face nears mine. "I'd never hurt you, Vi. Never."

I look into his blue eyes. His eyebrows rise slightly as he drinks in every inch of me, hesitating on the curvy parts of me that I know he likes the most. He's so incredibly handsome that the effect is nearly blinding. At a foot taller than me he oozes raw, masculine power. It used to thrill me, and at the same time it made me feel safe—to be held in his arms—so wanted—so beloved. A part of me is desperate to feel his touch again, even after everything that has happened tonight. Loving him is slowly unraveling me.

"Everyone thinks I'm crazy, Matt. I must be crazy," I say in a self-effacing way with a small hitch in my voice, "because the Mattie I knew would've told me who he was."

"I wanted to tell you." His hand reaches out, leaning forward and tucking my hair behind my ear. His fingers linger in it.

"Why didn't you?"

"I calculated the risk and it was too high. Losing you was something I couldn't afford."

"Why were you even with me? We're clearly not meant to be together."

He frowns at that. "Do you remember the day we met?" he asks, his finger moving from my hair to the sensitive spot behind my ear. The feeling of his skin on mine is primal; it causes my heart to skip a beat with a growing ache for him.

"Yes," I murmur. "I brought my students to tour your gaming facility at Source Products."

"You did something else. You brought a gift with you."

I color in embarrassment and look away. "I didn't know what to get you to thank you for the art grant you gave the school. I mean, what does one give a billionaire?" I ask softly.

He smiles for the first time and I have to reach out and place my hand on his outstretched arm to steady myself. He leans a bit closer to me, saying, "I was about to go into a meeting with several heads from the automotive industry when my assistant brought your box into my office. I told Fitch to keep whatever it was without even opening it, but he said he'd already seen what it was and that I might regret it. He was right. "

"It was just a small piece from the collection I was working on. It wasn't valuable," I say, thinking of the glass sphere that I'd made. I chose the orb for its symmetry and beautiful blue coloring; it had stratospheric cloud patterns woven into it and bursts of silver—my eyes open wide as a thought occurs to me.

"Yes," Mattie nods intuitively when he hears my deep intake of breath. "The piece of blown glass you made is the mirror image of my light."

"It's a coincidence," I breathe in a whisper, thinking about the light that grew in his palm this evening.

"I calculated the probability; let's just say it's not even in the universe of coincidence."

"Is that why you started pursuing me for a date?" I ask.

"No. It's why I skipped my meeting to find you in the building. I had to interrogate several of my employees to locate you. Everyone who played a part in transporting your gift from the front desk in the lobby was questioned thoroughly. I didn't really start stalking you until after we met on the tour."

"You mean when you pretended to be just another person taking the tour," I state, remembering how he had struck up a conversation with me as we walked from the lobby on the tour. He was charming and intelligent and so absolutely virile that I missed a lot of what the guide was saying, distracted as I was by his provocative gaze.

"It's a good thing I did," he smiles ruefully, "I had the hardest time talking to you after you found out who I was. It was like you swallowed broken glass."

"Extremely powerful men aren't really my type," I murmur.

"I know, you told me several times. I've never had to work so hard to get a date." He squeezes the back of my neck gently, triggering a carnal shiver to slip through me. I missed him so much. Him. This Mattie. Not the scary one at the lake.

"But you're so much more than what you've shown me, aren't you?" I challenge. "You're a ruler—you own slaves!" I say with tremendous disdain because it may be the worst offense in the litany of violations I've discovered.

"I own one slave," he corrects me. "Clyde. And I only bought him to protect him. If I hadn't, he'd be dead now. If I free him, they'll kill him without my name to protect him."

"Why?"

"He's the heir to another district. His family, the Parishes, were unseated. He's a threat to the new ruling family there. They want him dead. He's my friend; I'm not going to let that happen." The corner of his lip tightens with contempt for the situation.

I raise my hand to his face, smoothing the spot near his lip with my thumb. The action is completely involuntary. When I realize it, I drop my hand. I exhale a long breath before I shake my head. "This is all so crazy. You're like—" I struggle for a word.

"An alien," Mattie provides softly. "We prefer to be called 'Willas.'"

I nod solemnly. "Right...you're a Willa and I'm—what do you even see in me?"

"You're kidding, right?" he asks, like it's an insane question. When I just stare at him, he says, "You showed me how to love, Vi. I thought I was incapable of it."

My eyes narrow perceptibly. "That's because you'd been with May."

71

He shakes his head slowly, "No. It's because I hadn't met you—I wasn't with you. You're the variable in this scenario. You're everything I could want. You're creative, intelligent—you have the best sense of humor. You're extremely beautiful and brave—loyal. After I found you, I would've done anything to protect my secret from you until I was positive you'd be able to handle it."

"What if I can't handle it?" I ask in a tormented whisper.

His legs spread to either side of mine. Heat warms me through my t-shirt as he places his hand on the small of my back. His fingers on my nape move to entangle in my hair. Leaning down, he rests his forehead against my brow. "You'll handle it. We're connected, you and I. You heard me calling for you. You came to find me. We're meant to be, Violet."

His forehead lifts from me as his lips draw nearer; mine part in response to their proximity. His mouth hovers a fraction away, but he doesn't kiss me. He waits.

A need inside me builds. I crave him so much it's a physical ache. It's more than lust. When he died, something shattered inside of me. Now that he's here, there's hope that what's broken can be mended.

Slowly, I inch forward. My breath catches when I feel the firmness of his lips against mine. It weakens my knees. I place my hand on his chest to steady myself; the strong beat of his heart plays for me beneath my fingertips. My face flushes. "Mattie," I say against his lips.

He deepens our kiss, pulling hard on my bottom lip so that I feel it in my core. "Don't ask me to let you go, Vi," he says with sultry roughness against my lips, "I won't."

Sliding his hand over me, he bends down and hooks it around the back of my knees, lifting me in his arms. He continues to kiss me senseless as he carries me over the threshold of my room, closing the door behind us with his foot. His elbow turns on the light. He walks unhurriedly to the bed; he's seemingly enjoying holding me in his arms as he devours my lips with his.

He lowers me to the mattress gently; my head rests with seductive comfort against the plump pillow. He sweeps loose strands of my brown hair back from my face; his body lingers decadently above mine, teasing me with his proximity. He lies beside me on the bed. We face each other. I know that I must have a starry-eyed look because, without him touching me, I'm having a problem again believing that he's real.

Mattie's hand reaches for mine; he brings it to his lips and kisses it tenderly. Tears brighten my eyes instantly. He pulls something from his pocket, and before I know what it is, he's slipping it onto my finger. "I found this on the floor beside your purse back at my house. It must've fallen out."

I lift my hand to see the round-cut diamond engagement ring he'd given me. It sparkles with blue fire when I hold it up to the light.

Mattie pushes up from the mattress. He hovers over me as his legs rest on either side of mine. Looking down at me, his eyes smolder as he says, "Promise me you'll never take it off again."

A tear spills from my eye. His thumb reaches down to gently wipe it away. My hand moves to cup his cheek, and then it slides into the black, silky strands of his hair. I pull gently, bringing his face closer to mine. When he's a hair's breadth away, I whisper, "I promise."

With a soft, sexy groan, Mattie kisses me again and says against my lips, "I love you, Violet."

In that moment, I have no trouble believing he's real; we're reunited. I'm whole again.

Monsters of Earth

By Tammy Blackwell

For information on other titles

Visit the author's website:

http://www.misstammywrites.com/

Monsters of Earth

"Earth?" Helem looked at the assignment etched on his com-sleeve. "This is a joke, right? Because it's my first solo trip, you're messing with me."

Commander Sotiri didn't even look up from the massive console where he tracked reports from the Raimondas who were in the field. "This is the Raimann. We don't joke, Helem."

"But it's Earth. What the hell am I supposed to do there?"

This time the commander did look up. The stony glare made Helem's pulse jump erratically in his throat, but he didn't let it show. Raimondas never showed fear, and Helem was a Raimonda. Had been for all of three hours now.

"What you're supposed to do is your mission. Unless you don't think you can handle it." The commander tilted his head and cocked an eyebrow, a look Helem knew well. He'd been on the receiving end of it since the day he was born. "Maybe I made a mistake in graduating you too soon. You're young to take on a mission of your own, but I thought you were ready. Perhaps your mother was right and you should train for another year before going out solo."

"Dad—"

"Commander Sotiri."

"Commander Sotiri," Helem said between clenched teeth. "You know I'm ready to take assignments. I scored higher on my exit exams than anyone else."

"Then you should be perfectly capable of handling this assignment."

Of course he was capable of handling this assignment. It was Earth, for the stars' sake. There was a reason they sent students there on their first training mission. Earth was safe. There are no monsters on Earth.

And Helem's job was to fight monsters.

"You don't trust me," he said to his father, breaking all sorts of protocols and not caring. This was bullshit. If he'd been any other newly uniformed officer, he would be going off to Yabets to fight giants or Phobos to slay dragons. The only reason he was being sent on a cakewalk mission to Earth was because he had been unfortunate enough to be the son of the Raimann's commanding officer.

Golden brown eyes, the exact shade as his own, narrowed on him as if looking into his mind and measuring his worth. It was useless, of course. His father always found him lacking.

"I do trust you, Helem. Otherwise, I wouldn't send you on this mission."

"To see to a fern? You trust me with a plant? That speaks volumes, Dad. I feel deeply respected."

A muscle in his dad's jaw twitched, and he knew he'd gone too far. But instead of ripping into him like normal, his dad squared his shoulders and dropped back into Commander-mode.

"You will complete this mission. If you're successful and willing, you will receive others. If you do not choose to complete this mission, you can return your uniform to Penelope in Human Resources."

Helem considered it, but only for a second. Being a Raimondas was all he'd ever wanted. If it meant wasting his time with a mission on Earth, then so be it. What was the worse that could happen? Becoming bored to death?

Without another word to his father, Helem strode to the mission deck and keyed his identification number into the console.

"Helem Sotiri reporting for duty."

"Destination?"

"Earth."

A high-pitched noise threatened to split his eardrums apart, and then a flash of white light blazed across his eyeballs as he felt his body being thrust across the universe.

Helem double-checked his location with the coordinates on his com-sleeve.

Yep. This was it. He looked around, searching for his charge. There were a few flowers sitting in vases, but no ferns to be found. He opened a plain, wooden door, but only found a bathroom on the other side.

"Where are you hiding?" he muttered, looking around the small, austere room. There weren't exactly many places for a plant to hide. The flowers sat in a windowsill along with balloons, pictures, and various toys, mostly of the stuffed creature variety. There was a small area with a sink and a rolling table of sorts, but they were both bare. Other than some machines, the only thing in the room was a bed and the girl laying on it.

"I don't suppose you know where a fern is?" he asked the girl who watched him as he paced around the room.

The girl pushed up on her elbows, although she didn't make it far off the pillow. Helem noticed her skin was puffy and an odd shade of gray-white.

"Ungh agh ewww."

"I'm sorry, I didn't understand that," Helem said, double-checking his translator to make sure it was working. "Try again?"

The girl licked her lips and closed her eyes as if talking took all of her concentration. "Who. Are. You?"

"I am Helem of the Planet Iskander. I have come on a sacred mission." A lame mission, but all Raimann missions were sacred, so it wasn't exactly a lie. "Perhaps you can help me?"

He waited for a response, but the girl was back on her pillow again. She seemed to be breathing a bit harder than entirely necessary, and she somehow managed to look even paler than she had just moments before.

Understanding dawned slowly.

"You're sick?"

The girl didn't answer. She probably thought the answer was obvious. It might have been to another human, but not Helem. There was no such thing as illness on Iskander. He'd never seen a sick person before, although he'd read about them in his studies of other planets and their cultures.

"I'm not sure this will work," he said, digging in his pack as he walked over to the bed, "but it's worth a try." He pressed three small metal discs onto her right temple before slipping the receiver in his ear. "Okay, think something at me."

"Think something at you?"

Her mouth hadn't moved, but he heard her as if she'd spoken aloud.

"Excellent. The neuro-translator works on humans. Now we can have a proper conversation."

The girl's eyebrows crinkled together. "Who are you? What are you doing here?"

"I'm Helem." Didn't he already cover this? Was forgetting things part of her illness? Or maybe she had trouble with comprehension. He spoke slowly, just in case. "I come from the Planet Iskander on a sacred mission to guard the fern. Have you seen a fern?"

There was a strange noise on the neuro-translator, which Helem thought might have been the device's attempt at interpreting a laugh.

"Only when I look in the mirror," she said.

"In the mirror...? But you are not a plant."

"No, just a human girl with a plant-like name." Her eyes followed him around the room as he studied her from a different angle, trying to figure out what kind of mission his father had sent him on. "You know," she said, "you would think when my brain finally fried and hallucinated a teenage alien boy it would have had the courtesy to at least make him hot."

Helem froze mid-step. "Hot as in temperature?"

"Hot as in attractive. You know, six-pack abs, dreamy eyes, wicked smile... Hot."

He was afraid that was what she meant.

"I'll have you know I'm considered quite good-looking on Iskander."

"And good grief. The cancer must being eating away my creativity. I mean, you look like a human. Not alien-like at all. No funny-shaped head. No antenna. Very boring."

Helem felt his face growing warm. How dare this girl, charge or not, call him unattractive and boring?

"Everyone looks like this, across all the galaxies. Everyone except the monsters."

"Monsters?"

"Monsters: Werewolves. Unicorns. Fairies. The universe is filled with all sorts of horrible creatures." He'd studied them all, and had even seen a few on training missions. One of these days, he would kill them to protect the innocent. It was his job. It was what he'd trained for. What he was doing here…

What was he doing here? Surely there was something he was supposed to be doing with this girl called Fern, but he couldn't figure out what it might be.

"Unicorns and fairies aren't monsters," she said, interrupting his thoughts.

"Tell that to the inhabitants of Planet Fraizar where young girls live in constant fear of being stabbed and devoured by evil horned beasts or the citizens of Planet Bachai where a family of unchecked pixies left an entire country without a single bite of food to eat."

"Evil unicorns and fairies, huh? How come I've never seen one?"

"Because this is Earth. There are no monsters on Earth."

"Are you sure? Because I'm pretty certain the guy on the second floor with a gunshot wound is a werewolf."

Helem snorted. "On Earth even your Shifters are lame and half-human. I wouldn't worry about it."

With so little else to look at in the room, Helem wandered back over to her collection of flowers, toys, and pictures. Someone had decorated a poster with snapshots and hung it next to the

81

window. It took him a long time to find which person was Fern. The smiling girl with wiry reddish-brown hair hardly resembled the Fern who watched him through heavy-lidded, slightly unfocused eyes.

"What is wrong with you?" he asked. "What kind of sickness do you have?"

"I'm in a juvenile cancer ward. What kind of sickness do you think I have?"

Helem's study of diseases had been intense, but with so many illnesses on so many worlds, he wasn't familiar with everything that could affect Earth's humans. He pulled out his com-sleeve and did a quick search. It only took a few minutes of reading to understand the seriousness of Fern's condition. He checked what he could observe against the information on the com-sleeve, and finally understood his mission.

Helem was to watch Fern die.

It wasn't an unheard of mission for a Raimonda, but an unusual one. People died alone every minute of every day across the galaxy. It was impossible for the Raimann to help all of them make the transition from the land of the living to the afterlife. No one was quite sure why a handful landed on the Raimann's list of charges, but it did happen on occasion. The Raimonda who took such an assignment always considered it one of the deepest honors of his or her career. Protecting life was their job, but honoring life was their duty.

"Where are your parents?" he asked, noticing the man and woman who appeared in many of the pictures scattered around the room.

"I'm going to die tonight, so I sent them away."

82

Helem's forehead wrinkled in confusion. "What? Why would you do that?"

"Because I don't want to watch them cry. It's hardly comforting to know I'm breaking their hearts."

"Don't you think that is a little selfish?" Surely the woman whose smile was a carbon copy of Fern's would want to participate in her child's final moments.

"I'm sixteen and dying. I think I have a right to be selfish."

Helem couldn't argue against her logic, so he said nothing, focusing on the items in the windowsill instead. Through them he was able to piece together a picture of the person Fern was before the illness ravaged her body.

Dancer. Scientist. Frog lover. Friend. Daughter.

All of them would be lost forever when she finally succumbed to the disease.

"Do kids die from cancer on Iskander?"

Helem nearly dropped the music box in his hand. He'd been so absorbed in his thoughts he'd somehow forgotten she was still in the room and connected to the neuro-translator.

"We don't have cancer on Iskander," he said.

"I wish I would have been born there."

"Me, too." And he did. He wanted to get to know this girl who smiled back at him from the photos around the room. He thought that given the chance, they might have been friends.

"I don't want to die."

Even through the neuro-translator he could hear her fear and grief. The sound of it got caught in his chest, growing and mutating until it became his own. Tears stung his eyes, and he had to remind himself Fern didn't need his anger. She'd shut out her parents because she didn't want to be burdened with anyone else's emotions. She wouldn't want to deal with his either.

On Iskander, those who didn't die in the line of duty as a Raimondas died of old age. Somewhere in their tenth or eleventh decade their body would simply cease to function. For some it's a quick process. They live their lives as normal one minute and are gone the next. For others, it takes a few days. They feel themselves getting weaker and weaker until they finally fade out.

Helem's great-grandfather had been a fader. When he realized his life was slowly bleeding away he called in his family to be by his side. Helem's mother, who had always been her grandfather's favorite, stood at the edge of his bed, tears streaming down her cheeks as her hands danced over and around one other, unsure where they should be or what they should do.

"What do you need, Grandfather?" she'd asked. "What can I do to help you?"

His great-grandfather smiled, which Helem found odd. He was dying. What did he have to smile about? His life was over. Soon he would cease to exist. If ever there were a time to not smile, that would be it.

"Just hold my hand," his great-grandfather said. "Hang onto me so I know I'm not alone."

And so Helem's family had taken turns sitting by his great-grandfather's bed, holding on as the last hours of his life slipped away. The smile never left the old man's face the entire time.

Helem had always considered his great-grandfather odd and different, but perhaps on this point he was right. Maybe what someone needed most at the time of death was to know someone was hanging on, trying to ground them to this life.

He pulled a chair over to Fern's bed and took her hand in his own. It was cool to the touch; cool enough he watched closely to make sure her chest still rose and fell. After a few seconds, her fingers wound their way around his.

"It's not fair," she said. "I shouldn't have to die. I'm only a kid. There is so much I still want to do. There is so much left I can give the world."

"Tell me about them," Helem said. "Tell me about the things you would do if you have another eighty years. Tell me what Earth is losing by letting you go too soon."

It took her a minute to gather her thoughts, but then she was telling him about how she would go to college and become a doctor. How she would devote her life to finding a cure for cancer. She told him about the husband who would look like the member of a British boy band and think she was the most beautiful woman in the world, even if her face was swollen from the medication she had to take and her hair was all gone. She imagined the children she would have and how happy and healthy they would be their whole lives. She talked about all the social injustices she would work to right, of how she would eradicate the world of prejudice and hate.

Eventually her words came only sporadically and ceased to make sense. Still, Helem left the neuro-translator attached. Even if they were garbled nonsense, he wanted to hear whatever she had to say.

People in scrubs and lab jackets came in more and more frequently as the night wore on. Some of them questioned who he was and why he was there, but none of them made him leave.

At 2:32 am Central Standard Time on Earth, Fern died.

The woman who turned off the machines had twin streams trailing from her eyes, although she did not make a sound.

"Her parents?" Helem asked in a gravelly voice.

"On their way." She paused in her activities, her sad eyes finding his. "It's over now. You can go."

Helem looked at the shell, which was only moments before filled with love, hopes, and dreams. He thought about how cancer had taken it all away, and for the first time he truly understood the definition of evil.

"No," he said, pulling up a list of the planet's best medical schools on his com-sleeve. "I can't. I have a monster to slay."

THE HOUSE ON MAPLE STREET

By Amanda Havard

For information on other titles

Visit the author's website:
http://amandahavard.com/

THE HOUSE ON MAPLE STREET

You can still hear the screams.

Cliché? Sure. But clichés start somewhere, don't they? And here, they start at the Fentress County line, where you can still hear the screams.

I suppose I can hear them louder in my head than you'd hear them in yours because I was there. Traumatic memory is funny that way.

It started six months ago. My buddy Dana was hanging around while I closed up shop at the Dairy Queen one night. Dana loves ice cream, and DQ wasn't exactly hopping around closing time in January. She'd come keep me company and eat the large Heath Blizzard slowly — to savor it. Like it was the last one she was ever going to eat. But we both knew there'd be another Blizzard the next night. And the next night. She'd eat a damn Blizzard every night of her life.

Anyway, it was about five minutes till close and an 18-wheel moving truck pulls up in front. The door swings open, and the first thing I see is six-inch heels and a boot that goes up to someone's skinny ass thigh. Next thing you know, a Blonde Bombshell walks in the front door of my DQ.

Dana and I look at each other. Blonde Bombshell is the kind of chick who makes girls, like Dana, feel like shit because they'll never compare, whereas guys, like me, look at themselves and feel like shit for a whole different set of reasons. She's unattainable. Everything about her.

I set down the mop and wipe my hands on my apron. "Uh, can I help you, ma'am?"

"Do your products contain high fructose corn syrup?" she asks. Her voice is stiff, not the molasses drawl I'd hoped for -- one I could imagine being covered in.

From Dana, I hear an audible scoff. She's thinking: Of course, Bombshell can't eat what the rest of us do.

I'm instantly thrilled that the nights get boring enough around here that I've read the nutrition facts and ingredient lists, and, so, I know the answer to this question. "It's in all the sauces, and likely the candy you can put in the Blizzard, but technically the corn syrup in the ice cream itself isn't 'high fructose' per se . . ."

She tilts her head to the side. Weirdly. "That will do. Make me something. Large. Lots of candy and sauce."

"You want a large sundae?" I asked.

"Sundaes. Yes. I would like to order five."

It takes me a second to process, realizing most people ask the question about high fructose crap and then don't want to eat it. I shake off the confusion and get to making. I'm so distracted, I forget to charge her for them, but when she's gone, I realize there's a $50 bill sitting next to the register. Dana and I don't say another word.

She was the first one I saw. Dana drove me home that night and when we got to the shabby craftsman-house coated street I've lived on my whole life — Maple Street — we saw the moving truck was parked at the end of the block.

There were five of them, all adults, moving into a big square saltbox house that sits at the end of my cul-de-sac. Everything about the house always stuck out: different architecture, twice the size of everything around it. Vines covered the siding and bricks. The windows on the front looked like eyes staring at you. We pulled into my driveway, got out, and probably stood there for five solid minutes just watching them. Blonde Bombshell carried boxes on her shoulders, still in the heels.

"I think I'm going to go home," Dana said, neither of us able to wrap our heads around what we saw.

But I stayed out on the stoop, swinging on the porch swing, just watching. They unloaded that 18-wheeler in an hour, and at one point Blonde Bombshell carried in a leather recliner by herself.

Forty-seven new families moved to our tiny town in the next sixty days. And they all seemed drawn to the house on Maple Street, like a weirdo mecca. Maybe because it's the South and we're good at denial, or maybe because people like thinking everything is fine when it isn't, but whatever the case, no one said anything.

My mother, who lives in a uniform of mom jeans, nurse shoes, clunky sweaters from my childhood, and scrunchies, welcomed the mysterious group of five adults living in one house with a tray of chocolate chip brownies she made from a mix. I stood next to her as she introduced herself to the tall, suave man with caramel colored hair. While we exchanged pleasantries — well, while they did, and I watched awkwardly — he ate the entire tray.

Sugar. There was something about sugar. Blonde Bombshell with her apparent need for high fructose corn syrup. Suave Caramel dude with his brownie consumption. The more families that came, the longer the lines at the DQ got. I'd go into gas stations, and the candy aisles would be picked clean. Hostess treats — or whatever people started making after Hostess shut down — and candy, Icees, Cokes and Hi-C, Pixy Stix, and doughnuts, and so on. And so on. And so on. They ate it all. Sugar. The town was going crazy for sugar.

It took me three months to say the word "alien" out loud. I stayed up late reading about extraterrestrial encounters. Though it was safe to say my encounters weren't of the floating-faceless-object or little-green-men persuasion, there seemed to be a number of stories out there about people who just appeared, often to a small town, and then things began to seem . . . off. Just like they had in our tiny ass town.

I thought about an Are You Afraid of the Dark? episode I'd seen on Hulu — my older sister, Hanna, always reminisced about the show, and bored one night last summer, I'd watched them all online. You know the one I mean, right? With the aliens in the abandoned building, trying to take the twin or something? I don't know. They seemed like that. I decided the Maple Street sugar psychos — or fructose freaktoids, as I got to calling them (eventually shortened to fructoids in my head) — were certainly aliens. I just couldn't determine if the rest of the forty-seven families were aliens or were under some kind of spell.

Dana was the first person I spilled my hypothesis to. She'd rolled her eyes. She'd asked if I was high. She didn't even humor the thought past giving me the jeez-Fenton-how'd-I-get-stuck-with-you-as-my-best-friend-when-you're-so-lame face. I knew that face too well. The older we got, the more she thought it. And the more stupid shit I said out loud, the more serious she was in asking herself that question.

Too bad Dana was a mean, sarcastic, difficult-to-deal-with, chubby chick in small town Tennessee. She was outcast for the obvious, superficial reasons, which I could care less about. That clearly didn't keep me from befriending her, or liking her. But on top of that, she wasn't exactly a pleasant person. She wanted to know how she got stuck with me? I wondered how I got stuck with her.

People made jokes that we'd get married. That I'd be the pussy-whipped skinny husband who got elbowed around by the drill sergeant wife twice his size. You don't know that stereotype? You're lucky. There's a lot of that around here.

But all that brought a few things to light about my alien theory. One, this sugar obsession didn't seem to rot the population of Small-Town-Shithole, Tennessee the way you think it would. The girls were beautiful. The guys were athletes. They were all way too pretty in a really uncomfortable, Stepford or airbrushed or perhaps Kardashian sort of way. They were constantly overdressed and over-made and wearing clothes that might have passed in a big city — Nashville, maybe, or probably New York — but certainly did not pass here in the land of Walmart and oversized American Eagle jeans. And all they ever ate was sugar.

Secondly, no one seemed to know anything about these people. You'd ask questions of the kids in school, but they wouldn't be able to answer them. Teachers would call on them, they'd stay silent, and then the teacher would leave them alone, as if they had answered, or as if they'd suddenly been compelled — by alien mind melding, duh — to not require an answer of a student. I figured that one out pretty quickly after several of them showed up in Mr. Fence's third period American History class. Fence was a nervous man, in the Army once, and kind of jumpy now. Kids made fun of him, which was terrible. He always kept his dog tags on him. In the middle of class, he'd take them off, and then wrap them around his wrist, like a nervous habit. I kept a running tally of how many questions he asked the Fructoidss, and a count of how many they answered. One particular day, I looked at my rows of tally and hash and counted them as 0 for 47. He never once gave them a hard time. He'd just look at them, they'd look back, he'd wind the necklace chain around his wrist, clasp the tags in his palm, and then say, "Moving on."

Third, they only hovered about in little groups of Fructoids, but they'd say nearly nothing. My high school got 128 new students in the town's population influx — we had started at 400 — and yet the lunchroom got quieter. They'd be quiet and then people would be quieter, probably just to stare.

Fourth . . .

"Fenton, stop." Dana's voice. She'd had enough. (I'd been explaining this to her, my second attempt to make a case for aliens when she came in for her Blizzard. With things getting busy, she'd come right when it was time to close up shop, keep me company while I cleaned, avoid the line of weirdly pretty people staring at her while she ate.) "Tell me this is a lamely detailed April Fools' joke."

"You don't believe me," I said.

"Of course I don't believe you, you insane little fool. But I see a flaw in your theory," she said.

I sighed, rolled my eyes. With air quotes, I said, "Aliens don't exist."

"No, not that. That you don't believe anymore. And it's subjective. I see an actual hole in your logic." She licked soft serve

93

off the spoon. I idly wondered, if she'd been anyone else, would I have found that hot?

"I'm listening."

"It sounds like you're suggesting that they're playing some kind of mind voodoo on everyone. Like you think that's why no one cares what they're doing, or asks who they are. Right?"

"Right."

"Well, why isn't it working on you?" she said.

I hadn't thought about it. I'd been awake too long and thinking too hard, and somehow, I hadn't figured out my own strength against them.

A corner of that obnoxious smile of hers turned up, and she started to laugh. "You don't have an answer for that one."

"Maybe it's because I saw them first. When Blonde Bombshell—"

"Are we still calling her that?" Dana huffed.

I ignored her. "When Blonde Bombshell came here that night. I was probably the first person they spoke to here."

"So, what, that made you immune? Wouldn't that, by logic, mean that you were the first infected? Wouldn't that mean you were the most under their spell?"

"It's not a spell," I said. "You're thinking of the wrong kind of—"

"Mythical creature." She cut me off again. "Look, Fenton. You've always been weird. And you've always been my friend. So I'm telling you, as your friend, to let this go."

I crossed my arms, and stared at her. "Then what's your explanation? Fifty new families. A hundred plus new kids at school. Sugar bust?"

She looked me dead in the eye and said, "I don't need one."

"You don't understand."

"Stop being such a freak," she said. She got to her feet, not even halfway done with her ice cream, and she left.

That night I walked home since Dana had left me to fend for myself. When I got to the house it was dark - save for the glow of a TV coming from the family room, where my mom was undoubtedly asleep in a recliner.

When I rounded the corner of the house to come in the kitchen door, like I always did, Blonde Bombshell was standing there. Stiffly.

"Whoa," I said out loud, before I could stop myself. She was dressed like a sexed-up superhero sidekick in a comic book movie. Maybe like Scarlett-Johansen-as-Black-Widow-in-The-Avengers. Black bodysuit sort of thing. The same thigh-high boots. Hair big and all over the place. Red lips, dark eyes.

"Fenton Marsh," she said. Stiffer than the Siri robo-speak. It was so odd to hear her talk. You so rarely heard their voices.

"Yeah . . .?"

"Pleasantries suggest you should greet me with one of the acceptable phrases. And you should call me by my name, like I called you by yours."

"I never got your name," I said, which was true.

"Clarice," she said. Silence of the Lambs, I thought. She tilted her head to the side, like she had the night we met. A jerky movement. A robotic function.

"Hello, Clarice. What are you doing here?" I asked. My palms were sweaty. My hair stuck to my forehead.

"Do you like your profession at the Dairy Queen?" she asked.

"I wouldn't exactly call it my profession," I said. Surely I'd break out of the damn Dairy Queen. Surely this was my high school job, not my maximum potential.

"You do it for work, do you not? Professional denotes payment for service, a job. Am I incorrect in my linguistic understanding of the word, 'profession'?" she asked.

"No, you're right, it's just that . . ."

"What is just what?" she asked.

"Why are you talking to me about Dairy Queen?"

"We like it. It is a good source of food for us. Perhaps you will be useful for us, when the time comes."

My heart was beating out of my chest. When the time comes. Aliens! Invasion! Holy crap!

"Say aloud what you are thinking," she said, at my silence.

"What if I don't want to be useful?" I asked.

"Then we would have to take different measures with you," she said.

"Such as?"

"To start, we would need you to forget all that you think you have deduced about our existence," she said. "We only offered a select few that privilege. We would, of course, revoke it immediately."

As in: I was one of only a few whose perception wasn't being controlled by them. I was one of the few who had a chance to do something about it.

And though I'd never actually help them — though what were they seriously thinking I'd do, make them sundaes on a space ship for the rest of my life? — I knew better than to turn down the bit of wisdom I'd gained with them.

So I needed to play along. "Then I'm happy to be useful in whatever way you need." I put out my hand toward Clarice, to shake on it.

She stared at my hand and then back up at me. "I cannot place my palm in yours as is customary in your societal tradition. We try not to touch people. The salt in their sweat can hurt our epidermal layers. Your hand appears to be coated in residue of dried perspiration."

I looked at my hand and then back up at her. "Of course, I understand."

"Thank you for your compliance, Fenton Marsh. I will now inform the others it is safe to speak to you. They will likely choose not to speak, but if one speaks to you, speak back."

"Of course," I said.

She turned on her heels, like a German soldier, and she headed mechanically back toward the house at the end of the cul-de-sac.

"Hey, wait!" I called.

She stopped. "Wait on what?"

"Can I tell my friend? Dana?"

Head-flinch, as if a glitch in machinery. "No. You may tell no one."

"Oh. Okay," I said. Defeated. She'd still think I was crazy. I'd still be alone.

"That saddens you," she said.

"It's hard having no one," I said.

"You need a," she paused, "friend. That will be arranged. Good night, Fenton Marsh."

As I unlocked the house, wondering if I was dreaming, I realized she gave me the most valuable piece of information yet:

Sugar was sustenance; salt was a weapon. And she was to deliver on the promise of friend? She'd just given me one of them.

The next morning, a Fructoid stood at my locker. He was my height, about my skinny build. He had jet-black hair and ice-blue eyes to my sandy blond and brown. He had on a t-shirt and hoodie and Vans, just like I did. Most of them were a head taller than I was, with athletic bodies and everything else girls drooled over. But this one was just as forgettable, as short and small and normal as I was. They didn't just find me a friend. They found me a friend like me.

"Uh . . . can I help you?"

"Fenton Marsh," he said. The first Fructoid voice I'd heard other than Clarice's. "My name is Travis. I am your friend."

I laughed kind of. Looked around. A few kids looked at me, but not like I'd thought they would. No one noticed me. Maybe I could use that to my advantage.

"Nice to meet you, Travis. So she told you what's going on?"

"You make ice cream," he said. "And you'll be useful. And you need someone to talk to."

I slung my backpack over my shoulder, weighted down with my history and math books. Travis followed closely.

"What are you doing?" I asked.

"I'm going with you," he said.

"They aren't your classes."

"That won't present a problem," he said.

"Going to use your Jedi-mind tricks on them?" I said.

"I appreciate your Star Wars reference. It amuses me," he said.

I stopped and looked at him. "You know Star Wars?"

"We are assigned to study people. Culture. Colloquialisms. We are assigned to . . . fit in," he said.

"I see." He was so much more normal than Clarice. It irked me. Only I kind of liked it.

I got to my first period Trig class, and Mrs. Knots looked up with a furrowed brow when she saw Travis. He smiled back. Mechanically but warmly. Then she smiled back and looked back at her desk.

I took a seat, and he sat next to me. "Jedi," he whispered. He reached out a fist as if to fist bump me.

"What about the salt worries?"

He left his fist hanging there. "I sense no excess perspiration," he said. And in his most human-sounding voice, he whispered, "Clarice's strict. The rest of us are more . . . chill."

Chill. If they were supposed to be studying colloquialisms, he was doing a damn good job. I smiled, and fist-bumped.

It was nicer having a friend than I expected. I mean, I didn't know if Travis was really my friend, and I still felt a little weird being in with them — never mind how weird it felt that there was in fact a them -- but it was nice. Between classes, at lunch, after school, and even at the DQ, Travis was there. I asked a million questions. He answered some of them. I kept thinking it would get annoying, but it didn't. Which means I didn't know how lonely I had been until then.

Dana had more or less disappeared. She only showed up for Blizzards every few days, and she never spoke to Travis. She looked over her shoulder at him with a particular breed of bitchy disdain, and then she looked at me with about half as much. One night, when she came in, she managed to have an entire conversation with me while Travis hovered, and she never so much as looked his direction. When she walked out, he looked at me and said, "Does she like you or hate you?"

"Hate," I said. "Or something."

"I thought they were often one in the same," he said.

I raised an eyebrow at him. "Do you . . . like girls, Travis? Normal girls? Human girls?"

"Girls are girls, Fenton friend. I do not make a habit of analyzing DNA before checking one out."

Touché.

"Any particular type of girl?" I said.

He looked out to Dana as she stuffed herself into her tiny Civic. "Ones that might have an interest in talking to me," he said.

"No one talks to you," I countered.

"That doesn't mean I don't wish they could, you know?" he said. I did know. "Good thing I have you."

I nodded. "Good thing."

Even though things were starting to get interesting in my world, things were getting the wrong kind of interesting with the overarching Fructoid agenda. The next week, six teachers quit at school, and within a day or two, they were replaced by Fructoids. My Aunt Bonnie was a teacher at the elementary school, and I remember how long it took them to hire her into the system, go through the district paperwork, and all that. So six Fructoid teachers in a week told me their influence — mind-meld — was growing rapidly. It also seemed like their troops were mobilizing. But for what?

All of a sudden, kids started getting in trouble and were assigned to morning detentions. We'd never really had morning detention before, so that was particularly odd. Then I started noticing: kids who got in trouble started getting quiet. And after a morning in detention, they'd be silent, just like the Fructoids.

So they were starting with kids. Whatever the mission, they were going to infiltrate from the ground up. I thought of Travis, of his ability to fit in and sound so much more normal than Clarice. They were starting with their kids. They were starting with ours.

One Wednesday, three weeks after, (after what?) Travis and I were in the lunchroom eating questionable tacos and Butterfingers when I first heard the rumor. People said Mr. Fence had gone missing. A day later, it was humanities-hun Ms. Matter, and biology-biatch, Mrs. Kell. In a week, each of the six teachers who were replaced by the Fructoids went missing.

"Travis, what's going on?" I demanded.

He shrugged his shoulders, almost naturally. "They do not tell everyone down the food chain all the plans," he said.

"Why do they want to mess with the teachers? They already got them out of the schools and replaced them with—" I paused, "y'all. So why mess with the teachers who already left?"

Travis seemed to legitimately think this over. "Why do you assume the new teachers are here to educate," now he paused, "y'all, and not that they need your teachers to educate us?"

I sank back my chair. Why did I assume that?

"Trav, did they tell you what you could and couldn't tell me?"

He shrugged and licked chocolate off his fingers. "They just told me to be your friend."

Looking around the lunchroom, I wondered how much longer Clarice & co. could keep making waves without anyone else finding out.

"So does that mean you can tell me what the deal is with the house on Maple Street?"

He thought about it and then went back to peeling pieces of fun size candy. "It's the emergency way home."

My mind went wild. Home as in home planet? Way home as in vehicle as in . . . spaceship? I worried if I asked these questions, I'd go too far. So instead, I kept these spinning thoughts to myself and just asked the other question on my mind. "Trav?"

"Yeah, buddy?"

"How come no one's worried?"

He scanned the room and then met my eye. "Jedi," he said, matter-of-factly.

"Jedi," I said.

They may not be worried, but I was. That night, I went to that damn giant house on Maple Street, and I knocked on the front door, prepared to demand an audience with Clarice. I was a one-man army, but I wanted to know what the hell was going on. I thought about bringing Travis with me, but I didn't want to get him in trouble. He seemed so relaxed all the time, so genuine, really, for someone who was assigned to be my friend. I didn't know if there would be trouble. I didn't know what the danger would be for him, for one of them. He answered a lot of my questions, but in the end, I didn't know the basics: Where they came from, what they wanted, or what exactly they were.

No one answered the front door, though all the cars were there. I banged on that door for a while, and then I decided to snoop. I walked the perimeter of the house, and looked through the windows. I couldn't see much, but from what I could see, it looked like a nicely manicured home -- not so much like one that had been lived in but instead maybe like one you'd see in a magazine. I made it to the backyard gate, but it was locked. Convinced there was something I was missing, I hopped the fence. The backyard was dark, empty, and just as flawless as the house. Wooden steps with brick sides led up to a back deck.

But there was a noise. Quiet, reverberating, it sounded like the hum of an engine, and the gurgle of water. I walked around to get closer to the source of the sound. I put my hands on the wooden steps, and I felt the vibrations. On the far side of the steps, I noticed a faint glow. Coming around to it, there was a small door, maybe waist high.

I don't know if I should have been scared to be digging around like this, but I wasn't. I was just too intrigued.

I reached out for the latch, pulled on it a few times, but nothing. I was just about to give up when the door swung open. Caramel Suave — the one who so gluttonously delighted in my mom's brownies — emerged from the tiny door and I was bathed in a pale green light from inside. He swiftly moved to his feet, his eyes a head-height above mine.

"Why are you here?" he said. "You were not invited."

"I came to talk to Clarice," I said. "I am helping her."

"I am in full awareness of your compliance," he said. "But you were not invited here tonight. You must leave."

"What the hell is going on down there?"

"This is not your home, and you were not invited. You are beyond the bounds of your societal confines of politeness. You must go."

"Who's down there with you?" I demanded, growing hotter.

"Go," he repeated.

"Not without—"

He grabbed me by the throat and lifted me off the ground until we were eye to eye. You know how that looks badass in movies? In real life, it's just painful and terrifying and comes dangerously close to breaking your neck.

"Go!" he said again. He dropped me to the ground, and then he went back through the tiny door.

As I stumbled to my feet, something caught my eye on the ground by the stairs. I reached down and grabbed Fence's dog tags.

I ran back to my house and took my mom's station wagon keys off the hook by the door without waking her. I ran back to the car and got in and then realized: I had no idea where I was going. On the one hand, I could go to Travis, but on the other I could go to Dana. But she was so pissed at me! Yet she was pissed because she thought I was stupid, and now I had proof. Fence's dog tags in my hand were just what I needed.

I sped off toward her house. When I got there, she was in the backyard with her younger sisters, yelling at them.

"Fenton!" Emily, the littlest one, called as she ran to me. She was five years old, and she'd been climbing on me since she could stand up.

"What are you doing here?" Dana said.

"I kind of need to talk to you," I said.

"Well I'm kinda busy being a big sister here and all," she said.

Emily grabbed a hold of my shirt and was using it as leverage to climb up my legs, which I suddenly realized was a much easier activity when she was, oh, three and not five. Squirming and trying not to let her fall, I said to Dana, "It's important. I have proof."

"Fenton! Fenton! Fenton's here!" Emily laughed. She was koala-gripped onto my torso, reaching hands around my neck now.

"About aliens?" Dana rolled her eyes.

"Yes!" I said. "Exactly!"

She pulled Emily off of me. "Go inside, Em. Fenton and I need to talk."

"But Sissy!" Emily whined.

"Go!" Dana barked. When they cleared the porch, she looked at me and said, "You've got to be joking. I thought when you started hanging out with what's-his-face you'd given up on the alien theory. Are you telling me that you still think that's what they are and you befriended him?"

"It's a long story," I said, suddenly realizing I'd promised Clarice I wouldn't say anything to anyone. She'd even given me Travis to make that easier, but . . .

What the hell was I thinking? They were ALIENS! Why did I have any loyalty to them?

"They kidnapped the teachers!" I exclaimed, and I showed her the dog tags.

"Where did you get these?" she asked.

I told her the whole story. "And so, like I said, they've totally kidnapped the teachers!"

She looked at them long and hard and handed them back to me. "They did?" she asked. "Or you did?"

"What?" I blurted.

"That's what the police would ask. Probably what they'd say. You'd only bring speculation to yourself," she said.

I looked down at the tags. "This is bigger than the police, Dana. You see that, right?"

"This has gotten insane in your head, Fenton. You see that, right?" she mocked me.

"Forget it."

I got back in the car, but I didn't know where else to go. I drove down the street so Dana couldn't see me anymore, and then I sat and stared. And got angrier. And more worried. And then angrier again.

And then I decided to fight. I drove the long and winding road to the Piggly Wiggly — yep, those are real — aimed for a single thing. And lots of it.

Weirdly, I noticed a trail of cars behind me pretty quickly. And by the time I got to the parking lot, it was nearly full. Of Fructoids. I got out of the car, aimed for the spice aisle, and no one stopped me. They just stared.

Rounding the corner of the aisle, I ran into Travis. Suspiciously. His arms were full of Butterfingers. "Hey," he said. The store was packed, fifteen minutes till close.

"Hey," I said. "What are you doing here?"

"Sustenance," he said, gesturing with his candy. He didn't exactly show emotion yet, and but he looked . . . nervous? "Nestle trucks come in on Thursdays. What are you doing here?"

I deflected his gaze. I didn't really have a plan, per se, but I imagined whatever I was up to would cause some trouble. More and more Fructoids hovered near us. Listening. Watching.

"I just . . . needed something," I said.

"Oh, cool." He was waiting for me to say something. To tell him. To ask him something. He knew. The question was: did he only know what had happened with Caramel Suave? Or did he know what I was thinking?

I decided to go big or go home. I walked back to the front of the store, grabbed a cart, and went to the salt. I started pulling giant containers of Morton's salt off the shelf by the arm full.

Travis just stood there, watching, eyes wide. The crowd around us, though, pressed backward. Afraid.

He said nothing. When the cart was full, I headed to the register, walking right past him. "Fenton, wait," he said. I stopped and looked at him, hoping he could see the apology on my face. He took a flat row package of fun size Butterfingers and handed them to me. "A snack. For the road."

"Travis, I'm not—"

He cut me off. "Take them. You'll want them." I looked at them again: The plastic sleeve was open.

"Thanks," I said. I paid for the salt and candy and loaded it in the back of the wagon. Fructoids hung around the car and the parking lot like zombies. Waiting. Safely in the car, I slid the eight little pieces of candy out into my hand. Written on the white paper sleeve inside -- in what looked more like computer font than handwriting — read, They sent me to stop you, but I won't. Just be careful. And make sure you're not in the house when it happens.

When it happens.

I drove straight back to Maple Street, a line of cars ahead of me and behind me, people on the sides of rural roads, some walking and some running. All to the house on Maple Street.

The street was lined in parked cars, so I pulled down the center of the street and left the station wagon in the middle of the cul-de-sac. I opened the back of the wagon and brought as many cylinders of salt as I could. I left it open so I could run back.

The lights were on in the house this time, and I could see tons of people inside. All the zombie-walking Fructoids headed to the backyard, but I waltzed straight up to the front door. I kicked it, my arms full of salt. "Clarice!" I yelled.

You'd think the neighbors would come outside. You'd think they'd have been watching the pilgrimage. But they weren't. They were all mind-melded.

Clarice opened the door, looking just as unreal as she always did. She looked down at my arms. "Fenton Marsh, you were to be useful, not detrimental."

107

"I don't want to be detrimental," I said. "But you have to let the teachers go."

"They are to be useful too," she said.

"You kidnapped them!"

"We are preparing them. Their work will be more intensive than yours," she said, and I laughed maniacally, unable to believe I was involved with this over soft serve ice cream.

"Let them go," I said.

"I cannot acquiesce to your demands," she said. "You are not being useful, Fenton Marsh. I need verbal confirmation you will comply as you originally promised. The schedule of our mission has changed. I require your immediate compliance."

"For what?"

"For departure," she said. I thought of Travis. When it happens.

"Let the teachers go!" I screamed. I fumbled with the salt in my arms, peeling back the spout on one canister. I flung it in her direction.

She screamed, a high-pitched, foreign, tritone of a sound. The human skin façade burned right off, and beneath it she oozed green over what appeared to be black and purple insides. Fructoids descended upon me, but I went crazy, throwing salt all around. More screams and burns and sizzle and smoke and green and ooze. It was pandemonium.

And just like that, I was out of ammunition. Because I was an idiot. And I thought this was a movie, apparently.

"Restrain him!" Clarice called, and two of the burlier dudes strung me up against a wall. I began to struggle, but my resistance was futile.

Which I would normally laugh to myself about but . . .

108

The house filled quickly with them, wall-to-wall, shoulder to shoulder. And then a loud, reverberating sound came from underneath us, and the house shook. The lights in the house went off, and outlines of green came on. People stumbled down basement steps, cramming into what I was sure was a small space. But it was like a friggin' Mary Poppins bag.

Then I realized: the ship was underground. The house was merely on top of it.

They started talking to each other in another language. Weird sounds of hissing and electrical whines and that obnoxious high-pitched noise that a TV on mute makes.

Clarice, oozing and smoking and disgusting, made some clicking hissing noise that made people scatter to specific places. As if she'd called for places before a curtain rise.

Just then, Travis appeared in the doorway. "Fenton!" he called. He spoke to the burly men in a native tongue, but they ignored him. Finally, he just started beating their arms. "Let him go! Let him go!"

"There's more salt in the car," I said to Travis, not having the faintest clue whether he'd help me. He looked at me and then he looked all around the room, and then he bolted back out the front door. The house shook and groaned, and it felt like we were lifting. Travis tumbled into the doorway with more salt than I could have carried in ten trips, and flung it at the burly dudes first. They dropped to the ground, and so did I.

"You're helping me," I said to Travis in disbelief.

"We're friends," he said, like it was the most natural thing in the world that he was helping me rebel against his own kind. "We have to get you out of here."

"The teachers!"

109

Travis hesitated, and then said, "Come on." He bolted down the basement steps into the green room I'd presumably broken into earlier. There were eight tubes lining the room, each about three feet wide, spanning floor to ceiling, and filled with a green liquid. And inside them, each of the six missing teachers were floating, unconscious. Their names were inscribed on the bottom of the tubes. I looked back at the empty tubes next to me. At the bottom of the one closest to me read the words, Fenton Marsh: Sustenance.

Travis looked back at me. "There's no way. I don't know how to get them out. We can only save you."

"But . . ."

Travis grabbed me, dragging me away. "We can still save you."

We were fighting our way through Fructoids once we got back to the living room. They didn't care that I'd gone deeper into the ship. They cared that I wanted out.

Salt canisters littered the floor, and I grabbed them, threw them so they'd break open, spewed it everywhere. I made it to the front door, opened it, and hung out over the edge when Clarice grabbed me by the throat, pinning me against the floor, my body half in and half out of the doorframe. The burn on her body was spreading quickly, and I could see pearlescent white jawbone in her face. "Fenton Marsh!" she screamed angrily. The air around me burned cold on my face. We had climbed faster than I'd realized, the house literally moving on top of the ship. We were up in the clouds. There was no way out.

She saw the peril on my face. "Comply, and you will survive."

"Fenton, don't!" Travis cried. He barreled toward Clarice and me at full speed, and he threw us both onto the front stoop of the house, which was unbelievably still attached. I rolled down it,

110

hanging off the edge. Clarice did the same, but she quickly flung herself back up on the steps. She made another terrible noise, and more Fructoids came out of the house, lunging at me. Only, as if uncoordinated little lemmings, many of them went falling onto the ground. The most injured went first, as if on a kamikaze mission.

Travis made it to me, and he said, "You must trust me, friend." Then he ripped back the hands of the Fructoids grabbing me, and he peeled my own hands off the steps I had barely been clinging to.

And then? I was falling through the air. Falling and falling.

Travis's body sailed by me, and then I hit it, full force, in mid-air, and we were tumbling together. Screaming. I was probably crying. Dizzy, with the damn sounds of salt-burned Fructoids ringing in my ears.

Clarice's voice carried, "Fenton Marsh! Noncompliant!"

And many more seconds than you'd expect later, we hit the ground. And I was alive.

Travis maneuvered his body under mine, and took the force of the impact. Like Wyle E. Coyote, there was a Travis-shaped hole in the ground, and I had landed on top of him and hardly felt a thing, save for the wind being knocked out of me.

Who knows how long I lay there awkwardly on top of Travis's body, unable to process what had happened.

Beneath me, Travis laughed. "It worked," he said.

"You thought it might not?" I asked, getting to my feet. He hopped to his feet and then out of the cartoon hole. He reached down for me and hoisted me up.

"I hoped," he said. He looked up at the sky, a weird green and white blinking light rose higher and higher into the clouds before it straight up disappeared.

"Where did it go?" I asked.

"They reached the county line," he said. "Their Jedi only worked that far. Anyone else would be able to see what just happened, so they had to use the invisibility by the time they hit the county limits."

"Travis, does this mean . . . Can you not go home now?" I asked, realizing what he'd offered me.

He shrugged his shoulders, naturally. "There was not much for me to go home to," he said. "I have a friend here. Right?"

He reached for a fist bump, but I bear-hugged him. "Right," I said.

We walked back to Maple Street slowly. Travis had some minor burns. I'd fallen ten thousand feet. We were a little beat up.

When we got to the cul-de-sac, the house at the end of the street was now just a giant hole in the ground with a fence leading up to it. Abandoned cars still lined the streets.

"What are people going to think?" I asked him.

"That they were invaded by aliens," he said, his face sober.

"Really?" I asked, shock and surprise and a weird amount of relief overcoming me.

He laughed. "Nope! But it was funny to see you think that's the case. You'll still be alone in what you know."

I shrugged this time. "Not alone, man. I've got a friend."

And so, you can still hear the screams. It's weird, and who knows how long it will last, but these weird electronic alien noises mixed with people-screams still echo right when you get to the county line.

Am I traumatized? Yes. Sure. Can I believe it even happened? Pretty much no. Do I wake up every morning with the sinking feeling that it was only the beginning? You bet I do.

But do I have someone to sit with at lunch every day, who, using his Jedi mind powers, is sometimes pretty good at getting nice girls to sit with us?

Yeah, I do.

And all it took for that miracle to occur was the total alien invasion and eventual desolation of the house on Maple Street.

THE FORCE

By Heather Hildenbrand

For information on other titles
Visit the author's website:
http://heatherhildenbrand.blogspot.com/

CHAPTER ONE

My cheek slipped sideways from my arm to the bare mattress, jarring me awake. I looked down and grimaced at the pool of saliva that coated my skin. Did all humans drool in their sleep or was it exclusive to the male body I'd been issued? Gross.

I pushed myself onto my elbows and surveyed my surroundings. My eyes closed and opened again slowly. Maybe if I blinked enough, it would look different. It didn't. The suite we'd booked was trashed.

The bedroom floor was covered in a pile of sheets and blankets where I'd thrown them aside in my unconscious state. From my view through the open door, the common area looked worse. The couch was overturned, the curtains ripped from the rod, and the sliding door that led onto the balcony hung open. Cartons of takeout littered the beige carpet. Several of them were tipped on their side, noodles and chopsticks spilling out. Discarded clothing—jeans and a T-shirt that I remembered seeing on Dieben last night—left a trail from the balcony door to the second bedroom at the other end of the suite. The door was closed. I assumed he must still be passed out. I looked around once more and found my room empty of any other occupants. Bone must be in with Dieben.

I sat up, trying to piece together the previous night's events or how I'd ended up in this bed wearing nothing but a pair of shorts, but the details were lost. My head pounded with every movement. I slowed, carefully positioning my legs while pressing my palm against the thudding in my skull. This body didn't handle hangovers very well. Hopefully Dieben and Bone were better off.

Time to wake them and find out.

I made it three steps when my communicator beeped. Why did mothers always have the worst timing? A sixth sense, definitely. I hit the button and an image of her face projected itself outward, hovering three inches above the handheld device. On her end, an image of my face did the same.

"Hi, Mother," I said, running a hand through my hair at the last second. I couldn't even remember what my features looked like. Hopefully everything seemed normal in my expression. It was hard to hold a poker face when the face didn't belong to me to begin with.

"Hello, Axel." She gave me a tight smile, her smooth skin creasing at the edges of her mouth. It was strange to me how human-like our appearance seemed when our behavior was so different.

"Is everything okay?" I asked.

"Of course, I just wanted to say hello. How is your Rumschpringe experience?"

Rumschpringe. A one-week vacation where we could get away and not answer to anyone. A time to let loose before we went home and took up the life of a responsible adult of Panmera. During my time here, I'd learned the humans had something similar, called spring break.

116

Panmerans could choose any planet we wanted for Rumschpringe, but my best friend, Bone, and I had chosen Earth as sort of a personal challenge. It was the planet with the largest number of deserters. Our kind came for Rumschpringe and never went home. In our world, they called it the Force. The invisible thing that sucked us in. Made us willingly give up a home filled with higher technology, fewer diseases, and longer life spans. For … this. Earth. Being human. And every imperfection that came with it. No one knew what the Force was. Anyone who truly experienced it never returned to explain.

Deserters were considered the lowest of the low. Worse than criminals, not that we had many of those. Deserters were traitors. Even if they ever did try to return, Panmeran society wouldn't have let them. Only in death … and even then, it'd been luck more than anything that had brought my older brother Colryn's body home to its final resting place last year.

I wanted to show them all I was strong enough to resist the Force. I'd spent six days here, enjoying myself in the barbaric way only humans could, by over-indulging on food, drink, and whatever else this planet had to offer an eighteen year-old alien stuck in a human male's body, and soon I'd return home. Willingly. In one piece. With my friends. Nothing resembling a Force had shown itself thus far.

Even if it did, I would face it. I'd planned for this all year. When my tutor had asked which planet I chose for Rumschpringe, I'd answered "Earth" without hesitation. Because more than anything, I wanted to understand and actively resist the invisible Force that took more and more of our people each year. For peace of mind. For my parents. For Colryn.

117

It would help if I could remember what had happened last night.

The hologram flickered. My mother awaited an answer. Humans were obviously prone to daydreaming. "I'm having a great time," I assured her. At least, I thought I was.

"And the others? They are faring just as well?"

"Bone and Dieben are having a blast."

She frowned. "What is a blast?"

"It means 'a good time,'" I explained. "It's just something I picked up from my host."

"I see," she said, although her confused expression said otherwise. My mother had never inhabited a human host. I didn't expect her to understand.

"They're waiting for me in the other room. I have to go, Mom."

Her mouth tightened. I knew she wanted to ask me about what we were doing, but she didn't. And she wouldn't. It was against the rules. Thank goodness, since I didn't have an answer anyway. Human brains were a lot weaker than I'd expected. Why the heck couldn't I remember anything?

"I'm glad you've enjoyed yourself this past week. Your father is making preparations for your return. I'll contact you tonight with the pickup location," she said. "Be well, Axel."

"Be well, Mother," I returned. The hologram flickered and disappeared. I pocketed my communicator and went in search of my friends.

I stepped over a chair with two broken legs and zig-zagged around half a dozen overturned cartons of noodles as I crossed the common area. At Dieben's bedroom door, I turned the knob but nothing happened. I pushed harder and it gave a couple of inches then stopped.

"Dieben?" I called. No answer.

I shoved hard, putting my shoulder into it, and was rewarded when it gave, slowly, as something heavy on the other end slid aside. I entered and found a small writing desk overturned on the floor near the door.

"Dieben?" I called again.

I couldn't tell if it was a sleeping body underneath the mound of blankets lying in the center of the bed or just a balled-up sheet. I went over and poked it and it shot up. "Wha …?" Dieben blinked and looked around, his almond eyes scanning the room before landing on me. His dark eyebrows crinkled. "Axel?"

"This is me."

"Ugh. These bodies are weird. I can't tell them apart." He shoved the blankets aside and climbed out of bed, almost tripping when his foot caught on the edge of the sheet. "How long were we unconscious?"

"They call it sleeping."

"Whatever," he grumbled. Dieben was always grumpy in the mornings. His temperament didn't improve much in the afternoons or evenings, either. I tried to ignore it when I could. The only reason I'd brought him was for the numbers. Rumschpringe was always spent as a trio. We'd needed a third.

"Where's Bone?" I asked.

Dieben shrugged. "How do I know? I was sleeping."

I frowned, ignoring Dieben's sarcasm. It was against the rules to go out alone and Bone didn't have the smoothest host body to work with. His human was clumsy and awkward. So was Bone.

119

I tried using my communicator to call him, only to remember Bone had dropped his in the pool days ago and it shorted out. I tried instead on my cellular phone. We'd each purchased one when Bone's communicator had stopped working. There was a long pause and then, without ringing, his voicemail came over the line. I hung up. "He must've stepped out," I said, worry making my forehead crease. "We need to go look for him."

"Why would he leave? He knows better. Did you check the bathroom? The balcony?" Dieben took a step toward the door.

"Uh …"

I didn't have time to mention the mess in the common area before Dieben caught sight of it. He stopped and stared around the room before regarding me with wide eyes. "What the hell, Axel?"

"It was like this when I woke up. Do you remember anything about last night?"

Dieben cocked his head to one side in thought and then shook his head. "No," he said finally. "Why? Did I do something to Bone? Lock him out or something? If I did, it was just a joke …"

"No, I mean, maybe. I don't know. I can't remember anything either."

We shared a look. The limitations on the human brain were frustrating. And my alarm was growing. Number one rule of Rumschpringe: stay together. If anyone found out I'd lost my best friend, I'd be better off deserting than returning home.

We dressed quickly, Dieben forgoing his usual half hour in front of the mirror in favor of a quick hand-smoothing over his ruffled hair. Our true bodies had manes of hair twice as thick as our current hosts. Maybe Dieben had deemed this one manageable. Or maybe he actually gave a shit about Bone. You never could tell with Dieben.

The hall outside our suite was empty. I tried not to let the disappointment get to me. I'd half hoped Dieben's assumption had been correct, that Bone had just been locked outside as a practical joke, a habit Dieben excelled at. But he wasn't there, nor was he in the lobby when we arrived downstairs.

I waited while Dieben asked the front desk clerk for information. Females responded better to him, in either form. Something that always grated on me, mostly because of the way Dieben lapped it up and brushed them off when he was done. "Rude" was a trait he'd made intergalactic. While they chatted, I tried calling Bone again. Straight to voicemail. His phone was off.

"He has bright red hair, freckles on his face, skinny legs," Dieben said, describing Bone to a pink-cheeked young woman with too much paint on her eyes.

"I saw him leave with you last night," she said, smiling up at Dieben through her clumped lashes. "But not this morning when you came in."

We got back this morning?

Dieben ran a hand through his hair and the girl giggled. I rolled my eyes—this body's most common reaction to my self-absorbed friend.

"Did we happen to say where we were going?" I asked her.

She blinked, appearing to notice me for the first time. "No, sorry," she said, directing her answer at Dieben. She looked genuinely disappointed that she couldn't help. Dieben thanked her and turned away.

"What now?" he asked.

I felt the girl's eyes on us as we walked. Dieben either didn't notice or didn't care. "I don't know." I huffed out a breath and looked around, hoping for some idea or direction.

121

"Hey, what's that?"

"What?"

Dieben pointed at the left side of my pants. "That."

I looked down. Something metal protruded from my pocket. I pulled it out and turned it over in my hand, inspecting it.

"What is it?" Dieben asked.

I probed my host's mind for the answer. It took a moment, but I found it. "It's a ten-millimeter wrench."

"Why do you have it?"

"No idea." We stared at each other, both searching for memories that wouldn't surface. "Ugh. It must have something to do with last night. These are the same pants …"

"What does it do?"

"It's a tool. It … opens things." I cocked my head. "Your host doesn't know this?"

He shrugged. "They say you're given an appropriate match. I think this guy was more of a people person than a tool."

Something in my host's brain found that funny. I smirked as the joke dawned on me. "For once, the match was off," I said.

"Huh?"

"Nothing. Check your pockets. Maybe there's something else."

We both stuffed our hands into our pockets. My left hand closed around something small and hard. I pulled it out and held it up. "A bolt," I said, examining it. "You?"

Dieben squinted at a small scrap of paper in his hands. "A phone number. Score."

"Does it have a name or anything else?" I asked.

"Jane. Huh. This guy thinks she sounds plain," he said, tapping his finger against his temple.

Dieben's reference grated on me. I didn't particularly enjoy the way we invaded our host, mind and body, and then detached ourselves so suddenly upon exiting that our humans were left with short-term amnesia along with various other side effects. Panmerans, as a rule, didn't concern themselves with the damage we caused. The attitude was that since we didn't kill our hosts, we weren't wrong. My opinion on the matter felt a little grayer, though I'd never say so.

Still it was a shame Dieben's host didn't offer him an extra set of manners. I resisted the urge to hit Dieben—and his host. "Can I see it?" I snatched the paper when he held it out and sure enough, the name Jane and a seven-digit number were handwritten on one side. I turned it over. On the backside were several words printed in red, block letters. "Egg drop soup, four ninety-five," I read. I looked at Dieben. "It's part of a menu. A place called The Golden Noo."

"Golden Noo?"

"I can't read the rest of the word. Noo is short for something."

"Noo…" Dieben muttered, clearly at a loss.

Using both my host and my own knowledge database, I searched for possible words that began with Noo. "Something with food," I said. I stared at the piece of paper in my hand.

When nothing came to mind, my thoughts wandered back to the mess in our suite upstairs. Would they list something like that on our check-out statement? We'd have to clean it up so my parents didn't hear about it. And all those cartons of food … "Noodles!" I said.

"Noodles?" Dieben repeated.

I looked back at the menu, read the full name aloud. "The Golden Noodle. That's the place. We must've been there at some point last night. Come on, we'll start there."

I pocketed the wrench and bolt and headed for the door with Dieben close behind. A uniformed man with gray hair sticking out from underneath his navy blue cap nodded and held the door for us as we exited. I made it as far as the edge of the sidewalk, pedestrians parting around us as they passed, before jogging back to the man whose only purpose seemed to be to open and close a door all day. "Sir, can you tell me where The Golden Noodle is?"

"That Chinese place? Hang a left at the corner. It's about two blocks down. Right next to the vet's office." He chuckled. "Gets me every time."

"Thanks," I told him and motioned for Dieben to follow as I walked in the direction the man had pointed.

Progress was slow. The streets were crowded and the machines—cars—on the pavement just beyond didn't stop for anything. A heavy woman with a small, furry animal sticking out of her bag shoved me aside as she hustled past.

"Do you think he's there?" Dieben asked.

"I don't know, but it's the only place I can think of to look," I said.

Dieben's communicator beeped.

"What's that?" I asked.

He read the screen and then pocketed the handheld device. "A message. The shuttle home has been scheduled."

Worry for Bone spiked. I needed to find him, before anyone knew he was missing. Before something bad happened. Bone wasn't good in new places. He wasn't even that good in familiar places most of the time. He'd only come to Earth because of me.

124

Because he knew I'd wanted to meet the challenge it represented to our kind, and to me. If something happened to him, it would be my fault.

We made the left, sticking close on the heels of the two men in front of us, trusting the machines to remain stopped while the little white light signaled it was okay to cross the street. At the next block, I craned my neck over the heads of those in front of us, trying to see the place advertised on Dieben's scrap of menu.

"Do you see it?" Dieben asked.

"Not yet. Come on."

A yellow sign with the words "Golden Noodle" typeset in bold red letters floated into view above the heads of the couple in front of us. I skirted around them and perched on the edge of the curb with Dieben beside me.

"What's going on?" Dieben asked.

I simply stared.

Two four-wheeled machines—cars—with blue flashing lights on top were parked outside of the tiny restaurant. A man with a mustache and black uniform complete with a shiny badge stood outside the front door making notes on a clipboard. A short man in baggy pants and animated arm movements stood beside him, clearly excited about whatever he was explaining. The uniformed man nodded but never took his eyes off his clipboard as the second man talked. Through the front window of the shop, I spotted another uniform standing in front of a high counter. Across from him, facing the street, stood a girl.

None of the other humans I'd seen over the past week caught my attention like this one. I studied her, searching for the reason for my interest. She wore a white button-down shirt that contrasted with the "V" of brown skin left by her collar. Dark hair hung at an angle against her face, stopping just above her shoulders. Her eyes were dark and slanted—and trained on me.

"Are those police?" Dieben asked.

"Yes."

"Don't they come around when a crime has been committed?"

"Yes."

I continued to study the girl. Her lips moved—speaking to the policeman in front of her, I assumed—but her eyes remained locked on me. Most humans glanced at each other without even seeing, passing over as they travelled to the next destination or task. But this girl stared right into me. As if she knew me. Or wanted to.

I wanted to know her too.

I shook that last thought away. There was no time to know anyone. That's not what Rumschpringe was about. Anonymity. Fun. Temporary. These were the parameters of my Earthly experience.

"Should we go in anyway?" Dieben asked.

"Not yet," I said. "I don't see Bone. Let's walk around back."

We darted across the street between oncoming traffic. Someone honked as they slowed for us. Dieben scowled at them but I kept my attention on the officer with the clipboard. Something about being here with them made me nervous, though I had no idea why it should.

"...don't care if the window's not broken. I'm pressing charges if you find them," the older man said to the officer as we walked by.

Dieben and I passed the vet's office on the corner and found our way to the alley that ran behind the string of buildings. The air was stale here, smelling heavily of sweaty animals and excrement.

"It's gross back here," Dieben said, wrinkling his nose. We both kept to the center of the pavement, careful not to get close to the overturned garbage cans or piles of animal dung. The animal doctor clearly had no qualms about letting his patients relieve themselves wherever they pleased. Humans were filthy.

As we reached the restaurant, the scent of grease and noodles took over, blocking out most of the stench from the vet. Dieben went to the door and began to pull it open.

"Dieben," I hissed.

He stopped. "I was just going to peek in."

"Just wait a minute." I stopped in front of the small window level with my chin and pulled the bolt out of my pocket. It fit perfectly against the hole at the base of the lock. "Shit," I said, appreciating the punch of the word as it came out of my host's mouth. This part of the vocabulary felt colorful, perfect for expressing the way I felt at the moment.

"What is it?" Dieben asked, coming over.

I pulled the wrench out and twisted the bolt back into place, once again sealing and locking the window. When I'd finished, I regarded Dieben with a sinking feeling in my gut. I knew something about this place had felt familiar. Although, what had led me to such a horrible decision was another memory lost in the void of whatever had happened last night. Maybe the girl inside could explain.

"Axel?" Dieben prompted.

I looked from him to the window and back again. "I think we broke in here last night."

CHAPTER TWO

Dieben and I spent the next hour in the coffee shop across the street, watching The Golden Noodle and waiting for the policemen to leave. I consumed three cups of coffee while we stared through the shop's window. Something the cashier called "dark roast." By the time the flashers turned off and the police cars drove away, my knee bounced with poorly contained energy. I now understood the draw to such a bitter drink.

Dieben broke away from the table he'd stopped at on his return from the restroom. He held a small scrap of paper in his hand and a ridiculous smirk on his face. "We're going out tonight," he said, nodding at the blonde across the room. She waved, wiggling her fingers and sipping from a paper mug.

My lips pressed tightly together as I blew air out through my nose. "Bone is missing, we broke into a locked building, the police are looking for us, and you've got a date?"

"What?" he said, his shoulders rising in a shrug. "I'll only go if we find Bone." As if that made his behavior acceptable.

I rose and gathered my empty cups, shaking my head. "Nothing. Come on."

We crossed the street, dodging angry cars once again, and made our way to The Golden Noodle. The door was unlocked, the "open" sign lit through the large front window. A bell jingled as we entered.

"Just a sec," called a female voice from somewhere out of sight.

I walked to the counter, Dieben on my heels. "Give me that number," I said. I looked down at the paper he offered. "Not that one. The one from last night," I snapped.

"Oh, right." He fished the scrap of paper from his pocket and handed it over.

I flipped it over, momentarily ignoring Jane and the seven digits she'd provided Dieben. I turned the scrap of menu and held it over the full-sized one lying on top of the stack on the counter in front of me. It was a perfect match.

The door behind the counter swung open and the girl I'd seen earlier walked through.

"Mmm. We have a winner," Dieben said quietly.

I punched Dieben in the thigh.

He jerked forward, earning a confused stare from the girl. "Can I help you?" she asked.

"We're looking for our friend," I said.

She focused on me. There went those eyes again, that strange feeling of familiarity. "Axel," she said.

"You know me?"

Her eyes narrowed. "We met last night. You don't remember?"

"Um, not really," I admitted. I stole a look at her nametag, momentarily horrified as I remembered the number Dieben had earned from someone last night. The clip-on piece of plastic attached above her left breast said 'Becca.' I breathed out. Not Jane.

"We can't remember anything that happened last night," Dieben explained. "Surprising, though. You'd think I'd remember a pretty face like yours."

Even his host oozed with fake charm. I resisted the urge to punch him again. Usually I ignored him when he did this, but not with this girl. She was different. I wasn't sure how I knew that, but I did. And she knew me.

"Your attention was … elsewhere," she said wryly without more than a glance in Dieben's direction.

"Well, that's a shame," he returned. "Glad I'm here now to fix that."

I couldn't stomach this. "We're wondering if you've seen our friend, Bone. He has freckles and—"

"The redhead?" she interrupted.

"Yes. You've seen him?"

"He slept over at my house."

I tapped into my host's brain, trying to understand what that meant. My eyes widened. "Oh. I see."

"No, not with me," she added. "My roommate, Marnie. He went home with her last night. You really don't remember?"

I shook my head. "Sorry."

"You guys were at that after-hours club down on First. I came by when my shift ended to give Marnie a ride home. Your friend, Bone—is that really his name?"

"Yeah." Or at least the closest English translation. I didn't add that part.

"That's … different. Anyway," she went on, "he was with her and barely still on his feet. You guys didn't look much better off but some girl was already putting you in the back of a cab. She handed the driver money and you drove off before I could get your attention to take your friend with you. So I took him home with us."

"Is he still there?" I asked.

She shrugged. "He was when I left for work about an hour ago."

"Can you check with your roommate?"

"Yeah, sure—"

"Becca!" called a man's voice from the other side of the wall. "Give me a minute," she said with a grimace. She thrust a menu at us. "Here. Order something," she added before disappearing through the swinging door.

I scanned the menu. The thought of noodles made my stomach roll.

"Becca's pretty hot," Dieben said.

"Don't even think about it," I told him.

"Why not?" I didn't answer and Dieben's eyes widened. "You like this one? Oh man, there's a first for everything, I guess."

"Shut up," I said but Dieben ignored me, slapping a palm against my back.

"Wow, who knew you'd have a thing for humans."

"I don't have a thing for humans."

"Really? Name one girl from back home you've gone for."

The door swung open and Becca reappeared. Saved from answering. "Let's just get Bone," I muttered.

Dieben laughed under his breath.

"What'll it be?" Becca asked, her voice louder than before. Before I could ask about it, she jerked a thumb behind her.

"Oh. Um, soup?" I said.

"What kind?"

I picked the first thing I saw. "Egg drop?"

131

"What size?"

"Um."

"Two large bowls of egg drop," Becca yelled over her shoulder.

Pans banged together in answer.

Becca lowered her voice and leaned in. "I called Marnie. She's bringing Bone, but you guys can't stay here."

"What? Why not?" I asked.

Her expression was an accusation. "Are you seriously asking me that? Marnie told me what you guys did last night." My blank look only seemed to make her madder. "You broke in here and stole two hundred dollars' worth of noodles! Mr. Wu is furious! What were you thinking? Are you some kind of criminals?"

"I have no idea what we were thinking," I said.

"Probably that we were hungry." Deiben snickered. We both glared at him.

"Tell Marnie and Bone we'll wait at the coffee shop across the street," I said.

"One hour." She nodded.

My feet should've moved me toward the door, but I found myself standing still, caught up in those dark, slanted eyes of hers. She stared back at me, her gaze reaching far enough inside I was afraid she'd recognize I wasn't who—or what—I pretended to be. "You're not from here, are you?" she said finally.

I didn't answer. Dieben cleared his throat. "No. We're from … out of town," I said. "Why?"

"Some stuff Bone was saying. And—" Pink flooded her cheeks, causing a heated reaction in my stomach that confused and excited me all at once.

"And?" I prompted.

"And your eyes. They're violet and ... really pretty."

"Thanks."

A bell dinged behind the counter. I looked up and found a pair of beady eyes watching me through the gap in the two-way serving rack. Becca reached back and grabbed the two Styrofoam cups and set them on the counter in front of us. Behind her, the beady eyes blinked once and then disappeared.

Dieben slung an arm around my shoulders in a rough gesture. "We'll see you later then?" he asked, eyeing Becca.

"I have to work, and you guys really shouldn't come back in here." She pressed a flurry of buttons on the cash register, each one beeping in rapid succession. "Ten forty for the soup," she added.

I counted out the necessary bills and handed them over the counter. Money hadn't been a problem, thanks to Dieben's host. His host's parents had apparently given him a bank account large enough to provide for a pretty cushy Rumschpringe. Hence, the hotel suite.

"You should come to us," Dieben said. "Later. When you get off work. We're staying at the Imperial. Room Nine-Twenty."

It was the only thing Dieben had said all day that I agreed with. I wanted to see this girl again. I wanted to figure out this draw I felt—and whether the feeling came from my host or myself. Dieben was right. I'd never been interested in the girls back home. There wasn't a particular reason. I had many friends, including females, but none of them had sparked any sort of attraction before. Becca, however, intrigued me. I found myself admiring the curve of her neck, the smooth skin of her shoulder where it disappeared underneath the fabric of her shirt. Her long, slender fingers and the graceful way she moved as she counted the money and bagged our soup.

"I'll think about it," she said, her voice clipped.

I almost pursued it, but stopped short. Something in my host's mind said she didn't intend to show and pressing the issue wouldn't change her mind. Human girls didn't simply show up to strange hotel rooms. Or at least, the smart ones didn't. And Becca was smart.

Instead, I gave her my best smile. "Thank you for all your help. I hope I see you again," I said before following Dieben out.

CHAPTER THREE

Dieben was relentless. We sat at a small sidewalk table in front of the coffee shop while he baited me about Becca. First, trying to get me to admit I liked her. Then, when that didn't work, he went on about how hot she was, trying to make me jealous. I gulped coffee and tried to think of a way to shut him up.

"I can't believe it took coming to Earth to get you to recognize hotness when you see it. Wait'll I tell the guys back home. They're going to—"

"Do you think it's weird that we don't remember anything at all from last night?" I interrupted.

Dieben shrugged. "Doesn't that happen to humans? They call it a hangover."

"It just seems strange that it happened to both of us. I didn't think we consumed that much alcohol. And we broke into a Chinese restaurant? That's really stupid. We're supposed to be keeping a low profile."

Dieben seemed lost in thought and then said, "My host has been known to do that sort of thing."

Of course he has. "We need to find out if anything else happened," I said.

"You think breaking into The Golden Noodle wasn't our only dumb idea?"

"Bone went home with a human," I said.

"Good point. I can call that Jane chick whose number I got. I have a feeling that's who got us a cab. I can see what she knows."

I'd been thinking the same thing during Becca's story. "Yeah, do that."

Dieben pulled a small, black phone from his pocket and punched in the number. His expression lit as someone picked up. "Hello, Jane? It's Dieben. We met last night ..." He rose and wandered down the sidewalk while he talked.

I scanned faces, searching for Bone. The more time passed without him beside me, the more I worried. His hour was almost up. I cast a glance into the front window of The Golden Noodle. Becca stood behind the counter bent over a book of some kind. She seemed deep in concentration, her bottom lip stuck between her teeth. I stared at her mouth, remembering the warm feeling I got in my chest when she'd smiled.

"Axel, bro." I looked up at the sound of my name and found a red-haired teen approaching me from the other direction. I rose to meet Bone and he pulled me into a one-armed hug before swinging around to stand beside me. "Marn, this is Axel, my best friend. Axel, Marnie."

"Nice to meet you." A willowy girl with purple hair and narrow-rimmed glasses wrinkled her brow at me. "So, he's from Panmera too?"

I whipped my head around to gawk at Bone. "You told her?"

Bone grimaced. "Yeah, it was an accident. Sorry."

"An accident? Man, what the hell?"

"I was drunk and—"

"Wait, do you remember last night?" I asked.

"Not much," Bone admitted.

136

Before Bone could elaborate, Dieben returned, sliding the phone back inside his pocket. Over Marnie's head, our eyes met. Dieben's brows knitted and his mouth opened to say something. I nodded toward Marnie and then shook my head. Thankfully, he understood. "Bone, you made it back alive," he said, clapping Bone on the back as he rejoined the group.

"Yeah, sorry we got separated," Bone said, looking mostly at me. I knew he felt bad about deserting me. Dieben, not so much. "Marnie took good care of me, though. Oh, and Becca. She was cool. Gave us a ride home and everything."

"Yeah, Becca's real cool," Dieben said with a wink at me. I ignored him.

"Dieben, this is Marnie. She and Becca are roommates," Bone said.

"Marnie, nice to meet you." Dieben stuck his hand out in a human gesture of hello. A ritual I'd skipped due to my shock.

Marnie shook Dieben's hand, her mouth open in awe. "I can't believe you guys are—" she paused, casting a quick look over her shoulder before adding, "aliens" in a loud whisper.

My shoulders went rigid as I searched the faces of those passing by, but none of them reacted to her words. Dieben retracted his hand from Marnie's and then used it to smack Bone in the back of the head. "You told her? Idiot!"

For the second time today, Dieben and I were on the same page.

"Relax," Bone said, stepping to my other side—out of Dieben's reach. "She won't tell anyone. She promised."

"I'm not going to give away your secret," Marnie assured us. "Pinky swear."

"Pinky swear?" Dieben repeated, clearly having already worked out the meaning of her words. "That's how you seal your word here? With your smallest appendage? Great." He threw up his hands. "We're dead."

"We're not dead," Bone insisted.

"What did Jane say?" I asked.

"In front of her?" Deiben jerked a thumb at Marnie.

"Not like it matters now," I said.

"Right."

Across the road, a police cruiser sped by and pulled to the curb in front of the Golden Nugget. The Asian man I'd seen earlier— who I could only assume was Mr. Wu—came out, baggy pants now grease stained, and began talking animatedly to the officer as he got out of his car. I watched the pair of them while I listened to Dieben explain.

"She said she remembers us," Dieben said slowly. There was something off in his tone. Something uncertain and guarded.

"And?" I prompted.

"She said we danced for a while. I bought her drinks. At the end of the night, she found out we didn't have a car or a ride home and she called us a cab."

"That's it?" I asked. "Did she say if we …?" I paused to glance at Marnie. "If we told her anything?"

"She didn't ask if I was from another planet, no," he said.

I sighed. "Fine."

I checked on the scene across the street. The policeman had his pen poised just above his clipboard but was now paying close attention to Mr. Wu. A decided change from earlier. At that moment, Mr. Wu squinted across the street, eyes scanning the sidewalk, and pointed in our direction.

"We need to get off the street," I said without taking my eyes off the finger aimed at me. I was hyper-aware of the wrench still in my pocket. I couldn't take it out now but I knew, without a doubt, if I was caught with it, I was finished.

The policeman followed Mr. Wu's outstretched finger, scanning the sidewalk where we stood. "Now," I added.

The others finally broke off from their conversation. "Crap," Dieben muttered as he found the object of my attention. He took a step back. "Let's go," he said.

Marnie stared across the street, her expression transforming from blank to alarm. "Uh, guys, Axel is right. We need to go NOW."

"Who is that guy?" Bone asked.

"Mr. Wu. He owns The Golden Noodle and I think he just spotted your friends," Marnie said, tugging him down the sidewalk.

"The ... Is that the place you broke into last night?" Bone's eyes widened. "I remember! You called me from inside. Said you came looking for Becca, but she was gone. Dieben, you said you couldn't remember ever feeling so hungry. So Axel here swiped a wrench and got you inside. You said you ate so many noodles ..."

I stopped walking, listening to Bone's recounting of the event. Maybe his explanation would trigger something and I could remember ... but no, nothing. "I thought Jane put us in a cab home," I said, frowning.

Bone shook his head. "She might've put you in a cab, but you came here. Said something about when you saw Becca, the world stopped, and you had to know her. Said you saw this place on her nametag. I tried to tell you she wasn't here but my battery died before I could. Sorry, dude."

When Bone got to the part about the planet failing to spin properly, Dieben hooted. I did my best to ignore him, more confused than anything else. "If that's true, how did Dieben get Jane's number written on a scrap of menu from this place?"

Bone shrugged. "No idea. Maybe she came with you?"

I shook my head. "Becca said she saw Jane put us in a cab and paid the driver to take us home while she stayed behind."

"Strange," Bone said.

Very.

Across the street, the cop tossed his clipboard on the hood of his car and started walking in our direction. A car honked. His gaze was drawn to an approaching vehicle and he halted abruptly.

Good. Let him deal with the angry drivers. But instead of darting back out of the way, the officer pulled a shiny metal badge free of its clip on his belt and held it up. The car slammed on its brakes and came to a stop. The policeman hurried across.

"Time to go," I said, motioning for the others to follow.

I picked up the pace, speed walking. Something in my host's mind cautioned me against a full sprint. It would only draw attention. And maybe even alert pedestrians we should be stopped once they saw a policeman in pursuit. I hurried at the fastest walk this body could produce.

Bone was still oblivious to our pursuer. "Hey, do you want to bring your food?" He pointed to our table where I'd set the paper bag.

"No time," Marnie hissed, pulling him along. "Now, come on!"

"What's the hurry?" he asked, stumbling when she yanked.

"That," I said, pointing behind us. The uniform was on our side of the street now, eyes intent on the four of us.

140

"Well, shit," Bone said, plucking the best word I could think of from his host's vocabulary. "Let's go."

"Where?" Marnie asked.

"The hotel. But only if we can lose him," I said, darting left then right again as I slid between pedestrians. Marnie, her hand locked on Bone's wrist, did the same. Up ahead, Dieben disappeared from view.

We were almost running now, weaving in and out of bodies, cutting people off. A few cursed under their breath. One tried to trip me but I managed to hop out of reach.

Somewhere behind us, I heard someone yell. The policeman was getting closer.

Where was Dieben? I couldn't even see him anymore in the sea of heads bobbling in front of me.

"We have to run," I said.

"It will draw more attention," Marnie argued.

"I know, but he's catching up." I skirted around a stroller and rejoined them.

Bone grabbed me, his eyes wide, his hair wild. "This is bad, isn't it?"

"No, it's going to be—"

"You there!" I heard from not far behind. "Stop!"

"Split up," Marnie said, adjusting her grip on Bone's wrist. I opened my mouth to argue but she beat me to it. "Our hair is recognizable a mile out. Bone and I will lead them away. Where are you staying?"

"The Imperial, but I can't leave him again."

She shook her head. "I know the city like the back of my hand. Don't worry. Nothing will happen to him."

I hated that she was right. This stranger, this human girl, was our best shot.

"Three hours," I said. "The Imperial. Room Nine-Twenty."

"Got it." She yanked Bone's hand and they jerked right, disappearing down a side street before I could say another word.

I was alone.

Behind me, the policeman yelled again. I didn't catch what he said and I didn't wait around to hear him repeat it.

I took off at a sprint, scanning for Dieben as I went. Hopefully he'd already made for the hotel. At a run, he could almost be there by now. I didn't have that luxury. This man was too close. I couldn't lead him there. And I couldn't afford to get caught.

When I reached the intersection, instead of turning right toward my hotel, I ducked left. My shoulder caught on a handful of bags. They were knocked free of the grasp that held them and scattered behind me. A woman yelled. Footsteps pounded.

I ran faster.

CHAPTER FOUR

City blocks gave way to long, squat buildings my host knew as warehouses. There was less and less foot traffic and then none at all. Even the streets emptied. Fewer cars travelled here and those that did were built with rectangular boxes on the back. Tractor trailers.

My lungs burned. My chest heaved in an attempt to suck in enough oxygen to calm my racing heart. It wasn't enough. I couldn't keep this pace up much longer. Black dots danced at the edge of my vision.

Still, I ran, listening for sounds in the shadows.

When I was positive I would lose consciousness if I didn't stop, my feet slowed and then halted. With my back to the wall of a deserted building, I bent over at the waist and sucked in air. I stayed that way until the dots in my vision disappeared. Far in the distance a dog barked. I needed to move again.

I started walking, keeping to the shadows and the overhangs along the building entryways. When crossing the street couldn't be avoided, I sprinted. Otherwise, I crept slowly.

Eventually, warehouses gave way to a river. The bank was sharp and rocky, the murky water swirling and pushing empty soda cans and other garbage along its edge. Humans were filthy.

I followed the current until I found a bridge, crossing swiftly. The sun was at my back now. I wasn't sure how many hours had passed. It felt like several. I wondered if Bone and Marnie had made it back to the hotel. Or Dieben.

I had to get to them before the shuttle arrived to take us home. First, I had to figure out where I was.

With the river behind me, the scenery changed. Rows of houses with lawns full of dead grass lined the street. A dog barked, this one much closer. Children played and rode bikes along the crumbling sidewalk. No sign of a police car anywhere.

When I reached an intersection with a stoplight, I paused and turned in a slow circle. In the left distance, high-rise buildings rose into the sky. I headed toward them, careful to keep an eye out for police. Traffic picked up again, including pedestrians. I tried to blend in, move with them. Despite that fact that I'd slowed to a walk, my breath came in short gasps. My host identified it as panic. The Imperial felt impossibly far away.

Inside my pocket, my communicator buzzed. I bit back a yell as I reached inside my pocket and switched it off. Talking to my mother was not on the list of things I was capable of at the moment. Up ahead, the crosswalk light switched to red. The crowd stopped. I shifted my weight, antsy to be moving again. Not far off, a police siren sang to life and I darted into the alley, crouching there until the siren faded.

"Pssst!"

I froze at the noise and a hand closed over my wrist. I swung out, my host reacting out of pure reflex.

"Ow," someone muttered. "Axel, it's me."

I straightened and stepped toward the figure hunched in the shadowed awning. "Becca?"

144

"Holy hell. That hurt." She rubbed tenderly at her shoulder, still wincing.

"I'm so sorry," I said, reaching toward her only to awkwardly drop my hands at my sides again. Humans didn't touch each other often, not unless you were very close. "I didn't know it was you. I'm so sorry," I repeated.

"It's fine, I'll live," she said. Her hand still held her shoulder but her expression cleared and she threw a glance up and down the alley. I did the same. It was empty.

"I think I lost him," I said.

"For now." She bit her lip and tilted her head, studying me. "Come with me."

"Where?"

She didn't respond except to turn on her heel and disappear through the doorway behind her. I hesitated for all of two seconds before ducking inside behind her.

I pulled the door closed behind me and waited. "Where are you?" I whispered into the darkness.

"This way. Up the stairs."

"There's no light."

"One foot in front of the other. You'll be fine. Come on."

Haltingly, I made my way up the stairs in front of me. Halfway up, a beam of light appeared as a door was opened. I hurried the last few steps and found Becca waiting for me on the landing. A scarred wooden door hung open behind her, which she promptly closed and locked behind me.

"I have to get back, make sure the others are safe," I said.

"When it's dark I'll take you," she said.

"Where are we?"

Like before, she seemed to debate before answering me. "My place."

The space was open and full of light from long, narrow windows that ran along the ceiling. The walls were paneled in dark wood. Cherry? And the furniture sat low and scattered. It was inviting in a relaxed, "no rules" sort of way. "You live here?" I asked.

"Me and Marnie. And sometimes a third. She's out of town right now."

"It's nice."

"Thanks. You want something to drink?"

"Water, please."

I followed her to the kitchen, separated from the rest of the room by a long counter with stools. I sat on one and drank deeply from the glass she set in front of me. When I set it down again, I found her staring at me.

"I'm sorry about the cops. Mr. Wu set up a couple of surveillance cameras a few months back when a place down the road got held up. I forgot all about them until it was too late. He must've seen the footage and then you came in … Well, I just wanted you to know I didn't rat you out."

Rat you out? I took a minute to understand the meaning. "Actually, it never even dawned on me that you would've given us up. But thank you for explaining."

She frowned. "Huh."

"What?"

"Nothing." She waved her hand as if to dismiss it and began refilling my glass. "I take it you and your friends split up."

"Yes, Marnie went with Bone."

She nodded. "And the other one?"

146

"Dieben. He went on ahead." It was my turn to frown. "I think …"

"I'm sure they all made it back just fine. From what I saw, the cop was alone and he pursued you, not them."

"I hope so. I can't let anything happen to them."

"You're not responsible for them."

"Trust me, I am."

She eyed me. "I think it's pretty obvious I trust you a lot already." At my blank look, she added, "I brought you here, didn't I? You could be an axe murderer for all I know."

"I promise I'm not an axe murderer," I said, swallowing back the urge to laugh. If she only knew what I was … maybe she'd prefer an axe murderer. At least then we'd be the same species.

"It's not funny. I mean, how do I know?"

"I pinky swear I'm not an axe murderer."

Her eyes narrowed but I could see the hint of a smile. "You've been talking to Marnie, haven't you?"

I laughed and she gave in and smiled back at me. "Fine. I believe you're not a killer. But you are a criminal."

My laughter died and heaved a sigh. "I can't believe I broke into your restaurant. It's so unlike me."

"We all do crazy things when we're drunk."

"That's the thing. I don't remember drinking. Or anything else about the night."

"You and Dieben looked pretty trashed when I saw you getting into that cab. Dieben would've face-planted if it weren't for that chick you were with."

Jane. She was the only thing that still didn't make sense. "Did you happen to notice anything about her?" I asked.

"Like what?"

"I don't know. Anything out of the ordinary."

Becca tilted her head in thought and I found myself staring once again at the curve of her neck, the fullness of her lips. She stuck them out when she concentrated. It was fascinating and made me want to trace them with my fingertips.

I shoved my hands in my pockets and looked away. I'd never, not once, had those thoughts about a girl before. Human or Panmeran. Dieben was right. It'd taken coming to Earth to awaken my hormones. I'd never live this down.

"She was a little older than us. That was all."

"How old?"

"I don't know. She looked around twenty-five or so." Becca shrugged. "I figured she must've assumed you guys were her age. I mean, you're close, right?"

"I'm eighteen," I said.

"Yeah, so, not a big deal—"

"How old are you, Becca?"

She blinked, clearly thrown off by the question. Frankly, so was I. I hadn't intended to ask it aloud, but the urge to know more about her even in the short time we had left was too strong to ignore. "Me? Seventeen."

"And you live alone in this apartment? Where is your family?"

Her mouth tightened into a thin line. She didn't like my questions. "Marnie is my family. She's all I need."

"Of course. I didn't mean to imply—I just wanted to know you better."

I watched as she breathed deeply, relaxing her shoulders and then the rest of her, the action very deliberate. "And how is it you're staying in a hotel suite downtown with two friends? No car, no job, no family."

"Spring break," I said, giving the answer I'd been trained to give.

"Uh-huh and where do you go to school?"

"I ..." Suddenly, I couldn't remember the name I'd been given. Nor could I remember anything else about the lie I was supposed to perpetuate. For reasons I couldn't explain, I wanted to tell this beautiful girl the truth. Is that what'd happened to Bone? Is that why he'd told Marnie? "It's far away," I said, skirting the truth rather than giving it. "My parents let me come and stay for a few days before I go home and take over the family business."

"And what sort of business is that?"

"Politics?"

"Is that a question?"

"No, it's my answer." My dad is the viceroy to a consulate that governs half a solar system that would take your people eighteen hundred years to reach in a man-made space shuttle. I will one day take over and rule those planets in his place. In the meantime, I will eat a bunch of boring dinners and give a bunch of boring lectures to a bunch of boring constituents that chose plant-based life-formed planets for their Rumschpringe. This day will forever be the greatest adventure of my life.

I couldn't say any of that. "It's just ... complicated," I added instead.

"It always is." Becca's lips quirked up in amusement. "And then you went and stole noodles."

"The plot thickens," I agreed, using a term I'd gleaned from my host.

"Is that a food pun?"

"Huh. I guess it is."

149

She giggled and I grinned back at her. I enjoyed the sound of her laughter—especially knowing I'd been the one responsible for it. I wanted to do it again and again.

"Speaking of noodles ... You hungry?" she asked.

"I could eat. As long as it's not noodles."

She smiled. "Deal. How about pizza?"

"Pizza?" I was so absorbed in her smile, the way her whole face lit when she really meant it, that I fumbled in my host's mind for the meaning of what she'd suggested.

"I can do something else if that's not ..."

"Pizza's great," I said.

"Good. I need your help. Come around here." She began pulling things out of the fridge and handing them over her shoulder. I took the items and set them on the counter, reading and cataloguing each one in case she asked about them. I needed to concentrate, to be more careful. No more slip-ups.

Pizza was surprisingly similar to a Panmeran meal. Not necessarily the ingredients themselves—dough was such an odd, sticky thing to hold on to—but the ritual, the movements involved in preparing food. Colryn had loved cooking. We'd spent many nights, he and I, in the kitchen together, preparing food and horsing around before our parents returned from work. I hadn't attempted it without him. The idea had been too painful. But here, now, with Becca, it felt good.

The memories it triggered were bittersweet, but the scent and sight of her as we stood shoulder to shoulder over the counter distracted me. It was fascinating to know this species and mine enjoyed a common task.

"Here, use your palms to push it out at the edges," Becca said, showing me how to work the edges of the dough into a circular shape. "Make the edges thicker for the crust," she added.

I did as she asked while she sprinkled flour over the surface. "Like this?" I asked.

"Perfect," she said.

Becca's face crinkled as she attempted to twist open a jar of tomato sauce. After a failed effort, she held the jar out to me sheepishly. "Will you?"

I took the jar and was careful to exert only the necessary strength. The jar opened with a pop and I handed it back.

"Thanks." Our fingers brushed as she took the jar, and the soft tingles left behind distracted me. Becca seemed distracted by it a well, her gaze lingering on mine. I tried to think of something to say, but like before, nothing I was allowed to say felt authentic enough for someone like her. She deserved the truth—the one thing I couldn't give. I remained silent as she poured the sauce. When it was spread, she handed me a can of mushrooms and we took turns dropping ingredients over the pie.

"You're good in the kitchen," I said as she slid the pizza into the oven.

She shrugged. "It helps when I feel blocked." I cocked my head, trying to decipher her meaning. "I'm an artist," she explained. "The paintings along that wall, they're mine. When I feel blocked and I need an outlet or inspiration, I cook."

"You painted those?" I pointed at the framed canvasses hanging across the room. They were images of landscapes, but with such vivid color, I knew they weren't anything from this world. Becca's imagination was rich. Even after only a week among humans, I appreciated that about her. Most of them seemed

151

so stuck and limited in their view. Their minds were so closed. It's why no one even noticed Marnie's outburst on the sidewalk earlier.

"They're amazing," I said after studying each one. It seemed the more I learned about Becca, the more I wanted to know.

"Thanks. It's more of a hobby for now but maybe someday ..."

"They're fantastic. Why wouldn't you share them?"

Her cheeks reddened. For the first time since we'd met, she seemed uncertain of herself. "I don't know. I have a lot to learn," she said quietly.

I shook my head, determined to leave her with something. Even if it was only a shred of the confidence she deserved. "An open mind is always learning, or willing to. Doesn't mean you can't also be great."

She blinked at me. "Wow, that was deep. And true. Thank you, Axel. You're different than I expected."

"Different how?"

Her lips curved upward. "Most criminals aren't nearly as thoughtful as you are."

"What can I say?" I shrugged. "I'm well-rounded."

She laughed.

CHAPTER FIVE

Cooked pizza dough was nothing like the smushed, uncooked version I'd pressed out earlier. It held just the right amount of crunch and flavor to be delicious despite the pre-packaged, stale ingredients we'd added on top. Panmeran foods were always fresh. Earth's foods were either boxed or sprayed with so many chemicals, it was a wonder it didn't all resemble cardboard. But this, I enjoyed.

Becca seemed impressed when I collected the empty plates and carried them to the sink. Although it was decidedly different from the way we cleaned at home, the ritual was enjoyable. Becca stood nearby, her hip propped against the counter, drying the dishes as I finished washing. Again, I was reminded of Colryn. The way he used to do the same, hovering over me and pointing out when I missed a spot. I'd scowl and he'd laugh good-naturedly. Who knew, a year after his death, washing tomato sauce from plates with a human girl would give me the closest connection I'd had since losing him.

"Hello? Earth to Axel? Are you there?"

"Hmm? Oh. Sorry." I found Becca watching me, lips pursed.

"I lost you for a moment. Where'd you go?"

I debated for a split second before forging ahead with more truth. "Doing the dishes, preparing a meal—It reminds me of my brother, Colryn."

"I didn't know you had a brother. What's he like?"

"He was ..." It wasn't easy explaining Colryn in only a few words. "Thoughtful. And kind. And a jokester. And a loner. A secret-keeper and ... a writer. He was a lot of things. But mostly, he was my best friend."

"Was?"

"He died last year."

"Oh, I'm so sorry, Axel. How did it happen?"

Again, a hesitation even as I made the decision to be honest—or as honest as I could be while still maintaining the lie of being human. The more time I spent with Becca, the harder that lie became. I didn't want to bother with it. I wanted her to know me. But that was impossible. "We aren't sure, exactly. He came to—He came here. For spring break, like me. When his time was up, he decided to stay. He told my parents it was to pursue his writing, but no one really knew. My parents were ... not happy with his decision to remain."

Understatement. Try livid. Furious. They disowned him. Disconnected his communicator.

"They stopped speaking to him and forbade anyone else from contacting him as well," I went on. "A few months later, a group of our friends came here for a short vacation and ran into Colryn at a sidewalk café. He was hit by a car crossing the street as he left them."

"Oh, that must've been so horrible." Becca's eyes filled with tears and her face reflected my thoughts as I recounted the parts of the story I could share without raising her suspicions.

154

I cleared my throat, pushing away the images in my mind. I hadn't seen it for myself, but after spending the week here watching angry drivers and reckless cabs, I could imagine. "Yeah, it's been rough."

The truth was, Colryn had taken one look at the three Panmerans here for their Rumschpringe and fled. He'd been killed out of sheer panic—and I had no idea why.

Why would he run from his own kind? It was a question that still had no answers. One of many.

But seeing Becca's sympathetic reaction to my story dulled the frustration I carried of not knowing. For once, it was simply about Colryn. And how I'd lost my best friend that day. No. Not that day. I'd lost him months earlier, when he'd chosen Earth instead of Panmera. Instead of home—and me. He'd cited his writing, going on about humans and how fascinating their behavior was to him.

"They spend millions of dollars on war and weapons and killing each other in a way they can call civilized so they can sleep at night. But in the same day a battle is waged over motor oil, a man who drives his house around raised enough money to provide sustainable energy and water to a village in Kenya."

"What's motor oil?" my dad had asked.

"And where's Kenya?" my mother added.

"You're missing the point," Colryn had said, so wrapped up in frustration and passion he didn't hear the disgust in their voices. "They are such a contradiction. Hating and loving in the same breath. I can't leave now. There's too much here."

"There's nothing there," my dad argued, his tone transforming from confused and irritated to stone-cold. "Your mother, brother, and I—we're here. Waiting for you to take your place as head of this family. There is no question of your return. You are Panmeran. Not human."

"Dad, I ... I can't," Colryn whispered in a pained voice.

"You can and you will. The shuttle is on its way. You must exit your host and—"

Colryn cut him off. "I've already done the ritual. My body is permanent."

My mother gasped. I'd never seen my father so still. Not even during his rest-cycle. More words were exchanged, but I hadn't heard them. My mind had reeled. Colryn had chosen to stay. We'd always been told stories of this and how the one affected would like victimized somehow. Hollow eyes, anguished faces, like the choice hadn't really been theirs. Like it was something forcing them—the Force. But from what I could see on the hologram projection hovering above the communicator, Colryn's only anguish seemed to come from disappointing my parents. And me. His eyes had pleaded with me for forgiveness, but I'd said nothing as my parents banished him and shut down the communicator. The shock had been too great. And then he was gone. I hadn't really lost him in the car accident. I'd lost him well before that—to the Force.

My thoughts drifted to Bone and how I'd almost lost him today, too.

"I really need to get going," I said, suddenly panicked as I remembered my agreement with Marnie. I wasn't sure how much time had passed since we'd split off, but I knew it'd been more than the three hours we'd agreed upon. "I promised Bone I would meet them back at the hotel a while ago. I know they'll worry."

"Right. Yeah. I'll get my keys." Becca pushed off from the counter and whatever moment we'd shared as a result of my story faded away. It caused an ache in my chest, knowing the strongest connection I'd made since Colryn was with this strange girl who, after today, I would never see again.

"I think it might be better if I go alone," I said as she disappeared into another room.

"No way." She returned with a set of keys in one hand. "You shouldn't be walking around on the street. And besides, I need to find Marnie."

I agreed.

She led us back down the set of stairs, closing and locking the door behind us. On the street, the traffic picked up as humans rushed home from work, but that was probably for the best. Made it easier to blend in. Neither of us spoke on the drive back. I wasn't sure what to say. Conversation seemed so pointless with my imminent departure.

I'd never had to say goodbye before. Well, besides Colryn, and he couldn't exactly hear me by the time I'd said my final farewell.

Becca parked in the lot behind the hotel and we rode the elevator to the ninth floor. I remained watchful, but there was no evidence of police or anyone else following us as we made our way to the suite. I hoped that meant everyone had made it back. I didn't want to think what would happen if one of us was missing when the shuttle came.

I inserted my key card into the slot and waited for the soft beep that signaled the lock disengaging. When I heard the click, I pushed the door open and entered cautiously.

"Bone? Dieben?" I called.

The common room looked slightly better than when I'd left it this morning. Someone had set the furniture upright although it wasn't in its original position. The cartons of noodles had been picked up and placed in the now overflowing trash can. The best part about going home would be escaping the smell that hung in the air. Old noodles. Gross.

Becca wrinkled her nose. "Next time, steal some air freshener too," she said.

I caught muffled voices coming from the far end of the space. I headed for the bedroom Bone and I had shared for the past week. "Bone?" I called, pushing the door open and stepping inside.

I stopped, my hand still on the knob. "Oh." At the sight of Bone and Marnie sprawled on the bed, arms and legs tangled, mouths mashed together, I stumbled back and pulled the door closed with a hard click.

Behind me, Becca laughed. "Looks like they weren't as worried as you thought," she said.

I was speechless. The host's brain explained the scene as kissing. Lots and lots of kissing. "Making out," he called it. But I'd spent the last few hours as far from my human's thoughts as possible. I'd wanted to enjoy my time with Becca as myself. If that was possible while inhabiting a foreign body. So, at the sight of Bone and Marnie kissing, confusion took over and I felt my mouth turn down in a frown.

The image pervading my mind had replaced Bone and Marnie with myself and Becca. My human limbs ached to touch her in the exact ways I'd witnessed a moment ago. The desire was so strong, I could feel its pull like a physical thing. A line, a wire, connecting the two of us, inching me forward. Closer and closer. If I reached out and touched her, would she touch me back? Would she—

"What's wrong?" Becca asked.

"Oh. Nothing," I said, blinking my way out of whatever pull had almost made me do something so completely forbidden, I felt like a traitor for even imagining it. Panmerans observed humans, used them for entertainment and distraction. Nothing more. And when we were finished, we left them and never, ever returned.

So why couldn't I stop wondering what it would be like to spend another day with Becca—a day not spent running from authorities?

"Becca, I—"

The bedroom door flung open and Bone appeared, wild-eyed and disheveled. Marnie was close behind, hair and clothing in much the same state. "Axel," Bone said, his face a contradiction of relief and worry. "I was scared that—I thought—Are you okay?"

"I'm fine. Becca found me and brought me back."

"That's good." The relief won over and his features relaxed. "We were worried."

"I can tell," I said dryly.

Bone didn't meet my gaze. Marnie giggled.

"Where's Dieben?" I asked.

"In his room last I checked. He got a call from home," Bone said, giving me a pointed look.

Dieben's bedroom door opened and he stepped out. I caught sight of his communicator as he slid it back inside his pocket. "You made it," he said. His level of relief was nowhere near Bone's. Typical Dieben. He either hadn't worried or hadn't cared.

"Just now. How long?" I asked.

"As soon as we're ready," he said.

I sucked in a breath. It was time.

"You have to go?" Becca asked.

"Yes, I'm … due home tonight," I said quietly.

"Oh. I see." Her expression mirrored my own thoughts. Neither of us was ready to say goodbye. "I didn't realize ... I thought you had more time."

Bone and Marnie slipped away and headed for the balcony, giving us privacy. Dieben returned to his room. Probably for the same reason. "Today was my last day. I have to get back," I said, not quite meeting her eyes.

"Sucky timing, huh?" she said, smiling in a way that didn't seem at all like a smile except for the curve of her lips.

"Horribly sucky," I agreed.

"Well. It was fun meeting you and hanging out today," she said, her voice bright with what sounded a lot like false cheer. "I mean, aside from the whole fugitive thing."

I chuckled. "Right."

Silence fell between us. I shoved my hands in my pockets to keep them from reaching out for her. Was it me or my host that couldn't stand the thought of leaving without ever touching her? I swallowed, unsure what else to say but unwilling to walk away just yet. Becca seemed just as lost. Her eyes darted from spot to spot on the carpet before finding mine again.

"Maybe you can visit again sometime?" Becca's brows rose, her expression hopeful.

I stared back at Becca, at a loss. "Maybe," I agreed. I'd spent the last week lying. Why stop now?

The door to Dieben's room opened. He stepped out and caught my eye, nodding once. I sighed. "It's time," I said.

Becca bit her lip, seeming to debate something. After a moment, she darted forward and wrapped her arms around my neck, pulling me into a hug. I took a step back to regain my balance—and recover from the shock of the unexpected contact— and then wrapped my arms around her in return, holding her close.

The simplicity of the gesture combined with the wave of pleasure it gave reminded me of Colryn's words. Their compassion and kindness ... He'd spoken of that with such meaning. Such force.

Force!

The Force that'd caused him to remain. Could it be this? And if so, what was this? Compassion? No, more than that. It was caring. It was feeling for another human. Love, said the host's voice in my mind. It's love.

I held on to Becca and buried my face in her hair, inhaling the scent of her body. Love. So that's what the humans called it. That force, that thing that pulled two people together so tightly they couldn't bring themselves to leave. Not for another human and not even for life on another planet. I wondered if Colryn had been in love or just discovered its existence and beauty as he observed it in others. Either way, there was no question in my mind this was it. The Force, the thing I'd searched for all week. I'd found it in a girl- -over pizza and dirty dishes.

And now I had to walk away from it forever.

As I let her go and followed Dieben and Bone out, the temptation to stay was tangible. It was more than a feeling; it left a taste in my mouth. But I couldn't let my family down. Not twice. Not after Colryn. I had to return. To take my father's place. To step into my future. Besides, I had my answer now. The Force wasn't some monster hiding in an alley, ready to attack. It wasn't violence or something to fear. It was compassion and kindness and above all, it was love.

161

And maybe, by some miracle, Becca would prove to be right. Maybe I'd be back—although probably not. None of my kind ever got a second trip. But one thing was certain, I'd never be the same.

ULTRA-CON

By Tiffany King

For information on other titles
Visit the author's website:
http://www.authortiffanyjking.blogspot.com/

CHAPTER ONE

"Are you sure we're not going to stick out like a sore thumb?"
I asked my friends as we climbed out of James's beat-up Ford
truck. How I had let them talk me into going to Ultra-Con was still
a mystery to me. Tara and James, and especially my boyfriend,
Bobby, were the sci-fi freaks, not me.

"Trust us, Jenn. You would have stuck out more if you would
have worn jeans and a tee shirt like you wanted to," Tara scoffed,
linking her arm through mine. "I mean, look around," she
continued, pointing to a guy dressed head to toe in a red spandex
ensemble with a lightning bolt on the chest. I couldn't help
laughing as he zigzagged through the long line of cars waiting to
turn into the parking lot. He would run past them, pumping his
arms to give the illusion that he was moving faster than he really
was. That was just the tip of the iceberg. Everywhere I looked, I
saw people dressed in costumes from their favorite TV shows,
movies, comics and video games.

"Sweet. Check out the dude in the Master Chief armor," James
crowed. "Come on Tara. We've got to get a picture with him."

"Holy geek. Are you serious?" I yelled after my friends who
tore away like they had seen a celebrity. "I guess you know what a
Master Chief is too?" I asked Bobby.

164

"Of course. Who doesn't know Halo? Well, except you, of course," he said, hugging me in his arms from behind.

"So, why aren't you over there getting a picture with them?" I asked.

"I like you better," he said, giving me a soft kiss on the neck. "How do you feel?"

"Except for feeling out of place in this nerd kingdom, I'm swell."

"No, I mean, you know—are we still on for tonight?" he probed.

"Oh, that," I said, turning around to face him. "Yeah. What about you?"

"Hell yeah," he said.

"Well, I'm happy to hear that," I returned.

"Hey, come on lovebirds. Let's get inside. I want to see everything," James said, sneaking behind Bobby and kissing him on the cheek. Bobby drew his fake sword and took off after James, who pulled out a laser gun from the holster on his thigh.

"Come on, children. You want to go inside, or fight out here?" Tara called as she hooked her arm through mine.

"Hey, remind me who I'm supposed to be again," I asked as we headed for the doors. I had on camouflage pants, a black tank top and mirrored aviator sunglasses. The cherry to my sundae was a fake plastic machine gun. I had nothing to do with any part of my ensemble. This was all Tara.

"OMG, for the hundredth time, you're Sarah Connor from Terminator Two."

"That's right. I've got it now," I said. I was just thankful she didn't try to dress me in skintight spandex or some kind of furry getup.

I knew my friends were into this hoopla, but for the most part, it never trickled into our everyday lives. When Tara begged me to come to Ultra-Con with them, I had grudgingly agreed, figuring it would be like the Twilight convention my mom and I went to a few years ago when I was in my preteen Twilight craze. We had seen a few fake vampires, but most people simply wore tee shirts declaring which team they were on. Of course, I was Team Edward, but after I met the actor who played Carlisle, I was ready to defect. For an older dude, he definitely had a cute thing working.

The more I looked around, it was clear this convention was far different than Twilight-Con. For one thing, it was so crowded we could barely walk without stepping on the heels of someone in front of us. Regardless, everyone seemed to share an odd camaraderie, so it felt like a big party. You would almost think the thousands of people here knew each other. I had to admit, some of the costumes were really pretty, but there were others that were downright scary. And I don't mean monster scary. I mean, "holy hell, that's just wrong for a grown man to wear that" kind of scary. Like the guy ahead of us, whose costume was so tight it left little to the imagination. I think you could literally check his pulse if you looked close enough. Not that I wanted to. Then there was another guy who had to weigh at least four hundred pounds. He was the biggest man I had ever seen in my life. Somehow he managed to fit his body into purple glittery spandex that even Bobby or James would have had a hard time fitting into. It was at that moment I realized I was going to need a mental guidebook to get through the day. Rule number one: try not to make eye contact with anyone. It only encouraged creepers like the purple spandex guy to start a conversation.

"See, I told you it would be fun," Tara said, taking how I clutched her arm as a sign of enthusiasm.

"Right," I answered, urging us to move forward.

Thankfully, the crowd at the entrance of the building swallowed us up, and I was able to escape my purple spandex-covered stalker.

"Cool, huh?" Bobby asked, taking in the large space we had entered. There were tables and brightly colored booths as far as the eye could see.

"Wow, it's like another world in here," I said. The inside of the convention center was huge, but it seemed like every conceivable space was being used. Booth after booth, selling everything from comics and toys to shirts and memorabilia, were all crowded with people. All I could think was how much money these guys had to be making, because it didn't look like people were hesitant to buy what they wanted.

I was still gawking at my surroundings when I noticed Tara and James had disappeared. "Where'd they go?" I asked Bobby.

"They took off in that direction. We'll catch up," he said, pointing into a never-ending sea of people. Rule number two: never take your eyes off your friends when you're in a large crowd of people who are dressed as characters you don't know. One minute Tara was beside me, and the next, she and James were gone. I linked arms with some poor girl to my side who looked at me like I was some kind of freak. After apologizing profusely while Bobby stood and laughed, I grabbed my phone from my pocket so I could give Tara a piece of my mind. She had sworn on a box of Godiva chocolates that we were hoarding for our next sleepover movie marathon that she would not leave my side.

Stepping out of the main traffic area, I put my finger to my free ear in an attempt to muffle the noise. It was only after the call went to voicemail that I noticed there was no signal to be had in the convention center. Great. I was going to kill Tara when I found her.

Standing on my tiptoes, I scanned the area for a glimpse of the red costume that Tara was wearing. "You're never going to see them in all these people. Come on, let's walk around. I guarantee we'll run into them eventually," Bobby said.

"Fine," I reluctantly agreed. It was during my third sweep of the crowd that my eyes landed on the most piercing stare I had ever seen. At first, I thought it was only my imagination—that our eyes just happened to meet as we were scanning the crowd at the same time. I pulled my eyes away momentarily, and then looked again discreetly in his direction, but this time it was clear. His eyes were deadlocked on me. It was creepy that he didn't seem to move. Even among the crowd of people jostling around him, his focus remained on where I was standing. "Bobby, look," I said, yanking on his arm to pull him close.

"What?" he asked, not knowing what he was supposed to be looking at.

"That guy over there. He's looking right at me."

"Where?"

"Over there," I pointed, but when I looked again, the stranger was gone. "He was over by that booth with the big wall of tee shirts," I said, pointing to a crowded stand about twenty yards away. "It was creepy. He was staring right at me."

"He was probably just acting like whatever character he was dressed as. Everyone here does that. Or, it could be you were imaging it, and he was looking at someone else," he teased.

"Why, 'cause I'm not cute enough to catch the attention of some random guy?" I asked, feigning being insulted.

"Oh, here we go," he said, grasping my hand. "You are gorgeous, especially dressed up like Sarah Connor. It's seriously hot. I'm just saying, there's like two thousand people in here, he could have been looking at anyone. Come on. Let's go see if we can find Tara and James." I hoped he was right, but for the moment, I still felt a little weirded out.

CHAPTER TWO

I couldn't get the stranger out of my mind as Bobby and I bumped our way through the herds of convention visitors. It was my own fault for breaking the first rule. After purple spandex dude, this was the second reminder why I didn't make eye contact with anyone in here. I probably wouldn't have even noticed if he hadn't seemed to be studying me so intently. Even his contacts made his eyes look like they were glowing. It had to be the lights in here playing with my mind. Either that, or the convention had sucked all common sense from my brain.

My current favorite song started playing on my phone, breaking the freaky trance I seemed to be under. "Hold up, it's Tara," I said to Bobby as I swiped the screen to answer.

"Jenn, I'm so sorry. One minute you were there, and the next you were gone. Where are you guys?" she asked, but I could barely make out what she was saying.

"We're by some guy selling comic books," I answered, looking around.

"There's like a hundred of those. You're going to have to get more specific."

If I had a flare I could have shot it up into the air. "Okay, right beside the guy selling comic books is another dude drawing big breasted women with, like, hardly any clothes."

Tara sighed heavily on the line. "Jenn, you're not helping. Every other booth has a guy drawing girls with big melons."

"Ew, don't call them that," I said, gagging slightly. Tara had a knack for painting a vivid picture when she talked.

"You're such a prude. Fine, stay where you are and we'll find you," she said, disconnecting the call.

"Goodbye to you too," I muttered, stowing my phone back in my pocket.

"Where are they?" Bobby asked.

"Who knows? She said to stay put and they would find us."

I moved away from the wall where I was leaning and debated forging ahead to look for my friends, but the crowd only seemed to have multiplied. It would be a nerd miracle if Tara and James were able to find us in this madness.

"Let's just look around here. If we don't stray too far, they'll find us," Bobby suggested.

We stayed in the same aisle walking from booth to booth as Bobby educated me on various action figures and graphic novels. I nodded my head every once in a while to make it appear as if I were really paying attention, but every time he looked away, I was scanning the crowd for Tara.

"And this issue is where they show Batman naked," Bobby said.

"That's cool," I replied without looking. "Wait, what?" I said, whipping my head around.

"Just getting your attention," he teased. "Hey, look," Bobby said, turning my body slightly.

171

"Jennnnnn," Tara greeted me like we had been separated since birth. "You would not believe how many guys are drawing chicks with big boobs," she screeched, louder than necessary. Tara had no shame. I loved her to death, but she wasn't the person to hang out with if you embarrassed easily. "Sorry about ditching you, but are you having fun?" she asked, keeping her arm around my shoulder.

"It's all right. Hey, did you know there's a comic that shows Batman naked?" I asked, looking at Bobby who laughed.

"Really, Bobby?" Tara said, looking at Bobby as he held up his hands in surrender. "As if it wasn't hard enough to get her to come with us today," she chastised him.

"Dude, it's Batman. Why would you even go there? That's sacrilegious," James said, punching Bobby in the arm.

"She knows I was kidding," Bobby said, pointing his fake laser pistol at James.

We continued our trek around the convention, together this time. I kept my arm linked through Tara's to make sure she wouldn't leave me again. I never would have believed it, but I was actually having a good time. I had to hand it to some of the people and their costumes. It must have taken hours to put them together. We rounded a corner to an area where people lined up in single file rows in front of empty tables. "What's up with that?" I asked Tara.

"That's where the celebrity guests sit. There's people from different movies and TV shows."

"Really? Anybody I would know?" I asked.

"Probably. The whole cast from Star Trek: The Next Generation is here, and I think the Weasley brothers from Harry Potter too."

"And don't forget about Stan Lee," James piped in.

"Who's Stan Lee?" I made the mistake of asking.

172

"No freakin' way. Did she just ask who Stan Lee is? Bobby, you gotta educate your lady, bro," James said, placing his hand on his heart like I had caused him pain.

"Stan Lee started Marvel Comics, babe. He's a legend. Well, more like a god actually," Bobby said, enlightening me per James's request.

"Well, excuse me. It's not like it's Ryan Gosling sitting there or something," I teased.

"Oh, yeah. Now that would be a convention. I would totally wait in line just for the chance to sniff him," Tara added.

"I have to give you that one. I'm not even a chick, but damn, Ryan Gosling is hot," James replied.

Bobby and James decided to wait in line for the opportunity to talk to Stan Lee while Tara and I waited close by. "So, I have something to tell you," I whispered to Tara.

"Is it juicy?" she asked. Tara was the queen of gossip. If you needed the 411 on anyone or anything at school, she was your connection.

"Bobby and I decided tonight's the night," I admitted.

"What!" she screamed. I forced my hand over her mouth and looked around embarrassed as she got the attention of everyone in a twenty-foot radius.

"Are you gonna chill?" I asked before removing my hand. Tara nodded with beaming eyes.

"Oh my god, Jenn. Why didn't you tell me?" she asked. "When did you decide this? Give me the deets."

"I did tell you, just now, and there are no real details. Things have been getting a little hot and heavy, and we just decided to do it. That's basically it," I said. I wasn't overly comfortable going any further in a crowded convention.

"You have protection, right?" Tara asked. "I can hook you up if not."

"Hey, remember—chill," I said, looking around again.

"Sorry?" she said, bouncing in place. "I'm just making sure."

"Trust me. We've got it covered."

"That's one way to put it," she said, wagging her eyebrows.

"What?" I asked confused. It took a second for her joke to register in my head. "Nice, Tara."

"I'm kidding. Bobby seems to be acting cool though," she observed.

"What do you want him to do, wear a shirt that says 'I'm getting some tonight,'" I asked, looking over my shoulder. I had an eerie feeling I was being watched again.

I turned around and my eyes zeroed in on the same stranger as before. He was standing near a booth about two rows over, looking directly at me again. I pulled Tara close so I was standing behind her.

"What's wrong?" she asked.

"There's a weird guy about two rows over who is looking at me," I said.

"Ooh, I want to see. Where is he?" she asked, scanning the crowd.

"Wait, don't look. I saw him watching me earlier when you guys ditched me. Bobby said it was my imagination, but this is too much of a coincidence. This guy is, like, stalking me or something."

"You mean Tall, Dark and Dreamy over there, looking right at us?" Tara asked, spotting the stranger, who just like before, stood without moving.

174

"Yeah, but don't point. I don't want to draw his attention," I said.

"Point? I'm going to go see what his deal is," Tara said, strolling purposefully in the stranger's direction.

"Tara, no!" I said, reaching for her arm. I reacted too late. Before I could stop her, Tara was weaving her way through the crowd.

A large group of costumed people walked in between the rows, and my view of the stranger became somewhat obstructed. I tried stretching my neck, catching a quick view of his eyes that were glowing like they had before, but he became swallowed by the endless sea of people. By the time there was a break in the crowd again, he was gone. Tara, who had reached the spot where he was standing, turned around in a circle to try and spot him. She looked back in my direction, holding up her arms for my confirmation. Shrugging my shoulders, I waved her back over.

"There were too many people in the way. I didn't see which way he went," I said to Tara as I grabbed her arm.

"Wow, ease up on the death grip. I think you're worried over nothing. He probably just thinks you're cute and is too much of a wuss to talk to you, you know? Besides, look at all the eye witnesses around if he really is a creeper," she said, trying to make me feel better in her own way.

"Oh, that makes me feel a whole lot better."

"I'm just trying to loosen you up. Look, as soon as the guys get through the Stan Lee line, we'll take a break to get something to eat, cool?"

"Yeah, maybe I just need something to eat," I said, although I still had myself convinced some freako was out to get me.

It took another thirty minutes, but Bobby and James finally approached us, proudly carrying their autographed photos. As we made our way to the food court, they chattered on in a star-struck manner. I gripped Bobby's hand tightly, scanning the crowd in every direction as we walked.

"So, Jenn is convinced some dude is stalking her," Tara announced.

"Ha, you told Tara about your admirer?" Bobby joked. "She was convinced he was looking right at her when we couldn't find you guys earlier."

"Yeah, well, when you and James were waiting in line for whoever's autograph, I saw him watching me again. Tara saw him," I replied, feeling like I was on trial.

"Don't worry, Jenn. If he tries anything, it'll be off with his head," James declared, patting the fake sword hanging off his belt.

"It's not funny. His eyes were creepy, the way they glowed," I said.

"Glowing eyes?" Bobby asked, stopping.

"Yeah. At first I thought it was contacts or maybe the lights, but the second time I saw him, I could tell they were definitely glowing. What's wrong?" I asked Bobby, who looked more concerned than I had ever seen him.

"Huh? It's nothing. Come on, let's get some pizza," he answered.

The food court was as busy as I expected, considering the number of people at the convention. We waited in the pizza line for what felt like forever. Tara and James passed the time by stopping people with extravagant costumes to take pictures. Bobby was unusually quiet and looked tense, which only kept me on edge. I was beginning to think we should call it a day and head home.

"Is anything wrong?" I asked, wondering if he was more worried about my stalker than he had let on.

"No, babe. It's cool. I'm just starving," he answered, rubbing my shoulders to try to reassure me. Tara and James waved to get my attention. They had seized the opportunity to grab an empty table that had just become available near an emergency exit door. I jumped slightly when Bobby removed his hands from my shoulders to order our food.

"Four pepperoni slices and four Cokes," he said to an elderly gentleman working the pizza stand. After paying, we each carried a tray as we walked to join Tara and James at the table.

"Sweet," James said, rubbing his hands together. "I should have told you to get me two slices. I'm freaking starving."

The others began to devour their pizza as I sat anxiously watching the crowds of people in every direction. It was like looking at a Where's Waldo picture, except I was searching for a set of glowing eyes. When I didn't see anything, I began to think that maybe everyone was right, and that my imagination was getting the best of me. It was easy to do here in this type of environment. I picked at the crust of my pizza, taking one last scan of the crowd.

"I'll eat that if you're not going to," James piped in, breaking my concentration.

"Jeez, sweets, why don't you go ask some of the other people sitting around if they are going to finish their food too," Tara teased him.

"No, it's cool," I said, sliding my plate in his direction. "Actually, I have to go to the bathroom. Will you come with?" I asked Tara, standing up from the table.

"You all right, babe?" Bobby asked, looking concerned. I'm sure the only thing on his mind was that he hoped it wasn't something that would ruin our evening plans.

"I'm fine. Just have to pee," I answered, pulling Tara by the hand.

We walked out into the main concourse of the convention center, finding a bathroom not too far from Hall F, where the food court was located. The concourse was just as crowded with people walking in and out of smaller rooms that held different panels and other events. Go figure the line for the ladies' restroom was about ten people deep. Tara and I decided to wait, figuring any other restroom would likely be just as packed. Tara claimed she didn't need to go, but changed her mind by the time we made it to the front of the line. She took the stall I finished with as I washed my hands.

"Hey, I'm going to wait outside the restroom, okay?" I said.

"Okay, don't rush me. I'll be right out," she answered.

After washing my hands, I stepped outside the restroom and pulled out my phone to check Facebook. I was in the middle of reading a post on my timeline when someone approached me from behind.

CHAPTER THREE

I turned around to find the stranger who had been stalking me on the main convention floor. Panic gripped me. My arms and legs refused to move, and I couldn't scream.

"Do not be alarmed. You are in danger, but not from me. You are unable to move because I have taken control of your muscular system and your nervous system. We will be returning to the table where your friends are sitting." At his words, the stranger and I began walking forward. The sensation was like nothing I had ever felt. I could see and hear like normal, but the movements of my body were not my own. It was as if I was being strung along like a puppet. We got to the table as Bobby and James were in the middle of a conversation. When they looked up, they were taken aback by the stranger who stood next to me.

"Who's this?" James asked. "And where's Tara?" he added, looking around me.

"This is Joe." My mouth moved, but the words were not mine.

"Okay—Joe? Can we help you with something?" Bobby asked, reaching for my hand. When we touched, he jerked his hand away as if he had been shocked.

"Damn, that's some serious static electricity," James commented. "So, what's going on here? Do you know this guy or something?" he asked, looking at me for confirmation.

"Yes, we are old friends," my voice answered again. Bobby sat staring at the stranger as if he wasn't sure what to do. The tension on his face was evident. Suddenly, the stranger began speaking directly to Bobby in a dialect that was completely foreign. It sounded unlike any language I had ever heard. It was as if he wasn't speaking words, but rather odd sounds that could not be pronounced. Even more shocking was when Bobby answered in the same sounds.

"Dude, what movie is that from? I don't remember hearing it before," James asked Bobby, who ignored him as he continued to stare at the stranger in some sort of standoff.

"Hey, why did you run off? I've been looking everywhere for you," Tara said, walking up from behind us.

At that moment, Bobby jumped from his chair with his hands in front of him. His eyes glowed just like the stranger's had. The table rose into the air in front of us and flew forward, crashing into the stranger and sending Tara and me flying backward. The crowd of people in the food court erupted into screams as everyone began scattering. I felt the control of my body return instantly. I looked up to see James reaching for Bobby, only to jerk his hand away. Bobby stood for an instant, watching me before barreling through the emergency exit door as the stranger once again rose to his feet. He rushed after Bobby while Tara, James and I jumped up and followed the surge of people now pouring out of the convention hall.

"Tara, are you okay?" I asked as we hurried along.

"I think so. My leg kinda hurts. What the hell was all that?" she asked.

"Yeah, what the eff was with Bobby? I think I shit myself," James piped in.

"I don't know. This is freaking insane," I said, shaking. We made it outside and ran as fast as we could to James's truck in the parking lot. There was already a long line of cars honking and inching forward to leave.

"Get in," James said, unlocking the doors.

"Are we just going to leave Bobby here?" Tara asked, looking at me.

"Screw him. Whatever the hell that was in there, he can walk his ass home," James answered.

"Tara's right. We can't just leave without him," I insisted, although I wasn't completely convinced myself.

"You said in there that guy was an old friend. Is he a cop or something? Why did Bobby run? Is he in some kind of trouble he didn't tell us about?" James asked, rambling on.

"I honestly don't know. I'm in the dark as much as you are," I answered. I was still confused over having my body controlled by some creepy stranger.

"What are we going to do?" Tara asked. She looked like she wanted answers from me that I didn't have. All I could think about was Bobby's eyes, glowing in the same manner as the stranger who started all the commotion. Neither Tara nor James mentioned seeing them, so I kept my mouth shut, because it couldn't be real. There had to be an explanation. I felt like we were living in some science fiction movie that was the reason for this whole stupid convention. I began to feel nauseous and cranked down the window for some air.

"Look. We're getting the hell out of here. If Bobby is in some kind of trouble with the police, he's going to have to call his parents. It's as simple as that," James proclaimed as he started the ignition of his truck. He backed out of the parking space and forced his way into the line of vehicles waiting to exit the lot. It took twenty minutes to make it out of the parking lot and another fifteen minutes to get to the highway. None of us said another word during the drive home. I think we were all in shock.

CHAPTER FOUR

James pulled up in front of my driveway an hour later. I opened the door to his truck, eager to get into my house. As I slid from the bench seat, Tara squeezed my hand and asked me to text her if I heard anything from Bobby. I nodded in agreement and shut the door behind me.

My parents sat on the couch in our living room watching TV when I opened the front door. "Hey, sweetheart. How was the convention?" my mom asked.

"Fine," I answered shortly without stopping as I took the stairs to my room two at a time. That was probably a mistake. I could already picture Mom rising from the couch and on her way to my room. I flopped backward onto my bed, and could hear her coming up the stairs. "Is everything okay?" she asked, standing in the doorway.

"It's fine, Mom. I'm just tired," I said, hoping she would accept my answer and move on.

"Honey, I'm your mother. You know I can always tell when something is wrong." She stood waiting for an answer for a moment before sitting down on the bed next to me when I didn't provide one. "Did something happen between you and Bobby?" she asked.

183

"You could say that," I said, not offering any more explanation.

"Well, just give it a little time. I'm sure things will be better tomorrow," she said, rubbing my head.

"Yeah," I answered.

"You want something to eat?" she asked.

"No thanks. I think I'm just going to take a shower and go to bed."

"Okay, honey. Let me know if you need anything." She walked out of my room, closing the door behind her. I grabbed my favorite pair of Victoria's Secret pajamas and headed to the bathroom. I cranked on the water to heat up while I got undressed. Standing in front of the mirror, I found the reason why the back of my arm felt sore, noticing the unattractive dark purple bruise just above my elbow that must have happened when I was thrown backward.

I climbed into the shower, letting the warm water cascade down my body as I contemplated the day's events over and over again. No matter how many times I played it out in my head, nothing made sense. I remember reading in a book one time at school that said when you eliminate the impossible, what remains, no matter how improbable, must be the truth. This was the problem with trying to rationalize what happened today. Breaking each individual moment apart to try to justify them into logical explanations wouldn't work because it is simply not what happened. The stranger did control my bodily functions, and Bobby didn't pick up the table with his hands. It rose into the air on its own and rocketed toward us like it had been shot from a gun.

After drying off and slipping into my pajamas, I climbed into bed, no closer to any reasonable explanation other than accepting the fact that something freaky was going on. I clicked on my TV with the remote, hoping to find some kind of distraction, if that was even possible. The last thing I remember before drifting asleep was an episode of Pretty Little Liars.

I was startled awake in a pitch-black room with a feeling of unease. Sitting up, I clutched one of my throw pillows to my chest and glanced at the clock on my nightstand. It was one thirty in the morning. The room was as silent as it was dark, but I could sense some type of movement in the corner near my window. My immediate reaction was to scream, but no words escaped my mouth. Suddenly, I was pushed back against my will into a flat position on the bed. The stranger stepped forward as his eyes began to glow, illuminating my room in a soft hue.

CHAPTER FIVE

I realize once again that this will come as a complete shock, but you must remain calm. Do not fear that I have control of your mind. I mean you no harm. My name is Kawise. Your thoughts are correct. I am not from your planet.

"What do you mean, my thoughts are correct? You can read my mind?"

"That is correct. We are speaking telepathically."

"What do you want?"

"Your mate has been taken as a host for Rakar, a dangerous criminal from our home planet of Xorpeen. Rakar is a fugitive who is being hunted for developing a type of biological weapon capable of destroying all life on any planet where it is introduced. I have been tracking him for quite some time, and found him here on Earth."

"Wait. Are you saying that Bobby is now some alien species?"

"No. We exist as a form of living energy. We are able to live within a host species, if we choose, by attaching ourselves to your central nervous system. Your mate is simply being controlled by Rakar."

"But we were going to—oh god, I almost did it with an alien?"

"Intercourse would have remained possible, if that was your intention."

"Don't say it like that. Just let me go and get out! I don't understand what any of this has to do with me."

"As I stated, my intention is not to harm you. This course of action is for your protection. I am afraid there are complications that you are not aware of that place you firmly in this equation."

"What does that even mean? You're not going to tell me I'm a host too?"

"Not in the sense that your mate is being inhabited. The weapon that Rakar developed is a mutated virus of our own species. He has placed it inside you in order to keep it stable."

"I have a freaking alien virus in me? What does that mean? Am I going to die? GAAAAH! I hope that scream sounds the same as it would if my vocal cords worked because I am freaking out right now!"

"Please remain calm."

"Remain calm? Are you out of your mind or whatever you have? How did this happen? When did it happen?"

"At some point Rakar took control of your bodily functions, just as I have, and placed the virus into your system. You would not have been aware of when it happened."

"No shit, Sherlock. How do we get it out before it kills me?"

"The virus remains stable as long as it is attached to a host nervous system. That is how Rakar keeps it hidden. The reason I found him on Earth is because my tracking devices are set to locate the virus. When he placed it into your body, my tracking system recorded a faint signal. The closer I get to the virus, the stronger the signal, even when hidden inside a host. It wasn't until I tracked you today that I was certain of what Rakar had done. He is the only one who can remove the virus here."

"So, let's go then. I assume you caught him today, right?"

"I am afraid not. He has escaped for now, but he will not leave Earth without the virus. His plan was quite clever actually. We could remove the virus on my home planet, but you would not survive the trip. If you die, the virus will become unstable. Rakar knows I cannot allow this to happen."

"Well, that's just great! What is the plan then, K?"

"To keep you close until Rakar comes for you. Even if he knows I am protecting you, he has no choice but to show himself in order to retrieve the virus."

"How do you know he's not coming now?"

"My tracking device will detect his signal. I will stay until morning, at which time you will tell your parental figures you are leaving to see your friends. We will then wait for Rakar to come to us."

"So, on top of everything else, I am now the bait? What happens if you somehow catch him and he takes the virus out of me?"

"I take him into custody and return to Xorpeen. You return to your normal existence."

"Yeah, normal. That sounds like a great plan."

CHAPTER SIX

There was no way I could get back to sleep after K's visit. He had left my room after our talk, but said he would remain close by. It took everything in me to keep from jumping out of bed and running to my parents and telling them to call the police—the army, hell, the freaking president or something. I realized there was no point. One, it was completely unbelievable. They would throw me in a loony bin before I could prove anything. Two, it wouldn't change the fact that I supposedly had some killer mutant virus inside me that could wipe out our entire planet. My only choice was to trust K and hopefully help him catch Rakar.

Not only could I not go back to sleep, it was Sunday and my parents always liked to sleep in until ten. I didn't want to raise their suspicions by waking them at six a.m. to tell them I was going over to Tara's house, so I had to lay there and wait. Wait for my parents, wait for Rakar, wait-wait-wait. I only hope the virus inside me didn't react to me freaking out, because it was happening—big time.

I was already hot on my parents' heels when I heard them walking down the stairs from their bedroom. "Hey, Mom. Hey, Dad. I'm heading over to see Tara, okay?" I said, already reaching for the front door.

"Hang on a second," Mom said, stopping me in my tracks. "So early?" she asked.

"We've been texting all morning about yesterday, you know? We're just going to hang out and talk a little."

"Uh-huh. Don't you want to eat something before you go?"

"I already had a cereal bar. I'll be back later, okay?"

"Fine, sweetie. Drive safely and let me know if you are going anywhere else."

"I will. See you guys," I said, closing the door behind me. I walked down the driveway with my head on a swivel, looking for K. I didn't know what else to do so I climbed into the car and backed out of the driveway like I was really heading to Tara's. About halfway down the block, but far from view of my house, K stepped out into the road from behind another vehicle. I thought for a second about running him over, but didn't figure it would do any good. "Hey," I said as he opened the passenger door when I came to a stop. I drove forward, waiting for him to give me some type of direction. "So, are you going to tell me where we're going or what the plan is? And by the way, no taking over my body or communicating telepathically. Just speak," I said.

"As you wish," he answered. "There is an abandoned storage facility off Route Seven, approximately thirty kilometers away."

"You mean the old tire factory?" I asked. "Why there?"

"It lies far enough outside the proximity of the surrounding residential area to not attract any attention."

"And what makes you think Rakar is just going to show up? Why would he do that if he knows you are going to try and capture him?" I asked.

"He cannot afford to wait. Now that his location has been detected, he knows it is only a matter of time before reinforcements show up. This is his best opportunity to reacquire the virus and escape. I am simply providing the opportunity."

"You're not worried that he will kick your ass and get away?" I asked. It was blunt, but a fair question. I didn't know who I was dealing with here. For all I knew, K could have been the joke of his police force.

"I have been in my position for many of your years. I am experienced in apprehending criminals," he replied indifferently. At least I hadn't offended him. Not that I would have cared. My life was on the line here too. I just wanted to get through this without losing my life or destroying the planet.

We pulled into the gravel yard of the old tire factory, which looked completely desolate as always, except for empty soda and beer cans scattered around. I knew the place because it was a regular weekend hangout for teenagers in the local area. We would congregate here on occasional Friday or Saturday nights and party. It was isolated and out of the way, so the cops would never show up to bust us. "Okay, now what?" I asked as I shut off the ignition.

"You wait here while I check the area," K answered. He climbed out of the car, shutting the door behind him.

"Wait here? Are you kidding me?" I asked, jumping from the car to go after him. He turned and held up his hand to stop me.

"I can make you stay if need be, but I would prefer not to do that," he said as he pointed me back to my car.

"What am I supposed to do if he shows up and you're not here?" I asked, not understanding his stupid plan.

"Remain calm, return to your vehicle and lock the doors. I will be close by," he insisted.

"Oh, sure. Remain calm. Go ahead, little worm. Just sit on this hook while I lower you into the water. Nothing bad is going to happen. Whatever," I said, grumbling all the way back to the car. I turned around to plead my case to stay with K one more time, but he was nowhere in sight. I had no idea how he was able to disappear so quickly, but he was gone. I continued backing up, looking in every direction for him until my rear end bumped into my car.

"Jenn?" Bobby's voice called out, causing me to whirl around.

CHAPTER SEVEN

He walked out from behind a nearby tree. I tried screaming out for K, but obviously Rakar had taken control of my vocal chords.

"Don't be afraid. It's me."

"Bullshit, Rakar. K told me everything and when he comes back, your ass is toast."

"No, Jenn, listen. Rakar is still controlling my body, but he is letting me talk to you. Kawise is lying to you. Rakar is not a criminal. He is a renowned scientist on Xorpeen. He was working for their government, trying to develop a cure for a mutant gene that affects their species, when he discovered the government had lied to him and were planning on using his research to develop a weapon. He couldn't allow it to happen, so he destroyed his data, took the only remaining sample of the virus and fled."

"If you're telling the truth, why didn't he just go to their police or whatever they have?"

"He had nowhere to go. They come from a hostile galaxy of planets whose ruling bodies are all battling for control over the precious elements they need to survive. Kawise works for the government. He is only using you to lure Rakar out, and then he will likely kill you."

"Oh, like that's not Rakar's plan too. Why won't he stop controlling me and just take his virus and leave?"

"He will if you will come with us. Trust me."

"Ha. I don't even know if it's really you talking to me, and you want me to trust you?"

"It is me, Jenn. Just come with us now. Rakar will take what he needs and leave, then we can be together, just like before."

"I want to, but I don't know who to believe."

"Believe me," he said, walking toward me with his arms outstretched. I held my hand out to take his when a booming sound like thunder cracked around us.

"Rakar, stop!" K commanded, flanking us from behind one of the abandoned buildings.

"Greetings again, Kawise. I assumed you would be joining us, a little later than I expected, however. I have already explained the truth to the female," Rakar answered. At least they were speaking in our language, so I was able to follow along.

"You mean your version of the truth. Regardless, you are coming with me, now," K said, holding up some type of gadget that didn't exactly look menacing.

"Do you really think I am going to willingly give up my host and allow you to imprison me in your little cage there?" Rakar answered, indicating the device that K held in his hand. I couldn't imagine what it was, but Rakar obviously did not want him to use it. Rakar reached quickly behind his back, pulling out a nine-millimeter pistol he had tucked into his pants. "I didn't want it to come to this, but I will kill the female and unleash the virus on this planet before I will let you take it back to Xorpeen. Now, step away and lower your entrapment device," Rakar said, pointing the gun at me.

K looked at me before returning his gaze to Rakar. He lowered the gadget he was holding to the ground and took two steps backward.

"You. Go retrieve the device," Rakar said, barking the order at me.

I walked over to K and reached down to pick up the strange contraption. His eyes remained fixated on Rakar.

"Very good. Now, if you will excuse me," Rakar said after I handed it over to him. He returned the gun to his pants, reached into his pocket and pulled out what looked to be a regular smartphone. After swiping the screen and tapping a few times, K suddenly dropped to the ground. The human host remained in a heap, evidently unconscious while K stood before us in his true form. He looked like the luminescent liquid inside a hot lava lamp. The only time you could make out his limbs was when he moved, at which point you could see that he had an almost human shape to him.

"I am sure you are curious as to what this little device is," Rakar said. "You see, what Kawise would tell you if he could speak in your language at the moment is that each of our species is embedded with a molecular code, a security combination, if you will, that enables us to inhabit and uninhabit a host without risk of being removed without our control. I have created an algorithm using your cellular technology that unscrambles our molecular code, allowing me to remove Kawise from his host."

"You did that with a cellphone?" I asked in disbelief.

"Indeed. 'There's an app for that,' as you humans like to say," Rakar replied, chuckling. "Now, we will get Kawise tucked away in the entrapment unit, and then tend to you, my dear," he continued, pointing it at K. Before he could activate the device, I grabbed him by the arm, sending me flying back, but also causing Rakar to drop the entrapment unit. K surged forward, grabbing Rakar as a struggle ensued. Bobby's body suddenly flopped to the ground and the two alien forms continued to attack each other. The air around them zapped and popped, and they became so bright I had to shut my eyes.

I struggled to my feet, reaching for the entrapment device that lay on the ground. I had no idea how it worked, but it had a trigger that looked like any other gun. K and Rakar continued to struggle. Even if I wanted to use the device, I couldn't tell their forms apart. I could just as easily trap K. Holding the device out in front of me, I pointed it back and forth at each of the forms, trying to discern who was who. "K!" I yelled to get his attention. In a split second, one of the forms shoved the other away and turned my direction. It had to be K. I pointed the device quickly at the other form and pulled the trigger. A jolt of energy shot from the gun, pulling the form into the entrapment device like a tractor beam. It became instantly hot to the touch, causing me to drop the device at my feet. K, who had once again inhabited his previous human form, rushed over to pick up the device and tapped some type of code into a small screen.

I ran over to Bobby, who was beginning to regain consciousness. "Bobby, are you okay? Can you hear me?" I asked.

"Yeah, I feel okay. Just dizzy," he said, trying to sit up.

"Do you remember anything?" I asked.

"I remember everything. Where is Rakar?"

"He's in the entrapment device," I answered as K walked over to where Bobby and I were sitting.

"My planet owes you a debt of gratitude," he said with a smile on his face. It suited him, even if it wasn't his true form. "By the way, what made you decide which of us to believe?" he asked.

"Well, K. I don't know how they do it on your planet, but here on Earth, we have what is called a bullshit meter, and mine is as good as you will find. I could tell by the way Rakar snickered after his corny app joke that he was full of it."

"Ah, yes. Speaking of which, I have examined this cellular device Rakar has devised, and I believe I can use it to remove the virus from your system."

CHAPTER EIGHT

The last thing I remember before blacking out is K tapping the screen of the cellphone. I woke up on my couch, lying in Bobby's lap as he stroked my head. My eyes fluttered open and began to adjust to the light.

"Hey, sleepyhead. How do you feel?" Bobby asked.

"Fine, I think. How did we get here?" I asked confused.

"You said you wanted to watch a movie, but you conked out like halfway through. Hey, by the way, did you tell your mom we had a fight? After you went to sleep, she threatened me that I better not hurt her little girl, or something. She looked like she wanted to tear my eyes out."

"Huh? No, I meant—where's K?" I asked, sitting up.

"Who's K?" he replied. He looked at me like I had two heads. "Babe, did you have a bad dream or something?"

"Maybe, I guess. I'm not sure," I said, shaking my head. It couldn't have been a dream. Everything felt so real. "I have to go the bathroom," I said, standing up.

"Okay. When you come back, do you want to go grab a cone from Rodeo Whip?" Bobby asked as I walked away.

"Yeah, sure," I answered, waving over my shoulder. I walked up the stairs, confused, but thoroughly convinced that none of this had been a dream. I walked into the bathroom, locking the door behind me. As I stood, staring at myself in the mirror, I felt something in my pocket. Reaching inside, I pulled out what looked like a bright green emerald about the size of a golf ball. I held it up to the light when suddenly an image appeared from the strange stone. It looked like a hologram of K and he began to speak.

"This message is for you and you alone. It will only play once and will not work for anyone else. I have cleared any memory of Rakar and the other events from Bobby's memory. The virus has been removed from your system, so feel free to continue on as if nothing ever happened. As I stated, my planet and I owe you a great debt. Perhaps one day I will figure out a way to show our gratitude, but for now, I leave you with the memory of our fascinating encounter together. I am certain that one day we will see each other again. Take care and farewell.

With that, the image disappeared. I caressed the stone in my hand. Even if he was wrong, and he never came back to Earth, I would always take pride in probably being the only person who ever spoke to an extraterrestrial. It was one heck of a story. I only wish I could tell it to someone.

Snow Globe

By C.A. Kunz

For information on other titles
Visit the author's website:
http://cakunz.blogspot.com/

Snow Globe

"Aliens freaking do exist," I whisper through cold chapped lips while approaching the back door to my house.

With the assistance of my cell phone's flashlight app, I can see the remnants of a pre-winter frost covering the screen mesh of the exterior door. It's only November 1st and we've already had at least four inches of snow, which has to be some kind of record.

It takes a few moments for the shock from what I just saw in the forest to wear off, but even now there's still some residual disbelief.

A bright light.

A crashed spaceship.

A flippin' gorgeous human-looking alien who can somehow speak English.

A flurry of thoughts race through my head as I try and comprehend the fact I just had a conversation with an extraterrestrial. A freaking extraterrestrial.

I close the flashlight app and stuff the phone into my jeans pocket before reaching for the flimsy metal door handle. I see my hand trembling from the adrenaline rush enveloping me, and it's literally taking every ounce of my self-control to not scream out, "Aliens freaking do exist!"

Ever since I was a little girl, I've been absolutely one hundred percent positive that other intelligent life forms were out there amongst the stars. I knew we couldn't be all alone in this universe. My nana was the only other one in our family who shared these views, and because of this, we spent many nights while she babysat me and my siblings, having X-Files and Roswell marathons. We'd discuss in great detail all of the conspiracies surrounding Area 51 like they were truths and not some made-up pieces of fiction. My parents would call us both crazy, but now I have proof. I just never thought my proof would be in the form of a hot alien guy in the woods behind my house.

I push open the interior door with a sense of caution as to not make my parents stir upstairs. It's almost one in the morning, and my dad has to be at work early today. He'll be seriously pissed if I wake him.

Moving into the kitchen, after easing the back door shut, I take a mental note of the things I want to grab before I head back outside. I have to hit up my room for some essentials first though.

No matter how quiet I try to be, it seems the house wants to wake everyone. With each step I take, the old floorboards creak in the foyer, causing me to cringe and constantly look up to the second level to see if my parents' bedroom light comes on. Luckily, my room is on the first floor, but unfortunately, so is my younger sister. We share a bedroom since our two older brothers called dibs on the other ones upstairs. It kind of sucks being seventeen and still sharing a space with your twelve-year-old sibling.

The door to my room is cracked open and I push it the rest of the way, all the while trying not to make too much noise. Thankfully, the doors don't squeak like the floors do in this old farmhouse. I scan the two walls comprising my side of the room and see all of the alien posters plastered across them. My eyes land on the three shelves where the majority of my sci-fi memorabilia I've collected over the years is placed with purpose and care.

Shaking my head, I think to myself, It's so crazy how totally accurate, and completely way off at the same time, Hollywood was about aliens.

I make my way over to the far corner of the room to the dresser my sister and I share. I become hyperaware of every little noise my winter coat makes as my arms brush against my sides with every step. When a small moan sounds from my sister's bed, I stop dead in my tracks. It's followed by some stirring about under the covers until she seems to find another sleeping position. I breathe an internal sigh of relief and continue toward the dresser.

Kyle, which is the name I gave the alien after he said his real name and it sounded like someone talking under water, told me he was on a peaceful reconnaissance mission around Earth. He's a part of his race's form of military and is called a, for the lack of a better word, scout. His job is to take routine scans of our planet and return to his officials with a list of findings. According to him, it was all going smoothly until his ship collided with one of our satellites, and he crashed into my backyard. I decided to help him in his task by collecting things from around the house that I love, at the off chance he might find them interesting too.

I pick up the novelty plastic snow globe from the dresser and watch as the white iridescent flakes swirl around the image of a stereotypical big-headed green alien giving a peace sign next to the words Area 51. I thought it'd be funny to show Kyle how some here on Earth perceive his kind. My nana brought this back for me after she took a trip to Roswell, New Mexico, two years ago. It was on her bucket list, and she almost wasn't able to do it once her cancer began to worsen. This snow globe is one of the few things I have left to remember her by. It means so much to me, and acts as a constant reminder of how much I miss her, especially now since she's the only one who'd completely understand how awesome my current situation is.

"Andi?" I hear a soft voice whisper behind me.

I spin around and see my sister, Abigail, sitting up in bed with the covers drawn back and her favorite tattered stuffed purple bunny nestled in her arms. She rubs her eyes and then says my name again when I don't immediately answer.

"Shhh. Yeah, Abbi, it's me," I reply as I move over to her.

"What are you doing?

"Don't worry about it. Go back to bed," I say, and then begin to pull the covers back up to her chest.

"Why are you dressed and not in your comfy pajamas?" she asks after rubbing her eyes again.

"The truth?"

"Uh-huh," she responds through a yawn while holding the covers at bay, and not allowing me to move them.

I think for a moment, and then an idea hits me. I'll actually tell her the truth. She'll never believe me.

"Well, the truth is, there's an alien in the woods, and I'm bringing him stuff that he's never seen," I explain with a smile.

Her facial features scrunch into a questioning look as she begins to lie back down. Pulling the covers up to her chin, she says, "You're so weird, Andi, you know that? I'm going back to sleep."

"Thanks, love you too," I say with a giggle. "Good night."

After placing a kiss on the top of her head, I back away in the direction of my bed to grab a couple things from the shelves above it before heading out of the room.

I retrace my steps back toward the kitchen, though for some reason the floor decides to creak even louder this time. I find myself cursing each and every one of the boards the second they decide to make a noise. Instead of continuing to take my chances by creeping across the loud-as-hell floor, I decide to leap from where I'm standing to the kitchen. After landing safely, and more importantly, quietly, I make a beeline to the refrigerator. Pulling it open, I search out the shelves in the door for the blue tube of Pillsbury chocolate chip cookie dough. An alien hasn't truly lived until they've tried some raw cookie dough.

Before I close the door, I see the corner of what looks like the orange wrapper of a Reese's Peanut Butter Cup sticking out from behind a six-pack of Diet Coke. Dad probably tried to hide this from Mom, since he's not supposed to have them. It's his favorite candy in the whole entire world, and he was crushed when his doctor told him he had to start watching his sugar intake.

"Consider this a favor, Dad," I say, taking out the Reese's and snatching up a can of Coke in the process before tucking both items into my coat pockets.

Through the little window in back door, I see snow swirling around outside in a whimsical flurry display. This is the kind of snow I love to see—winter wonderland snow, not snowpocalypse.

Pulling up the hood of my coat, I open the door and step out. The instant the cold night wind sweeps by me, I shiver and clutch myself in a tight hug to ward off the sudden chill spiraling throughout my body. Drawing out my phone again, I turn on the flashlight app and shine it in front of me toward the forest. It cuts a

205

path through the darkened backyard, illuminating my diminished footprints from earlier.

The snow crunches beneath my boots as I follow the faint tracks back toward the woods. Staring at the wall of trees in front of me, I feel like I'm about to walk into another world, especially knowing what's waiting for me in there. Excitement bubbles up inside of me with every step I take, and the anticipation of seeing Kyle's beautiful face once more is enough to make me all giddy— not to mention, he's a freaking alien. I really wish my nana was here to meet him.

Maneuvering through the trees, I push aside the many branches that impede the route back to the crash site. The fastest way is unfortunately through the thick shrubbery that lies off the manmade trail etched through the forest. I high step through the many bushes and continue to swat away the tree limbs that attempt to assault my face when I try to move passed them.

After a few minutes of trudging along through the snow-covered greenery, I finally emerge into the clearing that Kyle's spaceship created when it landed. Downed trees fill my vision, leaving behind a huge gap in the canopy of trees for the large full moon to shine through. The moon's light shimmers off something surrounding the spacecraft, and immediately catches my eye. When I move closer, I notice the thing surrounding the ship is giving off a faint neon blue glow.

"What is that?" I ask myself while inching toward it.

The front part of Kyle's spaceship slides open and he climbs out with a grin stretching from dimple to dimple. As he strolls over to me, I realize he's not wearing the breather mask over his mouth anymore. He was afraid that Earth's air wouldn't agree with his system, since his species has never actually landed on our planet.

His short hair is a beautiful mixture of brown, black, and blond strands. His piercing blue eyes become partially hidden as his smile widens when I move closer, but then it falters.

"Wait," he says quickly, holding his hands up. His deep voice mesmerizes me. It's odd, but I've never felt this kind of instant connection with anyone. Maybe it's like one of his alien abilities or something.

"Okay," I reply, feeling confused by his request.

"I had to deploy my ship's force field because the mask malfunctioned. If you were to cross over, you'd be deprived of oxygen," he explains. "I had to wait in my ship until the surrounding area was detoxified."

"Oh," I reply, analyzing the field he was talking about more critically. I can see a slight reflection of myself in the glossy bubble, and instinctively reach my hand out to touch it. The moment my index finger grazes the surface it sends a bright neon blue ripple across the section I touch while distorting my reflection in the process.

"Neat, huh?" he asks, moving to stand right in front of me.

"Yeah," I answer in a daze, fascinated by the light trail my finger is creating on the force field. Even though I can see right through it, it feels solid when I press my fingertip against it.

"You were gone so long that I didn't think you'd return." Kyle's voice brings my attention back to his face, and I drop my hand to my side. "I thought maybe I scared you off or something."

"I was only gone about half an hour," I reply, seeing his forehead furrow at my response.

"It seemed like sectors to me," Kyle says seriously.

"Sectors? Is that your version of time? Ours are seconds, minutes, and hours." I wait for his answer, as he seems to be mulling it over.

"Yeah, time. I remember reading about that. Our time is essentially no different except for the names. On our planet, we don't waste any of, what you call time, and we must account for it or be … I can't seem to find a word in your language to explain it."

I begin to miss seeing his smile, and I don't want to know what he was about to say, because it didn't sound like it was going to be good. To lighten the mood I begin to pull out the items from my coat pockets and take a seat on the ground. Kyle mimics my sitting position on the other side of the "bubble." I notice his eyes are intently focused on each item as I place them on the ground in front of me, one by one. A light breeze swirls a trail of snow around the objects after I've laid them all out. The iridescent snow pieces inside the snow globe are sent into frenzied motion when I shake it up to show Kyle what it does before setting it down again.

When I gaze up at the top crest of the bubble, I notice a mound of snowflakes have gathered there in a sizeable clump. A sudden gust of wind sends the snow showering down on where I'm sitting. It's like a reverse snow globe, I say to myself, watching the delicate snow slipping down the side of the force field.

"I see you brought back some interesting gifts with you. Is that what you call them? I also hear they're referred to as presents."

"What do you mean 'hear'?" I say, looking for an earpiece or something that might be helping him gain this intel.

"Hear? Oh yes, sorry. I forgot to tell you that there's what you'd call a microchip stamped into my earlobe. It translates my thoughts into your language so I can communicate with you. It also allows me to understand what you're saying. Sometimes it's, what you call, 'a little off.'" He laughs, and oh my goodness, his laughter is so warm. It sounds so deep and genuine. It's almost like he's human ... almost.

I wish I could get nearer to him. Where did that come from? Could I be somehow attracted to an alien? Of course he's beautiful, but he's also something more, sincere maybe? Or real?

"What are you thinking?" Kyle's voice startles me, and I'm so glad he can't read minds ... or at least I hope he can't.

I begin to feel a blush creeping up my cheeks. I know for a fact my face has completely turned thirty shades of red, and I just hope he thinks it's because of the cold weather.

"I was thinking it's a little chilly out here, and was wondering if it's warm in there with you," I reply, but then immediately feel silly for asking such a stupid sounding question. It's painfully obvious the cold is not bothering him since he's not wearing a coat, and his spacesuit, if you can call his body-hugging—and oh what a body it is—onesie, a spacesuit. Could my face feel any hotter right now?

"Yes, this field of energy maintains a comfortable body temperature for me. You must be really cold out there. Your face is becoming a deeper red color as we speak. My translator is saying you're blushing, but that doesn't seem right. Oh, okay, now it says human skin can become red from cold temperatures."

Whew, I could hug that translator of his. A couple of seconds ago I could've strangled it, but it's redeemed itself.

"Aren't you curious about the stuff I brought to show you?" I ask, desperately wanting to change the subject and switch his focus from my bright scarlet face to the items displayed in front of me.

"Actually, I'm very intrigued by these gifts you have here. Please explain them to me," he says, looking down at the row of items.

"Okay, so first up is a Reece's Peanut Butter Cup. It's a chocolate candy with peanut butter inside. See?" I explain while taking the single cup out of the wrapper and breaking it apart. "It's so delicious and sweet, along with being very addicting. In fact, my dad can't resist them. My mom won't let him have them anymore because he's on a diet, so he mopes around the house a lot." I find myself rambling because Kyle is sitting there staring at me while hanging on every one of my words. I can't explain the emotions that are starting to bubble up within me at this moment. I'm suddenly feeling warm all over, when I should be shivering from the freezing cold temperature.

"Umm, so, up next is a Coke. It's also sweet, and is quite a popular drink here on Earth. It can be quite addicting as well. I also have a fork and a spoon here. These are what we eat with. We also use knives, which are sharp, to cut things with. Am I boring you?" I see him glance down quickly as I point out the items, but then his stunning blue eyes return to mine.

"Never ... You could never bore me," he says, shocking the heck out of me. His smile is so sincere, and I wish I could touch his face and feel his arms around me. I shiver again, but it's still most definitely not from the cold.

"Ahem, and this is a snow globe. My nana brought this back to me from Roswell, New Mexico, which is a place where many people have claimed to see aliens. When you shake it up, it looks like it's snowing inside, like it is out here right now." I shake the globe and watch as his eyes seem to fixate on the glistening white flakes while they swirl around.

210

"What's the green thing?" He points at the cliché-looking green plastic alien inside the globe.

"Well, this is what most people think your kind looks like."

Kyle chuckles and gestures to himself. "Could we be twins?" I have to try and fight back the laugh bubbling up in my throat, but fail epically. The moment I begin to laugh at his question, Kyle sends me a cheeky smile.

"Maybe you're not the only beings out there?" I say after my little laughing fit subsides.

"Your assumption would be correct. There are others out there, but I've never seen them with my own eyes, only images. This is my first mission, remember. On our planet, we're what you'd call regimented. We obey every order, and never ask questions. It's not what you might refer to as a happy place." He dips his head, avoiding my gaze, and shakes it back and forth.

When he pans back up to me, I see sadness reflected in his eyes, and wish he'd laugh or smile again. What a miserable place his home must be. I mean, we have to obey laws and our parents, but I'd absolutely hate it if I couldn't feel happiness. I wish this bubble would disappear so I could wrap him up in a hug. I'm sure he doesn't get anything like that where he's from. He seems so lonely.

I bring my hand up and rest it flat against the bubble and watch as the neon blue color begins to outline my fingers. Kyle raises his hand and places it opposite mine. Mine is dwarfed by his, which shouldn't surprise me since he has to be at least a foot taller than I am. When I initially saw him, his height was the first thing I noticed. Okay, so I also noticed how perfect he appears to be— otherworldly. He resembles many of the models that grace the pages of magazines or are on TV. I wish Nana was here with me.

She'd be so excited to meet Kyle, and would probably ask him a million and one questions. I hope she's watching right now and sees that we were right all these years.

"Before I became a scout, I watched your planet, and when they sent me on my first mission, I knew this is where I wanted to go first. You humans are such wonderful and fascinating creatures. Each and every one of you is unique in your own way. Through observing your kind, I've learned about happiness and love. Like I said before, these feelings are lacking on my planet."

A loud buzzing sound erupts from the downed silver spacecraft behind him. "Excuse me," he says quickly before springing to his feet and moving toward his ship. When he reaches the front part of the spacecraft, a door slides open and he disappears inside.

The snow is still drifting down lightly around me, and I watch as another wave of flakes cascade down the bubble to the ground. As the snow touches the surface of the force field, it causes a myriad of blue hues to ripple across it. If this is a dream, I most definitely do not want to wake up.

I can't believe it's only been two hours since I decided to sneak out of the house and take a walk in the woods after having a little tiff with my mom. The argument was over a party I wanted to go to next weekend. The moment I slipped up and told her there wouldn't be any adults around, she nixed the idea. I reminded her I'll be eighteen in two months, and I'm far from the typical wild teenager. In fact, I pride myself on being a good girl. I get good grades, and I'm freaking third in my senior class, what's not to trust?

So, there I was taking a stroll through the forest, away from my house to calm down, when I heard a thunderous bang, which

212

shook the very ground beneath my feet. I did something that my parents would've deemed completely insane, and without thinking, I took off in the direction I thought the sound resonated from.

The first thing I noticed was the path of decimated trees leading up to a clearing with a huge metallic oval-shaped object lodged into the ground. It looked like an elongated, cylindrical egg with windows. I couldn't believe my eyes. I initially thought it was some kind of satellite that had fallen out of the sky. I've seen pictures of satellites, and though it didn't really look like any I had seen, I figured that maybe it was a top-secret one from the military or something. When I approached the large object, it was making this odd humming sound. I continued to creep through the trees toward it, but stayed in the shadows so not to be seen, just in case someone was out here.

While I was wondering if I should call NASA, the military, or Sheriff Johnson, which was a foolish idea since I'd definitely have no reception this far into the woods, the top front section of the cylinder slid open. I swear I was focused on the metallic object the whole time, and a door just freakin' appeared. I'm positive that if I looked in a mirror at that moment, I would've been met with the most shocked look that's ever graced my face. Every single thought left my mind the moment a figure began to emerge from the opening. I was surprised to see the figure was actually a male dressed in some kind of jumpsuit with something covering his nose and mouth. He had a small gold stick in his hand, and his eyes, which I swear were glowing deep neon blue, scanned the area and then fixated on me. The one thought that did cross my mind in that instant was I must be seeing an alien. At least that's what I was hoping he'd be. Even though he looked human, I just couldn't let go of the thought of him being a real-life extraterrestrial.

Pulling myself away from my musings, I glance over to the opening at the front of the large metallic spacecraft, wondering what's keeping Kyle. It seems like forever since he scampered off. Maybe he's getting ready to leave. I suddenly feel a sense of panic because I don't want this first encounter to end. I don't want him to go, but if he stays, there's a chance he could be found and stuck on a slab somewhere to be dissected and analyzed. The world isn't prepared for this kind of revelation, and I know for a fact that my small town is definitely not ready for this.

I sigh with relief when he emerges from his ship, and I see a pulsating red sphere in his hand. He looks up at me and then back down at the object he's holding. I get this feeling it's not a good thing. When he moves to stand right in front of me, he lifts his hand and places the sphere up to the wall of the neon blue field of energy. He removes his hand, but the ball stays there like it's stuck to it. I hear a slight ticking chime resonate from the small red orb, and it sounds like a synthesized version of the grandfather clock in our foyer.

"Kyle, what's that?" I ask, and he looks up at me with a smile, but his eyes look bleak.

"I have communicated with the main scouting vessel, and they informed me that Earth is on high alert after I hit one of your satellites. There will be no rescue. I am to be what you call terminated. This device will destroy all evidence of me being here, including me. My craft is unable to travel, and I'm deemed an accepted loss."

"What? How can they just leave you here? Our military has a code: no man left behind," I say, wondering what kind of monsters would leave him here to die like this.

"I told you, our species do not have the same emotions as you. There are so many of us that our military sees us entry-level soldiers as nothing but expendable. There's always someone right there to take our place." He shakes his head while his shoulders are slightly slumped, like he has accepted his fate.

"That's stupid. Really stupid. We have people on Earth that think like that, but to have everyone be so callous about life, that just sucks." I'm so angry I could scream.

"Sucks?" he says with a ghost of a smile.

"Stinks, rotten, unfair, not right, and I can't think of anymore words, but yeah, sucks."

"Ah, now I understand," he replies before going silent for a moment. "I have my orders though, and I must obey them. No one can know I was here. I could put my whole entire race in danger." His somber tone makes me think that maybe he's different from the rest of his species. Maybe he can feel emotion, which only makes this whole scenario worse.

"You don't have to obey this order. You can tell them to go shove it, and that I know and am not afraid to tell the world, so they'll have to rescue you." I know my face is red with anger, but it begins to fade when I see his beautiful smile return.

"You care about me. No one has ever cared for me. I've always been an outcast on my planet. I'm different, and I've always struggled to fit in. But I must obey these commands. I must die, and leave no trace of my existence behind. It's for the common good."

I feel the tears begin to roll down my cheeks, mixing with the fragile snowflakes collecting on my face. In this moment my heart feels like it's going to snap in half. I've just met this wonderful alien being and he's going to die because his people told him he

215

has to. I have to stop him. I'm not going to let him do this. No one should be forced to do this to themselves, it's barbaric.

"No, I won't let you. You will stay here with me. My parents can help you. Nobody will know the truth." I swipe away the tears of frustration and shoot up to my feet. My legs feel stiff from sitting on the cold ground for so long.

"I don't believe that will be possible. I have to follow orders. If I disobey, I might not be able to survive in your atmosphere anyway. I was only supposed to observe Earth from afar. My death is the only way to protect the rest of my race from discovery. Why are you crying?" I again angrily wipe away a few stray tears.

"I'm crying because I don't want you to die. I want you to stay here and live. We can do this together," I choke out.

I want Kyle to stay here. My emotions are so intense right now that I feel like I'm going to burst. Freaking hell, he looks human, so surely he can adapt to our atmosphere. Fate can't be this cruel.

"I wish I could touch your crying—wait, tears. I'm being told they are salty. I wish I could disobey my orders, but I cannot. Please stop crying … You are sad, and it's because of me. I'm honored at the emotions you are expending because of my imminent termination. Nobody will miss me when I cease to exist. Meeting you will make this bearable for me. We have only a short while, so can you sit back down and talk to me a little longer? Keep me company in my final hours? I want as much knowledge about you before I, well, you know. Oh, and I'm told your tears could freeze from the cold temperature, so please stop since I don't want you to be a frozen human."

Between my sobbing fits I feel the need to giggle, and a little one seeps out at his comment. I love the way he talks, looks, and makes me feel. Could I be having feelings for him? I so don't

216

believe in insta-feelings, but my emotions are raw at the thought of losing him. Maybe it's because he's an alien, and I'm just overwhelmed by the fact that they are actually real. Maybe my strong link to my nana and the thought of how I miss her so much and wish she was here to meet Kyle are increasing the intensity of my feelings.

"I find that your giggles make me feel … happy." Kyle's voice interrupts my thoughts, and I give him a watery smile.

"You feel happy?" I ask, smiling wider.

"Yeah, I guess I do. Well, at least I think this is what happy feels like," he replies, answering my smile with a grin of his very own.

"So, what do you want to know?" I ask, trying to reign in my emotions and gain some self-control. The least I can do is give him what he wants. The ticking noise draws my attention to the hateful red demon, I mean sphere, attached to the force field.

"You mentioned parents earlier, explain. All I can hear is that they are related to you."

"My mom and dad? Well, they made me and my sister." I'm not sure what else to say about them, or how else to explain it. I don't think this is the most appropriate time for a sex ed lesson.

"I'm told you are made through sexual reproduction. Do you partake in this sex?"

He didn't just ask me that question, did he?

"Hmm. Well, no, I don't. I mean, I've kissed boys and have made out with a few here and there, but never went all the way." Yeah, I definitely would've so regretted losing my virginity to Bradley Majors, aka the Jackass. In typical jackass fashion, when I wouldn't put out, he moved on to someone who would, and did.

"What exactly is love? I'm told it's a feeling. I've seen many of your human feelings in action, but I'm told love is one that you all seek."

My eyes meet his and I swear I'm experiencing the stirrings of some deep emotions, or maybe it could be frostbite of the brain or something.

"Love is indeed a feeling, but it has many meanings to many people. There's the love for your family. There's the love for someone you have an intimate connection to who's not related to you. There's also a love for an animal or pet that shares your life. You know, it's actually really hard to explain what love is exactly. I've never really thought about it in detail before, but I can tell you that it's a very complicated emotion." I see his smile slip as frown lines appear on his perfectly smooth forehead like he's thinking really hard.

"If I was human, would it be possible for you to love me?" His eyes—I swear they change to a different shade of blue—stare attentively into mine like he's willing me to say yes.

"Maybe, but I don't think you'd have to be human for me to love you," I say honestly, and I really mean it.

"That makes me happy. The definition of happy seems appropriate for this moment." He grins widely like he has just figured out some complex problem and is bursting with pride. "Will you do something for me? It's maybe a small thing for you, but I want one question answered before I … go. I want to know how it feels to kiss someone."

I'm struck speechless. He wants a kiss. A beautiful alien guy wants a kiss from me. I nod my head and then I realize to do this, the bubble must disappear. He might die before my eyes from exposure to our air. I don't think I can handle that.

"I'm sorry, was it inappropriate for me to ask this of you?" He looks at me intently, and I pull myself together.

"You'll have to remove the barrier for me to give you a kiss. What if you die? I don't want you to die," I say, my voice laced with desperation.

"At least I'll die happy. I'm told that kissing is an enjoyable experience, and I would like to feel true joy at least once in my life." He sounds like he's almost pleading with me, and I abruptly stand up before placing my hand onto the bubble. Kyle does the same.

"Yes, I will," I say boldly, even though I'm breaking apart inside at the thought of these being my last moments with him.

"I'll be back right back, don't leave, and please don't change your mind." He scrambles back to his ship, and within seconds he returns.

"I've made it so that the barrier will disappear in one minute, your time. Are you ready?"

No, I yell to myself, I'm not ready. I don't want this kiss to be my last memory of him. This isn't fair.

I nod, answering his question, and move closer to the bubble as it begins to flicker and pulsate a neon blue. My emotions are all over the place, and I find myself torn between wanting to experience my first kiss with an alien, and the fact it will most likely be the last.

The force field fades away and Kyle rushes forward, wrapping his firm arms around my frame, and pulls me close. His head almost immediately moves down to mine and our lips meet, causing my legs to feel like jelly. Swinging my arms around his neck, I wish I wasn't wearing my thick jacket, because I'd love to actually feel his body next to mine. With the tip of my tongue, I

219

boldly push my way into his mouth, and swear this is turning out to be the most amazing kiss I've ever had. He pulls me in closer, and I feel my heart pounding so loudly that I swear it's going to explode. His tongue is thoroughly exploring every inch of my mouth, and I feel like I've died and gone to heaven. I'm freaking making out with an alien, and I'm loving it. Then it hits me, he's taken a breath, I'm sure of it because I felt his warm breath against my lips. He's still alive, I want to jump up and down, but I don't want this kiss to end.

My hands comb through his soft hair, and I shiver as he reciprocates the gesture. When I open my eyes for the first time since our lips met, I see a bright red glow encompassing us, and reality sets in. When will that damn thing go off? I gently pull away from Kyle, which is almost impossible, because he immediately groans and tries to pull me close again.

"Kyle, that red thingy," I say breathlessly, wanting his lips on mine again, but someone has to face the problem lying at our feet.

"We must leave before it detonates." I see him glance down at the glowing ball, and then his eyes meet mine again. "That kiss was more than I ever could have imagined it could be. Happy doesn't even begin to describe what one feels during a kiss—that kiss in particular. As much as I want to continue, you must leave before ..."

"Don't say it," I say, grabbing for his hand. "We're leaving together. You're still alive, Kyle. You're breathing our air. Please come with me. I don't want to lose you." I watch him bite his lip as if he's grappling with what he's supposed to do, and what I know he wants to do.

After what seems like an eternity, I feel my nerves stretch tight because of his hesitation, but then relax when he nods his

220

head. OMG, he nods his head. My heart leaps. He's coming with me.

Kyle squeezes my hand as I lead him and his gorgeous grin away from his death sentence. As we hurry quickly through the woods, away from the crash site, a bright red light fills the surrounding area. I hear a high-pitched screeching sound behind us followed by a loud bang, and we're suddenly pushed forward by what feels like an intense wind. Kyle wraps me up in his arms as we tumble to the ground, taking the brunt of the impact himself. When I gaze up into his beautiful eyes, a smile grows on my lips and on his as well. He pulls me to my feet and we both begin to dust ourselves off.

"Thank you," I say while looking at him intently.

"It is I who should be thanking you," he answers with a thoughtful gaze. "So, have you given any thought to how you are going to explain me to your parents?"

I pause for a moment while letting his question sink in. "Well, I really haven't thought that far ahead yet, but I do know one thing."

"And what is that?" he asks while slightly titling his head to the side.

I sigh. "Life is most definitely going to get interesting around here."

THE BLACK STONE HEIR

By Sarah M Ross

For information on other titles
Visit the author's website:
http://www.sarahmross.com/

CHAPTER ONE

Krissy

"Oh come on! Don't do this to me, not now." I pressed harder on the gas, but the truck only slowed. "No no no no…" I whined. My old Ford pickup sputtered to a stop before it gave one final clunk and died. "Damnit!"

I pounded on the steering wheel not that it would do any good, but it did make me feel better. The 1963 Ford F100 pickup truck had been on its last leg—or wheel as the case may be—for a while now, but I was deep in denial. It had belonged to my grandfather before he passed. I tried hard to maintain it, but without access to the proper parts or funds for a great mechanic, I knew it was only a matter of time before it went to the great junk yard in the sky. I had really hoped the truck would last me through senior year because I couldn't afford anything new and wasn't looking forward to riding the bus with the freshman.

I yanked the door open and stepped out into the dark, empty street. Although I was in almost the center of town, I might as well have been in a graveyard. I spun my Converse-clad feet in a slow circle looking for a light to be on or a person walking by, but found nothing. I could call for help, but I had just been trying to charge my phone in the truck. Now, both were dead. I guess I'd just have to hoof it. Great.

The late August days in my tiny town outside of Roswell, New Mexico were unforgiving in their humidity levels. I was looking forward to the winter, when the air would be crisp instead of heavy and thick. It wasn't as bad as Florida or anything, but it aggravated my asthma. I was enough of a nerd without the constant puffing on an inhaler to remind people.

I knew I'd have to take this walk slow since I didn't have my inhaler with me. I was still a good three miles from my house, but I didn't make it two blocks before I could feel the sweat dripping down my neck and back. I paused at the next block and sat on a bench as I dug in my purse for a hair tie. Long, thick hair made for great fashion sometimes, but it was hell to manage. I often wanted to cut it all off, but my mom said she'd kill me. If I heard "but people pay to have hair like yours" one more time, I might say screw it all and pull a GI Jane. It wasn't as if I could get much more unpopular, and it would save me so much time in the morning.

As I dug, a car engine grumbled to a stop next to me. *Thank heavens*, I thought. *Finally something is going my way. Maybe I can get a ride home, or at least borrow a cell to call my parents for a ride.* I found the hair tie and pulled my dark brown hair up into a messy bun before standing up and heading to the car. The sporty car looked brand new, so I didn't recognize it. And the windows were darkly tinted, so I was unable to see the driver. No matter, it was a small town, so I was pretty sure I'd know whoever it was.

The window began to roll down, and I leaned over to peer inside. "Hey, thanks so much for stopping. Do you think you could..." I stopped, unable to get another word out when I realized who it was. My breath caught in my throat, and I stumbled back a few steps.

Sitting smugly slouched down in the seat, Tate McCallister formed a smile that slowly spread across his gorgeous face. "Well hey there Prissy Krissy. Whacha doin out here at this hour?"

I inhaled a deep breath and held it for a minute before slowly exhaling, trying to calm my irritation before I went off on him. Again. Of course of all the people to come by, it would be Tate.

I'd known Tate since kindergarten, and had a pathetic crush on him almost as long. He was gorgeous: tall, dark, and handsome. He was the star wide receiver on the football team, had all the muscles to back up his athletic abilities, and had the most piercing green eyes I'd ever seen. The problem was: he was a huge ass.

Throughout most of middle school, he tormented me. He'd pull my hair when he sat behind me in class, once he'd even drawn a dirty picture of me in art class, made copies, and passed them out to all the guys in gym class. I wasn't naked in the picture and he didn't put my name on it, but it was very clear who the drawing represented and the suggestive things I was doing in the picture. Worst of all, it was him who saddled me with the nickname Prissy Krissy in ninth grade after I went on one date with Joey Fishborne. I'd pushed Joey away when he sloppily shoved his tongue down my throat at the end of the night and slapped him when he tried to grab my boob. I wasn't really prissy, but c'mon! It was the first date and the guy was a terrible kisser. But Joey went and told everyone that I didn't like guys, starting the rumor that I was a lesbian. Thanks to my best friend, that rumor died quickly, but Prissy Krissy stuck to this day.

After ninth grade, I luckily fell off of Tate's radar and he ignored me, which suited me perfectly. I'd have the occasional class with him or see him around town and though he never said anything to me, I'd catch him watching. It made me nervous…and as much as I hated to admit it, excited.

"Ugh. Nevermind. You can keep on driving, Tate." I stood up straight and clutched my purse, turning away from Tate. I'd take the heat and humidity over him taunting me during a ride home— or worse, enjoying the ride home sitting next to him—any day. Yeah, his was a kind of heat I needed to keep bottled up and far, far away.

******

Tate

I almost hit the curb with my new car when I saw Krissy Montgomery sitting on that bench. We were in the middle of Main Street after eleven at night, so what was she doing walking around alone? It wasn't safe. It didn't matter, she wasn't alone any longer. I wouldn't let anything happen to her.

I still remembered the first time I saw Krissy way back in kindergarten. She wore a bright yellow jumper, which made her dark brown, almost black hair really pop. When the teacher told us to gather 'round the story-time mat, she noticed one girl hiding in the corner. Everyone ignored her and went to sit, but Krissy didn't hesitate; she walked right up, grabbed the girl's hand, and smiled warmly as she told the girl, "C'mon. You can sit next to me." I had gone home that first day of school and told my mom that I would marry that girl one day.

Krissy only got more beautiful as we grew up, but somehow I always managed to screw it up with her, and she'd hated me for years. I'm sure the nickname the punks at school gave her didn't help, and I know she blamed me for it though I didn't start it. I just couldn't get it right with her and always managed to make it worse. I finally decided to keep my distance, hoping to screw It up any more than I already had with the hopes I could make it up to her one day.

Maybe today was that day.

"Krissy, it's not safe for you to be walking around out here this late. Hey, will you stop for a second?" I put the car in park and hustled to catch up with her and heard her huffing in irritation in front of me.

"Take a look around, Tate. What exactly am I supposed to be afraid of? Mrs. Lopez's Chihuahua getting out? Or maybe Old Man Pollard shuffling out here with his rolling walker to get me?"

She spun away from me and continued down the street. She looked so good in her tight little shorts that I almost wanted to let her keep walking. The view was incredible. I shoved my hormones aside and remembered why I chasing her in the first place.

"Don't be stubborn, Krissy. Just let me give you a ride home. Do you hate me that much so you can't be in the car with me the few miles to your house?" She ignored me and kept walking, so I increased my stride and reached out to touch her arm. She shivered and stopped walking. "Let me take you home. You can continue to hate me tomorrow, okay?"

*****

Krissy

I stared into his pleading eyes, and just couldn't say no. Hell, I might have agreed to marry him and bear his children with that look his was giving me. I could drown in that look, but oh what a way to go.

This was such a bad idea, but I couldn't resist.

"Fine, you can drive me home. But don't touch me. Or talk to me." Because if he did, I wasn't sure I could keep hating him. And I really, really wanted to keep hating him. It was always easier to remember the reasons he was a total doucheburger when he wasn't standing so close to me, smelling of leather and soap and making me want to lean into the crook of his neck and never leave.

I took a breath of clean air to clear my head and began walking toward Tate's truck. His hand brushed against the small of my back, guiding me. The touch was like hot coals igniting me, and I hated that I loved it. I walked faster, but he still somehow managed to get to the car first and hold the door open for me. I started to slide in, but paused at the edge of the seat.

"Should I just plug my address into your GPS here or..."

I was cut off by a low wail coming from the alleyway behind the Quik Pick. "What the hell was that?"

The sound—the wail—happened again, louder this time. Tate spun around and pushed back against me protectively. "No idea. Sounds like someone's in a shit load of pain." He turned around into me, suddenly so close that we were breathing the same air.

I closed my eyes and leaned back. I needed away from the now almost overwhelming temptation. It was one thing when we were a classroom apart and I could remember why I hated him, but it was a whole other ballgame when he stood this close. My brain became mush and wanted to make up with him. And make out with him.

228

A crash brought me out of out of my head and I instinctively grabbed onto Tate's shoulders. "What was that? Did something fall? Someone has to be hurt; we need to help."

"No, you need to stay here. We don't know what that noise was. It could be a junkie comin' down from their high or someone trying to break into the store." He reached into his trunk and grabbed his hunting rifle. "You stay here and call 911 just in case. I'll go check it out."

CHAPTER TWO

Tate took off running before I could explain that my cell was dead. God, he was infuriating. I had no choice but to follow him. With each step I took down the alleyway, it became darker and darker. I could barely see my feet in front of me, and had completely lost sight of Tate. It had become as silent as it was dark, and chills ran down my spine.

"Tate?" I whispered, inching my way forward. "Where are you?" I waited, but heard no reply. Taking two precarious steps forward, I tried again. "Tate?"

Before I could take a third step, a large hand reached out of the shadows and grabbed my wrist, pulling me and causing me to stumble. I didn't even have the chance to scream before another hand covered my mouth, preventing me from making a sound.

"Shh. It's okay, Krissy. It's just me." I let go of the panic seizing my chest and sunk back into him. "There was something— or someone—over there behind the dumpster, but it just disappeared. Into thin air. It was the craziest fuckin' thing." He paused for a second, gently brushing the hair from my neck and leaning in. "Sorry, I forget my manners sometimes." I could feel his warm lips caressing my ear. "Something just feels off. Unnatural," he whispered.

"Are you sure?" I knew I should be frightened by the situation, but I wasn't. Not until his words began to sink in.

Tate's arms tightened around me. "Enough to tell you we need to get the hell out of here! Like, now."

I didn't stop to argue because even without the strange noise, an abandoned alley in the middle of the night still gave me the creeps. Tate's hand slipped into mine and he began to lead me out of the alley. We didn't make it ten steps before the wail sounded again, louder and more frightening. And this time, a small orange glow emanated from behind us, lighting our path. We stopped dead in our tracks, frozen by the grating and pained sound of the wail.

Tate cocked the rifle and pointed it down the alley as we slowly pivoted toward the sound, curiosity winning out over fear this once. A figure was huddled beside the dumpster. It was small, maybe a child, but the glow silhouetted him or her, and I couldn't make out much more than the vague, hunched-over shape.

"Oh my God, it's a kid. We have to help them!"

The glow disappeared, shrouding us in darkness once again. Tate passed the gun to me, but it fumbled in my shaking hands and I dropped it as Tate opened his cell, turning on the flashlight app so we could see. I shrugged out of Tate's hold and we both stepped toward the child, but as I approached I realized it wasn't a child at all. Although she was built like a child, she stood no more than three-and-a-half or four feet but had the features were those of an adult woman, full of wrinkles, grey hair, and all.

"Are...are you okay?" The woman-child's face was scrunched and her eyes were closed in agony, but I could see no obvious injuries.

231

The woman stilled, surprised as if I'd scared her somehow. When her eyes opened, they glowed bright orange.

*****

Tate

I'd never seen anything like it. Not in real life, not on TV, and not in any sci-fi movie I'd ever watched. I blinked repeatedly and rubbed my eyes, wondering if I was hallucinating. The creature's eyes—I wasn't sure I could call it a human—burned so bright they lit the entire area. I was simultaneously intrigued by their beauty and freaked out of my mind. What the hell was this thing?

With her eyes open and illuminating the area, I could now make out the extent of her injuries. She had been beaten, badly. I could see heinous purple bruises up and down her small arms and legs: several lacerations oozed thick trails of blood, and given her labored breathing and hunched position, I guessed she had a couple of broken ribs too.

"Ppp...please. Help me," the woman spoke, pausing to cough up blood.

Krissy didn't hesitate, leaving the safety of my side and rushing toward the creature. "You need a doctor. Should we call 911?"

"I don't need a doctor," the creature spoke. "My name is Anusha. I come from..." She paused for a coughing fit again before laying her head gently back against the wall. "It's not important. I need you—" Anusha sunk back to the ground,

232

grabbing her head in agony. Her eyes closed and immersed us in blackness before she opened them again.

I stepped up, no longer afraid. No matter who—or more aptly what—this woman was, she was severely hurt, maybe even dying, and I couldn't stand back and not do something to help. "What do you need? We can help, or at least try to."

The woman-creature smiled. "I need you to keep safe..."

"Keep you safe? From what?" Krissy asked, taking off her scarf she was using as a belt and gently wiping the blood from Anusha's mouth. It wasn't red like human blood, but more of a deep purple that beaded on the cloth like water on a duck's back.

"Not...me," the creature wheezed. "This."

She reached into her pocket and pulled out a small, silver dagger with an ivory-embellished handle. "Shit," I whispered, pushing Krissy safely behind me. She bristled and moved beside me, not nearly as concerned with the knife-wielding non-human as I was.

"Don't be afraid. I intend you no harm." As if to prove her point, the creature pointed the blade of the knife away from us and toward herself. *What the hell is going on?* I opened my mouth to voice my question when Anusha plunged the knife into her own gut.

We stood in horror, not believing our eyes. Why did this creature say she wanted our help, only to take her own life? It made no sense. We were motionless for only a few moments before we sprang into action. I shrugged out of my shirt to apply pressure to the wound while Krissy fumbled with the phone.

"It's password protected, Tate. I need your password!"

"One two three four," I told her.

"Seriously?"

I wrapped the T-shirt into a ball. "Yeah, well—"

"No, don't," Anusha cried as I bent to apply pressure. She held up her hand, and the next thing I knew I was laying flat on my ass several yards away. How the hell did she do that? She hadn't even touched me! Krissy ran to my side and helped me up, her eyes lingering over my bare chest. *She's probably just looking to make sure I'm not injured*, I reasoned. She'd hated me for years, no reason for that to change now.

"I'm sorry," Anusha whispered. "I meant you no harm."

I nodded and she continued. "Please, take this and hide it. Show no one and keep it far, far away from the Ruscors. A time will come, another will come. Keep our hopes for survival safe until then. Trust no one but the intended."

"What the hell is she talking about?" I murmured to Krissy.

"Not a clue. Maybe she's delirious from her injuries."

"Take this," Anusha repeated. She still had the dagger in her hand, so I assumed that's what she was referring to. I grasped the handle, but she pulled it away."No, not the blade."

Anusha placed the dagger on the ground, and then to my horror she shoved her hand inside of the gaping hole she created in her chest. Beside me, Krissy blanched, going green and swaying a bit on her feet. It was a horrific sight, seeing this woman digging around her own chest cavity. I was pretty sure even Hannibal Lector would find this disturbing.

After several long seconds of digging around, Anusha sighed happily and pulled out a goo-covered ellipsoidal object that just fit in the palm of her hand. It was solid, and deep black in color. Was it a tumor? Or some other sickness? Why would she want us to keep that?

She reached forward, grunting in pain, and handed it to me. The object was disgusting and I didn't want anything to do with it, but it was obviously important to her and I wouldn't be disrespectful. I also didn't want Krissy to take it in case it was dangerous.

Before she had any chance to explain what it was, Anusha took a deep, final breath and closed her eyes.

"Anusha?" Krissy called. When we got no reply, she bent down and went closer. "She doesn't have a pulse. She's gone."

CHAPTER THREE

Krissy

I was beginning to think I was in a dream. It was the only reasonable explanation for what was going on. Only in a dream would I be perfectly okay with some otherworldly creature pulling us into a dark alley and imploring us to keep some bodily object safe from an unknown alien. Oh, and even stranger? Tate McCallister was being nice to me. Tate McCallister who dumped chocolate milk in the baggie with my peanut butter and jelly sandwich in the third grade. Tate McCallister who pulled my braid until I begged and pleaded with my mom to cut my hair short in the eighth grade just so he'd have nothing to pull on any more. And Tate McCallister who plagued my dreams in all of his hard-muscled shirtless glory night after night. Yep, this was a dream.

"So what are we supposed to do now?" I tried to keep calm, but I couldn't hide the quiver in my voice.

"I don't know. I don't think there's anything else we can do for her." Tate pocketed the black object Anusha had given us before wiping his hands on his pants. "Let's go."

"We can't just leave her here."

236

Tate wiped his hands and placed them on my shoulders and brushed them up and down. "I wish there was something else we can do, but there's not. She was obviously in some type of danger, and exposing her to others could place them in danger too. Why don't we—"

His words were drowned out by a sudden and strong burst of wind. My hair fell out of the loose bun and whipped around my face, and obscuring my vision. My arms stretched out, reaching for something to grab on to. I ran smack into Tate's bare chest, and he pulled me down to the ground where the wind wasn't as strong. We clung to the ground and to each other as it felt like a tornado passed by. I was terrified and couldn't stop my hands from shaking. Tate's arms held me in a vice grip, and I could just make out his whispers of "shit, shit, shit." Several minutes later, just as suddenly as it arrived, the winds disappeared and the air around us stilled.

I slowly lifted my head and looked around. The streetlights came back on, which was a relief, but strangely nothing was out of place. All the garbage and debris from the alleyway was exactly where it was before the violent windstorm started.

"Look!" Tate whispered. "Over there, where we left the body."

I swung my head around to the spot where Anusha fell. Nothing was there. Nothing. No blood, no body, just…nothing. It was like she never existed.

"Your pocket," I instructed Tate. "Is the thing she gave you still there?"

Tate sat up and checked his pockets, pulling out the black, still-gooey stone-like object. "Yes, I've still got it. At least I didn't imagine the last hour."

He sat, fingering the object and flipping it over and over. Without saying a word, Tate stood, reaching down and helping me up. He never let go of my hand, instead leading me out of the alley. I followed willingly, hoping Tate had a plan. I slid into his car, silently watching him grab a towel out of his trunk and one of his game jerseys. Neither of us spoke as he drove, which was just fine with me. I needed time to wrap my head around what the hell was happening. It would take more than just a car ride to come to terms with everything, but I'd take what I could get.

I stared out the window, but paid little attention to the scenery shrouded in darkness. I absently noted turning off Main Street and passing the high school before closing my eyes altogether. It wasn't until the car stopped that I bothered to look around. "I thought you were going to take me home."

Tate shook his head. "We need to figure out whatever this thing is." He held out the object Aunusha gave him. "And we need to figure out that riddle she gave us as to what to do with this. My parents are on a cruise, so I figured my house would be the best place to talk for a bit."

"Oh...yeah. Of course."

Tate unlocked the front door and I followed him inside. He threw his keys in a large bowl by the front door before stepping out of his big boots and plopping down on the couch. "Make yourself comfortable."

Unsure if his family had a "no shoes on the rugs" policy, I took mine off as well and sat in the arm chair opposite him. "So..." I started. I was nervous. More nervous now than I was in the alley. Being in his house, alone, was awkward. We'd had such a tumultuous relationship for so long, to suddenly act like we were long-time friends was, well weird.

Tate seemed to be ignoring me, staring off into space. After several minutes of awkward silence, he stood up and left the room. "I'm going to wash this off. Maybe once it's clean we can figure out what in the world it is."

"Or out of the world..." I quipped.

If Tate heard me, he didn't reply. When he came back, he pulled the coffee table up closer to me and sat on it, straddling my legs. I tried not to focus on his nearness, and instead on the object in his hands. "Take a look. It's completely solid, like a stone, but shaped like an egg."

"Yeah, but it's way bigger than a chicken egg. I've never seen anything like it. Plus, it's not spotted or brown or anything. It's pitch black. What kind of egg would be like that?"

Tate shook his head slowly. "I have no idea. But I guess we can't really compare it to anything we know, since..." He paused, his next words on the edge of his tongue, but unwilling to come out. "It's not from here, right?"

I took a moment to process that. It was one thing to live so close to Roswell and hear the rumors all my life, but seeing it in front of me? Experiencing it? I didn't quite know how to deal with that. "So what do we do with it? Should we tell someone? Our parents maybe? They might know what to do."

"For now, I think we need to keep this between us. Anusha was pretty scared of something, or someone. Not to mention that she was beat to hell. We can't risk anyone finding out we have whatever she died protecting. It's too dangerous."

"So what do we do now then?"

"What was it that she said about someone coming to find it?"

"Let me think." I closed my eyes, recalling the words she'd said. "I think she said, 'A time will come, another will come. Keep

239

our hopes safe. Trust no one but the intended.' Or something like that."

Tate scooted closer, his jean-clad legs brushing up against my bare ones. The brief contact heated my cheeks, and while I wanted to move away, I had nowhere to go. I swallowed hard, glancing into Tate's eyes. They were wide and the pupils dilated. He looked....turned on? Surely it couldn't have been because of me.

"Well, there you go," he said. His voice had lowered to just above a whisper. His finger brushed my leg, tracing a pattern I didn't recognize along my skin. "We wait. We don't say a word about what happened tonight, and we wait."

I gulped, suddenly feeling very stupid. Of course he'd want to keep quiet about tonight. It's not like he'd want to tell all his popular friends that he was stuck hanging out with me all night. He'd probably just as soon forget the whole thing. I'd been stupid to think that he was being nice to me. Or worse, that he was turned on by me. Stupid!

"That's fine with me, Tate. We'll pretend it never happened. It's not a problem."

"To keep it safe. And us safe. I think it's best as if we go on like nothing happened. That way we don't arouse suspicion."

"Got it." I stood up, no longer caring if I was being rude. I just wanted out of there. "Can you take me home now? My parents are going to flip out that I'm this late. They expected me over an hour ago."

Tate looked startled, but he complied. "Yeah, no prob. Are you sure you're okay with this? If you have another idea, I'm all ears."

I already had my shoes back on and was heading for the door. "Nope. It's fine. I agree, we should just pretend like this whole thing never happened." I turned the handle on the door. "I'll be in the car when you're ready."

I didn't say anything to him on the drive to my house. He didn't ask me for directions, which I found strange, but he went straight to my house. I didn't think much about it, instead focusing on staying as physically far away from Tate as I could get. I didn't want to like him. I wanted to hate him. So staying away was the easiest way to do that. And tomorrow, I could wake up and pretend this really was all a dream.

CHAPTER FOUR

Tate

I wasn't sure what I'd done, but I knew I'd somehow screwed things up with Krissy again. She practically ran out the door and gave me the silent treatment the entire way to her house. I replayed the night over and over in my head, but wasn't sure what I'd said or done to make her angry with me.

Over the next week, I was swamped with football practice. School started soon, and our first home game was less than two weeks away. Coach was relentless with our conditioning training, and I spent the entire week either working out with the team or passed out from exhaustion. I didn't hear from Krissy once, and I didn't have the energy to call her.

But no matter how tired I was, I always paid close attention to my surroundings, vigilant to see if anyone was watching me, or if anything was unusual in any way. With both Krissy and me in danger, I took no chances, questioning everything. But I never came across anything or anyone suspicious. I didn't even see anyone that I hadn't known since I was in Sunday School. The one good thing about living in my small town: anything out of the ordinary would stick out immediately, and everyone would be talking about it.

I had placed the stone egg in my parents' gun safe, tucked away in a cloth handgun sleeve. No one would look there and if they did, they wouldn't see anything out of the ordinary unless they opened the sleeve. Plus, it was an added bonus that the safe locked with a five-digit combination lock, so whatever threat Anusha was worried about wouldn't be getting the object she fought so hard to save.

Monday morning rolled around, and I flew out of bed with an abnormal amount of gusto. It was the first day of school, and I was excited to see all my friends again. If I was being honest, I was excited to see Krissy. I hated the way we left things, and I hoped she'd give me a second chance. Well, at this point it would be like a tenth chance, but who's counting?

I left early and headed to Krissy's house to offer her a ride to school. I knew her truck was down for the count, and no one wanted to ride the bus if at all possible. I pulled up to her house without calling first. I was afraid that if I called and told her I wanted to see her, she'd reject me. So, better to beg forgiveness than to ask permission. I stepped out of the car, taking a deep breath before jogging up to her door and ringing the doorbell. Those seconds waiting for the door to open were completely nerve wracking.

"Tate? What the hell are you doing here?"

I looked all around, trying to figure out where the voice was coming from. I finally spied her in an upstairs window. "Hey! Can you come down and talk? Or I can come up?"

"No!" She paused. "I mean, I'll come down. Just...give me a minute to put on some clothes. I just got out of the shower."

She started to slam the window shut, muttering under her breath as she did. I stood on the stoop, rocking back and forth on

243

my heels and waited. And waited. And waited some more. *Geez.*
How long does it take a girl to throw some clothes on? What is she
doing up there? Reshowering? Okay, I should not be thinking of
Krissy showering. Naked. Wet. Soapy.

"…without calling first? Did something happen?"

Oh, shit. Krissy stood in front of me, talking, but I'd barely
heard a word she'd said. Damnit! I'd been with her less than two
minutes and I'd already screwed things up again. I needed to get on
my game.

"Hey. No, I just wanted to check in with you, make sure you
were okay. You haven't had anything strange happen this week?"

Krissy crossed her arms over her chest. *God she looks good*, I
thought, praying I didn't start sporting wood in front of her. In
barely there shorts that highlighted her tone, tan legs and a tee shirt
that hung off one shoulder, leaving it exposed, she looked
practically edible. "No. It's been pretty boring around here. No
alien sightings. You?"

"I've had football every day, so I haven't had much time for
anything else."

We stood there, staring at each other for what seemed like
hours. I didn't know what to say. Honestly, I'd come over here just
to spend some time with her. And it didn't seem like she was too
thrilled that I'd shown up.

"Listen, Krissy. About last week—"

She cut me off. "Don't worry about it. It had been a long night,
and I didn't mean to take it out on you. I know you were…just
being yourself." She took a breath and changed topics. "Is the
stone safe?"

"Yeah, I have it locked up tight and hidden away. No one's
getting to it." She nodded, leaving us both in an another

uncomfortable silence. I laughed to myself. I'd never had this much trouble with girls. They always made things easy for me; I never had to work to get a girl to like me. Maybe that's what made Krissy so appealing. "So, can I give you a ride to school?"

"Oh, um, I was just going to take the bus."

I reached out and wrapped my finger around one of her silky smooth curls. As a kid, I loved touching her hair; it was always so pretty. "C'mon Krissy, you don't really want to ride the bus with all those little kids, do you? Let me drive you."

Krissy pulled her hair back into a ponytail, preventing me from touching it. "You're right, I don't. But I'm sure you don't want to be seen pulling into school with me."

"Why would you say that?" Did she really have no idea how much I liked her? I always thought I made it abundantly clear.

"Never mind. Let me just go finish getting ready. I'll be just a minute."

We had barely pulled into the school when I realized something was off. Students were huddled into groups, whispering. This wasn't usual first day of school gossip, something major had happened. I glanced over at Krissy as I pulled into a parking spot. "What do you think all this is about?"

"I have no idea, but whatever it is must have just happened, otherwise our phones would be blowing up."

I checked my phone, but I only had one message from Will, asking me what time practice started tomorrow. "Do you think it's about..." I didn't even want to say the word out loud. How did I know if aliens had super hearing or anything?

"I doubt it. But something happened, that's for sure."

I turned off the car and we stepped out. Krissy's friend Tanesha rushed over to us, practically bouncing as she asked in an excited whisper, "Did you hear? Someone killed Vice-Principal Evans. And it must have been bad, because they brought in some big-shot agents from the FBI or something. They've been pulling people in to the office one by one and questioning them."

"They think it was a student?" Krissy asked.

"I don't think they have a clue, because they're questioning everyone: students, teachers, secretaries, even the lunch ladies! I just talked to Weston, and I guess he was one of the first people brought in since his mom works here, and they got here so early. He said the only thing the feds really wanted to know is where they were a week ago Thursday night."

My heart sped up when I heard the date they were looking for. That was the night Krissy and I found Anusha in the alley. Turning my head slightly, I eyed her reaction. She sucked in her breath and gulped. Shit. She realized it too. No matter, I wasn't going to let anything happen to her. But how the hell did I protect her?

"Wow, Tee, that's crazy. Did they say what happened to Mr. Evans?"

"No clue. The man was always a little weird, but he didn't deserve this. Rumor has it that his wife was killed too."

"Oh wow, that's horrible."

"Yeah. The cheerleaders are organizing a remembrance vigil tonight."

Krissy snorted. "Of course they are. Um, Tee, can I catch up with you later? I want to call my mom and tell her before heading into school."

Tanesha looked between Krissy and me, not buying the lie for a moment. "Sure, yeah. Go call your mom. Be sure to tell her I said hi." Tanesha winked at Krissy before sashaying away, repeating her story to a new crew of kids who had just pulled up.

"Do you think it's—" I started.

"Yes. I do. It's too big of a coincidence for it not to be. What do we do now?"

I stood, watching Krissy's lip quiver slightly and wanting nothing more than to wrap her in my in my arms. I leaned back against my car to resist the temptation. "First thing we need to do is get our stories straight. It's best to go as close to the truth as possible, so if they question you just tell them that your car broke down and I gave you a ride home. But we'll just change the timeframe. Tell them it was in the early evening rather than late at night. I'm sure they found your car in town the next day, so we can't lie about where we were."

*****

Krissy

I knew my head was nodding, but all I could feel was the tremble in my hands. Tate's confidence in our plan made me feel slightly better, but I was still terrified of being questioned. Would I crack under the pressure? I wasn't sure I could pull it off. I never could with my parents; they always saw right through me.

"Okay, I think I can do that. Piece of cake, right?"

Tate took a half a step toward me, raising his arms as if he were going to hug me, but before he could make contact, someone called his name from across the way. "Tate! You comin' or what?"

He cringed and balled his hands into fists. Yeah, he was pissed he got seen getting so close to me. I sighed. "Well, I should go. Make sure I can find my locker and all."

It was a bullshit answer; students were assigned the same locker all four years, and the freshman got the departing seniors' lockers. I didn't worry about it and turned on my heel, walking briskly away before I made the situation worse.

I made it to my locker, through homeroom, and was breezing through Spanish 3 when there was a knock on the classroom door. "Excuse me, Mrs. Cruz, but we need Krissy Montgomery in the main office please."

"Uh, uh, uh. En espanol, por favor," Ms. Cruz replied. The class chuckled. Only Ms. Cruz—who'd been teaching Spanish at the school since she came to the States from Cuba in the 1960s— would make other personnel feel like they were back in tenth grade. The secretary looked around the room, clearly startled by the request. She observed the stern look on Ms. Cruz's face and knew there was no getting out of it. Ms. Cruz didn't play.

"Okay, um. It's been years since I've used this. Let me try. Necessito hablar con Krissy Montgomery en la officina, por favor?"

"Muy bien, senora. Krissy. Apresurate para que no pierdas la tarea de hoy."

I gathered up my books and nodded, following the secretary out the door. "Si, senora. Hasta manana."

I followed the secretary silently down the halls. I tried not to read too much into it, but with each step I took, I felt as if I was walking into a trap. I'm sure I was being ridiculous, but I couldn't shake the feeling. Stepping into the office, I glanced around. Tate sat behind a closed conference room door, speaking animatedly. Two men in suits—FBI I presumed—sat opposite him, clicking their pens and taking notes. Crap! This was happening.

"Have a seat, Ms. Montgomery. They'll be with you shortly."

I sat, trying unsuccessfully to keep my legs from bouncing like a hyperactive two-year-old. Twenty-two minutes later (yes, I stared at the clock and counted), the door opened and Tate came out. "Thank you for your cooperation, Mr. McCallister. We'll be in touch if there's anything further. You may go."

Tate didn't answer them, keeping his gaze fixed on me. I could see the questions in his eyes. He was worried about me. Or maybe just about what I'd say. I smiled ever so slightly out of the corner of my mouth, just enough to reassure him but not enough to draw attention.

"Ms. Montgomery, we're ready for you now."

I stood, brushing by Tate as he passed, and entered the small conference room. Just that small contact reminded me I wasn't alone in this, and my confidence surged. "Shouldn't my parents be here if you're going to question me? Or my lawyer?"

"Do you feel you need a lawyer, Ms. Montgomery?"

I shrugged. "I have no idea. You haven't even told me what this is about, but I know that law officials can't question a minor without their parents' approval."

"Why don't we back up a minute. I'm Agent Rhodes, and this is Agent Samuels. We're with the FBI."

I waited to see their badges, but neither presented them. "Aren't you supposed to show me your credentials too?"

Agent Samuels huffed. "You've got a little mouth on you, don't ya?"

I shrugged again. "I'm a teenager. Don't we all?"

Neither man laughed, but they begrudgingly pulled out their IDs and held them in the air.

"I'd like to see them," I stated, before adding sweetly, "Please?"

249

I held out my hand and waited. Yeah, I knew I wasn't winning any brownie points, but I didn't care. Agent Samuels ground his teeth. I was really getting on his nerves. Oh, well. I smiled widely at him, but my smile faded just as quickly when I saw a flash of orange in his eyes.

Holy. Shit. He was an alien. I was sure of it. I swallowed, but kept my body very still. I could not give away that I knew he wasn't human. I glanced at the IDs, but didn't really process what they said after that. I needed to get out of this office and tell Tate.

"So, Ms. Montgomery, if you're satisfied with our credentials, could you tell us where you were last Thursday night?"

"I was babysitting for the Powells."

"And then what?"

I locked my eyes on Agent Rhodes, both wanting to see if he was an alien too and hoping the eye contact would make me seem more trustworthy. "I drove home, but my piece-of-crap car broke down halfway here. Fortunately, Tate was driving by and offered me a ride home. But you already knew that since he was just in here, so I'm not sure why you need to hear it again from me."

Agent Rhodes didn't even so much as blink. He was a tough cookie to crack. "And about what time was that, Ms. Montgomery?"

I blew out a long, exasperated breath. "I don't know, I didn't realize I was going to be questioned by the FBI, so I didn't take copious notes detailing my evening." I paused, but still I got no reaction. Agent Samuels clicked his pen rapidly, but I didn't turn my gaze. "It couldn't have been too late, maybe seven-thirty or eight. The sun was going down. Sorry, but that's all I can remember."

Agent Rhodes wrote my answers in his little book as I waited impatiently for him to finish so I could get the hell out of there. "Is Tate your boyfriend, Ms. Montgomery?"

"What?!" I shrieked. "No! Why would you ask that?"

Agent Rhodes looked up and smirked. "You sure?"

"Yes I'm sure. I'd think I'd know if I had a boyfriend." He didn't respond, but the smug look on his face told me he thought he had something on me. "This is stupid. You're not even asking me about Vice Principal Evans, and my personal life—or lack thereof—is none of your or the government's business. Can I go back to class now?"

"Suurreee," he drawled. "But we may have a few follow-up questions later."

I didn't wait to hear anything else, gathering up my things and practically sprinting out of the room. I flew out of the office and headed straight for the girls' bathroom, locking myself in the handicapped stall. I dropped all my books and hoisted myself up on the window ledge, using the toilet as a footstool. It was the one spot in school that had good cell reception. I pulled out my cell and began furiously typing. Not even three minutes later, I heard the bathroom door open and Tate calling, "You in here?"

I hopped down from my perch. "Yeah, but let's not talk here."

Tate nodded and grabbed my hand, entwining our fingers as he pulled me out the door and toward the student parking lot. I tried not to read too much into the gesture, but my heart sped up a bit. He was acting nothing like the Tate I'd known him to be, and I didn't know what to make of that. Maybe it was just the situation that was bringing us together, but I liked this sweet side.

Once we reached his car, I slid in the passenger seat as he started the engine. We were a good five miles outside of town before either of us said a word. He pulled into a small parking lot for an abandoned feed store that went out of business a few years ago. Now, kids used it as a kind of hangout, building bonfires in the large field behind the building or sneaking into the side entrance to drink or whatever if the weather was bad.

I leapt out of the car, needing fresh air and to move.

"Krissy, what the hell happened in there? You're freaking me out!" Tate tried to pull me to him, but I shrugged away. My emotions were all over the place, and I needed to sort out the thoughts racing through my head before anything else.

"Just…give me a minute to think. To decompress. That—whatever that was back there—freaked me the hell out and I need a minute to deal with that."

Tate seemed to understand, letting me have my space. After several minutes of soul searching and attempting to make sense of the last few weeks of my life, I was no closer to acceptance or understanding. I wasn't sure I ever would be.

"Tate, I'm pretty sure those guys weren't with the FBI."

"No shit," Tate remarked, kicking at a rock. "I'm betting some secret government agency out of Roswell and Area 51."

I paused my pacing and faced him. "The one agent was an alien. I'm sure of it. I don't know about the other, but it's entirely possible. I'm pretty sure they know or at least suspect something, and it wouldn't surprise me if they were tailing us right now."

"Woah. Back up for a minute. One of them was an alien? Are you sure?"

"Yeah. His eyes glowed just like Anusha's did, just for a second."

"Holy shit! This is crazy. Do you think they're the ones who hurt her? Or are they the ones that she told us to give the stone to?"

"They gave me the creeps, and I don't trust them."

"Don't worry, Krissy." Tate stepped forward and wrapped me in his arms. "I won't let anything happen to you."

As if my head wasn't already swimming enough, now I had Tate—warm, delicious-smelling, sexier-than-hell Tate—not only being nice to me, but also being wonderfully protective and affectionate. I'm pretty sure if I looked up, I'd see pigs flying.

We were still embracing when a voice startled us. "Not your boyfriend, huh? What else have you been lying about, Ms. Montgomery?"

CHAPTER FIVE

Tate

My eyes flew open and Krissy gasped, stumbling backward. How the hell had Agent Rhodes found us here? I hadn't heard anyone approaching, there wasn't a car around, and we were a good five miles from the school.

"You have what I'm looking for, don't you, Krissy?" Rhodes snarled, his hands fisting as he flexed and unflexed.

"Shut the hell up! You have something to say, you say it to me!" I growled. Krissy clung to my shoulders and back and I could feel her shaking. I didn't blame her, I was scared too. I remembered what Anusha looked like, and I knew whoever did that could—and would—probably do a lot worse to us.

"How sweet. Your boy here is defending you. Maybe it's he who has it. Is that what it is, Mr. McCallister?" He paused to look at me, eyeing me inquisitively, like he was reading my mind. "Yes, I think so."

"I don't know what you're talking about. We just came out here for some privacy. You know, just a little alone time." Krissy took my hint, snuggling closer to me. I wrapped my arm around her and kissed her temple, using the opportunity to whisper softly in her ear. "Reach in my back pocket."

Agent Rhodes smiled, holding his hands up in surrender. "I don't want to hurt you kids. I think you got yourself mixed up in a situation that is far beyond anything you could have imagined. So it's time to stop playing and let the grown-ups handle it. Now, where's the heir?" Agent Rhodes took several slow steps toward us as he spoke, causing Krissy and me to back up—straight into the warehouse. We were trapped.

"I really don't know what you're talking about. Please, you can take the car. Just leave us alone."

Behind me, Krissy had taken the knife out of my pocket and pulled the blade open. It wasn't much of a defense, but it was all we had.

"Here, take it." Her voice was shaking as much of the rest of her.

I shook my head once. "Keep it, just in case."

"I'm only going to ask one more time. And then you'll force me to do something I really don't want to do. Where. Is. The. Heir?"

"What the hell are you talking about? What heir? I can't give you something I know nothing about."

Agent Rhodes' nostrils flared, the veins in his forehead popping. "I'm tired of these games!" His fists pounded the hood of my car, crushing the hood like a tin can. "Give me the fuckin' heir!"

Rhodes charged at us, closing the distance with each angry step. I turned, pushing Krissy toward the highway. "Run, Krissy! Now!"

255

I never saw the first blow coming. Agent Rhodes picked me up and tossed me like a ragdoll onto the hard, cement parking lot. My body ached, but I didn't think anything was broken. I rolled onto my stomach, struggling to stand. Rhodes picked me up again, pulling me to his face. My eyes burned looking into his, like looking into the sun. I slammed them shut, but I could still feel my skin boiling—bubbling up as blisters formed where he held me.

"Your mistake was underestimating me, little boy. I gave you so many chances, and now—"

There was a loud "thwack," and suddenly Rhodes' grip loosened. I looked around and couldn't believe what I saw. Rhodes was on the ground, and Krissy held a large two-by four like it was a baseball bat. She raised it over her head and swung again with a grunt, striking Rhodes across the shoulders.

She dropped the piece of wood and helped me to my feet. "C'mon! We need to get out of here. God only knows how long he'll be out."

"Where's the knife?"

"Here, it's here." She pushed the closed blade into my hand. I grabbed it and pushed passed the pain, running without feeling, not stopping. Driving my car was no longer an option, and we didn't even slow down to try. We ran for a good mile without stopping, neither of us saying word. It was times like this when I craved city life. The ability to get lost in a crowd and blend in.

Krissy slowed, bending in half and placing her hands on her knees as she tried to catch her breath. "Wait, Tate. I just need a minute."

I rubbed her back. "Take slow, deep breaths in through your nose and out through your mouth. We only have a minute, that thing could be back any—SHIT!"

256

Rhodes came out of nowhere, grabbing a hold of Krissy by her arms. "You little bitch! You're gonna pay for that stunt."

Krissy screamed, kicking and struggling to free herself from his hold, but he never budged. I looked around for something— anything I could use as a weapon, but we were standing the middle of a street, surrounded by nothing but desert.

Until I remembered the knife.

I pulled it out and flicked the blade open with one flick of my wrist. Rhodes' arms were squeezing the life out of Krissy—I could see her turning blue from the strain and lack of oxygen. My only clean shot was to go for his back, maybe strike his kidney. That might be enough to get him to loosen his grip so she could get away—or at least breathe.

Rhodes' focus wasn't on me, and I used his distraction to approach him from behind. I gripped the blade and withdrew a breath. I knew I'd only get one, maybe two shots at the guy. I couldn't afford to miss or only knick him.

With one quick thrust, I jabbed the knife into the left side of his back, just below his ribcage. The knife sunk in to the hilt. I expected Rhodes to scream or grunt in pain. At the very least, I thought having a four-inch blade jammed into his side would make him loosen his grip, but he barely budged.

"Tsk, tsk, little boy. Did you really think your mortal weapon could stop me?" He slowly turned his head and glared at me. "As if I could ever be that weak."

One glance at Krissy, who was no longer conscious in his arms, and I backed up a few steps and charged at him like a linebacker, aiming my shoulder directly where the blade was positioned. Blinding, white-hot pain rain through my body as I struck, traveling down my arm and back. I knew the impact from the knife's hilt tore something, but I got back up. Rhodes had stumbled slightly, but not enough to lose control of Krissy. I readied myself for a second run at him when the sound of squealing tires turned both of our attentions.

The car never slowed, aiming directly for Rhodes. I dove out of the way as did Rhodes, who dropped Krissy. I scrambled to her side and dragged her to me, thankful for the car that now idled between us. "Krissy! Wake up, beautiful. Please wake up." I checked her neck for a pulse, thankful to find one though it was weak. I watched carefully for the rise and fall of her chest, but it never came, so I started mouth-to-mouth. I'd spent years imagining the moment my lips would finally taste hers, but never thought it would be to save her life. "Breathe. You gotta breathe for me."

After several arduous moments, she sucked in a deep breath, coughing.

"Oh, thank Jesus." I cradled her in my arms, only then remembering the mysterious car and Agent Rhodes. "Just breathe, and try to stay quiet. I'm going to check out what's going on."

Krissy only nodded, still coughing painfully. I stayed low, listening for sounds of movement. Besides some rustling, and a grunt every now and then, it was silent.

Eerily silent.

Creeping behind the rear bumper of the Dodge Charger, I peered around the edge. Even with all of the amazing things I'd seen and experienced over the last week, the sight still managed to shock me.

Agent Rhodes was bloody and beaten—but not from my knife or the car. Standing in front of him—and beating the crap out him—was a little girl in braided pigtails and a Dora the Explorer romper. She spun, landing a roundhouse kick to his face. Rhodes spat black, oozy liquid onto the ground, and then spoke in a language I'd never heard. The little girl replied in the same language, giggling like he told a joke.

I turned my attentions back on Krissy. She hadn't moved but to wrap her arms around herself and shiver—though I doubted she was cold. I pulled her back into my arms, keeping my voice low. "I know you're hurting, but we need to try to get out of here. The keys are still in the car; we may be able to escape. I don't see another way. There's some crazy badass little girl kicking the crap out of Rhodes, so it's now or never."

Krissy's eyes widened a bit. "You said a little girl? And he hasn't killed her yet?"

I scoffed. "I know, right? I tried everything I could think of and he wouldn't budge for me. This little kindergartener comes out of nowhere and suddenly she's like Jackie Chan crossed with Chuck Norris out there."

"Tate, Anusha was like that too, remember? Looked like a child but she wasn't. I bet that's who we're supposed to find!"

"Holy crap! You're right. I didn't even put the two together. So what then? Should we go see if she needs help or something? Though, from what I saw, she was holding her own and then some."

Krissy stood on shaky legs. "We should at least try."

Seeing Krissy attempt to breathe, and the pained look on her face she took with every breath, made up my mind. I scooped her up and carried her. "Right now, you're my priority. He squeezed the shit out of you, and it wouldn't surprise me if he cracked a rib or two. I'm not worrying about anyone else. You're more important to me than anyone or anything. Now I'm going to put you in that car and drive you to the hospital. No arguing!"

She laid her head on my shoulder in quiet capitulation. I stood up straight and peered over the hood of the car. The little girl was now straddling Rhodes, her whole body glowing bright orange. The longer she glowed, the brighter she shone, and the dimmer and more translucent Rhodes became. Mesmerized, I didn't move. I just stood watching in awe. The sight was both beautifully fascinating and frightening.

"My God," Krissy exclaimed. "He's fading away as if he never existed."

It took only seconds before Rhodes was gone. The little girl shuddered and closed her eyes, allowing the glow of her body to fade away as well. When her eyes opened again, she looked over at us and smiled. "You need not be afraid. I will not harm you."

The adult words and tone coming from the small child were off-putting, and I didn't know whether to believe her or not, but that wasn't important. "I need to get her to the hospital."

"Please," Krissy added.

The little girl stood, reaching her arms out to us. "Bring her to me."

"I don't think so. Just let us go, and we won't tell anyone about you or what we saw."

The little girl shook her head. "Please, let me help. It is what I do."

"Just let her try," Krissy whispered. "If she wanted to hurt us, there's nothing we could do to stop her. Besides, for some reason deep in my gut, I trust her. She reminds me of Anusha."

The little girl's eyes widened. "Anusha? You knew my sister?"

"Anusha was your sister?"

260

She smiled, wistful longing twinkling in her eyes. "Yes, my name is Abhaya. I was sent here to find her, but when I arrived, I knew I was too late. I could not feel her light."

Abhaya strode toward us and placed her hands on Krissy's midsection. When they began to glow brightly, Krissy sighed in relief.

"Are you okay?" I asked Krissy, concerned that somehow the light was making her injuries worse.

"That feels so much better. Thank you, Abhaya."

Abhaya bowed slightly. "It is my pleasure to help friends of my sister."

"I'm so sorry for your loss," Krissy said.

"Thank you. But please, tell me, did the heir survive? Is he safe?"

I shook my head. "I'm so sorry; I have no idea what you're talking about. Rhodes asked us the same thing."

"Anusha never gave you anything?" She tried again.

I eyed Krissy and she nodded. "Well, yes, but it wasn't a person."

Abhaya inhaled sharply. "Please, take me to it."

We piled in Abhaya's car, although it was incredibly weird to let a six-year-old behind the wheel. She even had a booster seat with pedal extensions so her feet could reach. When she saw me staring, she giggled. "I realize how this must look to you, but I promise I'm perfectly competent behind the wheel and am a very safe driver."

I let Krissy take the front seat, safely clicking her seatbelt into place as she lowered the seat to a reclining position. She might have been healed, but her body was exhausted. I kissed her forehead before buckling myself in, whispering the directions to Abhaya along the drive.

CHAPTER SIX

Krissy

"Hey, beautiful. Time to wake up. We're here." Tate's husky voice tickled my ears, causing me to emit a happy sigh. Yeah, I liked this dream. "She's out. Let me carry her," I heard him say before being scooped up in powerful arms. Realizing where I was, I know I probably could have opened my eyes and walked on my own, but this felt way too good to protest.

Tate sat me on the couch and I reluctantly opened my eyes, leaving my happy cocoon of denial. Abhaya sat in the club chair across from us.

"I'll be right back," Tate said, before turning to me. "You okay? Need anything?"

I shook my head. "No, I'm feeling much better, thank you."

Tate hurried into the other room, presumably to get the stone Anusha had given us. As I watched him walk away, I couldn't help but shake my head at how much had changed between us. I wasn't sure if it was just going through this together or if his feelings had genuinely changed toward me, but for the first time in years, I was happy. With Tate. Who woulda guessed it?

263

Abhaya smiled, swaying her Ked-clad feet since they couldn't reach the floor. "Your union is a strong one. I can see it in each of you—that tie connecting you is strong. You'll go far together."

Heat rose up my neck and into my cheeks. "Oh, um. We're not together. We're just friends."

Abhaya winked at me. "For now."

I didn't get to ask her what she meant before Tate came back in the room carrying a padded handgun sleeve. Abhaya scooted forward in her seat as he approached, looking like a kid on Christmas awaiting her presents.

"I'm sorry, but this is all Anusha gave us. It's just a stone. I don't know anything about an heir."

He held it out and Abhaya reached for the stone reverently. Tate sat next to me, wrapping his arm around me as I sunk into his side. Abhaya opened the bag and pulled the stone out. It began to glow in her hands and her eyes closed and she sighed happily. "I can't tell you what this means to me and my people." She held it to her lips and kissed it adoringly, then opened wider and swallowed it whole.

"Oh my God!" I scooted to the edge of my seat, disbelieving what I had just seen.

Tate was furious. "We went through all of that for you to have a snack?"

Abhaya ignored Tate's comment, her face lit up in pure ecstasy. When she opened her eyes, she stood rocking on her heals. "When the Suryti destroyed my planet, a few of us were lucky enough to escape, including some of the royal family. My sister and I were a part of the Royal guard, assigned to protect the King and Queen." She paused, sighing. "But we failed, and they died.

264

But not before passing us their heir and begging us to protect him and keep the hope for our race alive.

"We travelled for years, but never found a planet that could sustain us. Until we reached Earth. You have a beautiful planet, and we lived here peacefully for years, searching for others of our kind. But the Suryti found us, and found us once again."

"But why? Why do they keep trying to kill you?"

"It didn't start that way. The Suryti's planet began to self-combust. It's just the nature of their being: they are consumers. Of everything. And after a while, they consumed so much, they consumed everything they needed to survive. They were our closest neighbors, so they came to our planet and began to consume it—and us! A war ensued, and many lives were lost. But we are a gentle people, and were no match for the Suryti. They destroyed us easily.

"We thought they'd leave us alone once we got here, but their appetite for our light only grew. They craved it. We are able to stay hidden in places with much light—like your New Mexico here. But Zaket was a hunter, and he found us."

As Abhaya answered, an amazing thing happened. She began to grow—both up and out. It was like watching a time-lapsed home movie of someone through the years. But it wasn't only that. With each word she spoke, her abdomen grew.

And grew.

And grew.

By the time she finished, a young, very pregnant woman stood before us. My jaw dropped to the floor and Abhaya grinned shyly, rubbing her swollen belly.

"Thank you for keeping the heir safe. His Highness will be here soon, and we will have a leader once again."

"As a baby."

Abhaya chuckled. "Yes and no. Our race can save and transfer memories, and those of his parents have been stored away. He'll be a sage ruler, I assure you that. I cannot thank you enough."

I glanced at Tate, who, like me, was at a loss for words. "Um, what will you do now?"

"Zaket did not work alone. Others will follow, so it is time for me to move on until we can find a way back to our true home so the heir can rule. Perhaps Florida." She pushed her now full body up and out of the chair. "I hear it is known as 'The Sunshine State.'"

Abhaya made her way to the front door, Tate and I in tow. Just an hour ago she looked to be barely in elementary school, and now she looked older than us—and she was pregnant! If I hadn't seen it with my own eyes, I never would have believed it.

We hugged Abhaya goodbye, wishing her luck on her journey. I knew it would probably be the last time we ever saw her again.

"I wish you much happiness, my friends, and much light. But, judging from the light that emanates around you two, I don't think you'll need any luck." She winked, before waddling down the stairs and down the street.

"What do you think she meant by that?" Tate asked me.

I shrugged. "No idea. She said something very similar before as well. I think she meant..." I bit my lip to keep the embarrassing words from escaping. Tate might have befriended me, but that didn't mean he wanted anything more.

"She meant what, Kris?" He stepped closer, until his warm, soft lips were mere inches away from my own.

I gulped, and pulled up my big girl panties. I couldn't look back and regret staying silent in this moment. "I think she meant we should be together—romantically."

Tate moved even closer as my eyes slid shut. "That's the best idea I've ever heard."

His lips closed in on mine, causing me to moan. I wrapped my hands around him, gripping his hair to bring him closer still. His kiss started soft, exploring and tasting, before turning heated and passionate. I couldn't get enough of him—his smell, his taste, his touch.

He pulled my bottom lip into his mouth, biting down gently. The bite of pain sent a wave of pleasure straight through me. My tongue swept into his mouth, tangling with his own. We stayed lost in the pleasure of each other, not even caring that I was growing lightheaded from not pausing to take a breath.

Tate's lips left mine, traveling down my cheek and along my jaw. "God, Krissy, I've wanted to kiss you for so long."

"You have?" I breathed, barely able to concentrate on his words as he nibbled his way to my ear, sucking on the lobe. I wanted those lips everywhere, and never wanted this to end.

"For as long as I can remember. It's always been you, Krissy. Always. I just always managed to screw it up, and never knew how to make it right."

I pulled back, needing the distance to focus. Though, staring into his lust-filled eyes only made me want to resume kissing. "I thought you hated me? You did so many mean things..."

Tate placed his hands on either side of my face so I looked him in the eye. "I could never hate you. I'm just an idiot. I was a stupid punk kid who never knew how to make you see how much I loved you. The hair pulling? I just wanted your attention—your

267

eyes on me. The drawing? I drew it so I could always see your beautiful face. It was that asshole Joey Fishborne who drew nasty things on top of it. He stole it out of my backpack and passed it around. And Prissy Krissy? Joey was going around telling everyone you were a lesbian because you wouldn't put out. I told him you had better taste than to be with a jerk like him, so he said if you weren't a lesbian, you must be a priss. He started the nickname. I kicked the crap out of him after gym class for that, but by then the damage was done. The whole school had heard it and it stuck. I'm so sorry, Krissy. I never wanted to hurt you. Never."

I blinked, replaying every incident from my childhood with Tate in my head, but my mind kept focusing on one thing. "Love? You loved me?"

"No, Krissy. I love you. As in, present tense. I always have."

I didn't need any more words, any more apologies. I went to him, kissing him feverishly. My hands roamed over his broad shoulders and strong, defined arms. He picked me up, and I wrapped my legs around his waist. He led us into the house and onto the couch, setting me down like I was delicate china.

"Are you sure I'm not dreaming? Aliens? Being chased and almost dying? And now this? You? Here with me? I must be dreaming."

Tate wrapped a strand of my hair around his fingers, pulling gently like he used to as a kid. "No, Krissy, this is just a dream come true. A long, overdue dream come true. We've heard the rumors about aliens our entire lives living so close to Roswell, and I never believed it. I always thought it was a pain in the ass with all the damn tourists and crazy lunatics who came here for them. But I swear, I've never been so happy to have found evidence that other life forms exist, because they brought me closer to you. And my life? It's complete now that you're here."

"I couldn't agree more."

From that moment on, every time I saw a falling star in the sky, I'd think of Anusha and Abhaya. And thank them. Tate and I may have saved their future, but they saved ours in return. And I couldn't be happier.

The Ascendant

By Raine Thomas

For information on other titles
Visit the author's website:
http://rainethomas.com

The Ascendant

Jason Ringsted was a colossal butt-munch.

That thought pounded through Kyra's head in time with the blades whipping across her windshield. Her knuckles whitened as she gripped the steering wheel and struggled to focus on the road. It was a toss-up whether her inability to see clearly was due to the monsoon currently drenching the township or the hot tears pouring from her eyes.

She should have known. Hadn't she wondered why a hot university freshman had invited her—a nobody seventeen-year-old—to a party? Hadn't she asked herself why Jason would suddenly show interest in her? In the three years they'd lived down the street from each other, they'd barely exchanged ten words between them.

Yes, she had asked herself those things. But in the end, she'd decided that it was possible that he was just shy. Maybe he'd secretly wanted to ask her out for a long time, but hadn't known how to approach her.

So she'd agreed to attend the party with him. She'd begged and pleaded with her parents to let her go, agreeing to an early curfew in a form of compromise. She'd spent far too much of the money she earned at the local diner to buy an outfit that she thought made her look more sophisticated. And she'd taken extra time to get ready, really wanting to impress Jason.

She offered to meet him at the party, not wanting him to have to leave after just two hours due to her early curfew. Her nerves nearly got the better of her when she parked at the large home where Jason told her to meet him. Boisterous people spilled out the open front door, mingling on the wide porch and vast lawn with drinks in hand.

Who was she kidding, thinking she could do this?

Jason knocked on her window before she could drive back home. His smile gave her a boost and she finally dared to step out and join him.

He introduced her to a number of his friends and their dates. She had expected the university girls to be more standoffish and, well, spectacular. Although she met some girls like that, most of them were nice and friendly. Jason's friends also went on and on about how perfect she was for him, calling her a real prize. For the first time, she felt like she was holding her own in a social situation.

About an hour after she arrived, she visited the bathroom. The door was so thin that she could hear everything happening just outside of it. It was awkward, but it turned out that it was how she found out why Jason invited her.

"They do it every year," a female voice said. "They call it Dog Days."

"I don't get it," another female said. "Why would they deliberately choose to go out in public with such ugly girls?"

Kyra's face paled as their words registered. She considered the many plain girls she'd met that evening. Heat rose in her cheeks as she dried her hands and stared at her own unremarkable reflection in the vanity mirror.

"It's a contest among the freshmen. They all contribute. The guy voted as having the biggest dog of a date wins the whole pot."

It had taken Kyra a couple of minutes to compose herself enough to leave the bathroom. She avoided the gazes of the girls standing outside the door when she walked past, but she heard their snickers.

She got soaked running to her vehicle, but she was beyond caring whether her new outfit got ruined. She'd probably burn it now, anyway.

Once she tore out of the parking area, the vehicle moved on autopilot. She had no idea where she was going, but she had to get away from Jason and the awful party. She wasn't ready to return home and face her mortification by telling her parents what had happened.

It took about ten minutes for the numbness of shock to ease and the tears to come. The extent of her humiliation had her wanting to leave town and never return. How could anyone be so mean to another person? Sure, she'd experienced her share of being picked on as a kid, but this went far beyond that. This was a boy telling her that he thought she was the worst possible date he could get.

Is he right? she wondered.

Pain lanced through her as she questioned her self-worth. She knew better than that. The true "dog" in this situation was him, not her.

That was easier to think than to believe.

After a while, she tried to stop crying long enough to concentrate on her driving and figure out where she was. It was dark…much darker than usual for this time of night, even with the storm clouds filling the sky. She registered that there weren't any lights or other vehicles driving down this particular stretch of road. Where in the world was she?

As she strained to read a passing road sign, the vehicle skidded over a deep puddle. Water shot up and over the hood, completely coating the windshield and obscuring her view. Adrenaline shot through her, making her skin prickle. Her foot eased off the accelerator and her grip tightened on the wheel. The last thing she wanted to do was hydroplane.

The rain began falling even faster, battering her windshield in heavy sheets. This was crazy. She would drive to the next intersection and turn around.

She wiped her cheeks with the back of her hand and swallowed a sob. When she glanced at her reflection in the rearview mirror, her foot inadvertently pressed against the accelerator. God, she looked awful.

A dark figure darted into the road. She barely saw it in the flash of her headlights. It moved fast, but stood tall on two legs. Impossibly tall.

She was too terrified to even scream. Her foot slammed on the brake. She jerked the wheel to avoid hitting the shadowy figure. The vehicle hit another patch of water and started to spin. When she saw a thick wooden pole racing towards her, her paralyzed vocal cords finally eased enough to free her scream. She braced herself for the impact and prayed the vehicle's safety features kept her alive.

Something large and solid leapt in front of the wooden pole. Her door impacted it. The vehicle propelled away from whatever she'd hit. The action hurtled her forward and to the side, causing

274

her forehead to strike the steering wheel. After another brief second of spinning, the vehicle came to a shuddering stop in the middle of the road.

Kyra stared straight ahead, oblivious to the blood trickling down her face from her hairline. Her choppy breathing filled the vehicle. The engine had cut off, but the headlights still shone and the wipers continued to slash across the windshield.

So she saw the incredibly tall, lithe shadow approaching, and she saw that it wasn't alone.

This can't be happening, she thought, even as she tried to turn the key in the ignition.

Nothing happened. Whatever had been done to stop her vehicle had totally killed the engine. She was a sitting duck.

She fumbled for the latch to her safety harness. Although the dark figures moved cautiously, her intuition screamed that they sought to harm her. Her eyes didn't move from them. They reflected no light even in the beams shooting from the front of her vehicle. They wore some kind of camouflaging clothing that allowed them to blend seamlessly with the night. She'd never seen anything like it.

Just as her safety harness released, her door opened. Another scream lodged in her throat as she was yanked from the vehicle. She was tossed backwards like a bag of refuse, landing in a muddy puddle with an impressive splash.

"Stay," growled the large male who had thrown her.

Fear and insult made her want to snap out an argument, but she realized he was now surrounded by the dark figures. Although he stood about six feet, four inches tall, his opponents towered over him. He was dressed much like the guys at the party had been, wearing a short-sleeved shirt, black pants, and boots. He was also apparently unarmed. Despite that—and the fact that he was seriously outnumbered—it was the shadowy creatures who hesitated.

"You know the routine," he said over the rain, his back to her. His deep voice was accented and familiar, but she couldn't place it. "If you want her, you have to get through me."

The figures paused. Their heads twisted as they looked at each other, as though they were communicating without words. Kyra watched in frozen silence as the rain pelted her. Her heart thudded heavily enough that she felt it in her throat. She tried to rationalize what she was seeing.

Who or what were these creatures? Who was this warrior-like male with the dark hair and such calm assurance? What did any of them want with her?

Run, you idiot! she thought. But she couldn't move.

Instead, she watched as the shadowy figures moved as one, surging towards the male. Long, dark weapons suddenly appeared in the hands of the attackers. Kyra couldn't imagine where the sword-like objects had come from, as she hadn't seen any type of sheaths or harnesses around their waists.

I'm dreaming, she realized. *This is just a nightmare. I'll wake up any moment.*

But the rain felt cool and wet as it struck her skin. The sharp grit beneath her hands bit into the tender skin of her palms. The bright light of the weapon produced by the dark-haired male hurt her eyes.

She knew she wasn't dreaming.

The tendons in her neck stretched taut as she watched the male fend off his attackers. She counted seven as he met each strike with either his sword-like weapon or his fists. A couple of them were brought down by his powerful legs. He used whatever means necessary to defeat his enemies, who were much more slender and clearly less trained than he was.

When the last one fell, the male let out a vicious curse. Her eyebrows shot up. Though she didn't know how, she sensed that she was in danger.

Strong arms seized her from behind and dragged her from the ground even as the male turned in her direction. For the first time, she saw his eyes. They were the purest silver she'd ever seen, gleaming almost white in the light from her vehicle. Although he was focused on the enemy, the look in those eyes made the hairs on the back of her neck rise.

"Release her if you want to live," the male said.

It sounded like a cheesy line, but Kyra sensed the power behind the words. She guessed her attacker did, too. Its grip tightened around her ribcage, making her cry out. The male's eyes flickered briefly to her, then once again focused on her assailant.

She tried to grasp the arms around her in order to escape, but the material of whatever clothing the creature wore wouldn't allow her to get a handhold. Undeterred, she kicked backwards as hard as she could. Her heels met with solid matter, but she hurt herself more than her attacker. Pain shot up her calves.

The hold around her ribcage cinched tighter. Her breath left her in a quick whoosh, as though the creature was stealing it.

The male's silver eyes flashed like diamonds catching sunlight. The creature flinched, then froze. The male charged with his weapon poised to strike. Kyra screamed, certain she was about to die.

The next thing she knew, she was on the ground, covered in filth and dark, chalky residue that blended with the rain. She stayed

277

on all fours, trying to figure out what had just happened. One
moment, she was in the shadow-figure's grasp, and the next it just
dissolved into nothing. Did that mean she was covered in the
thing's remains?

"Rise," the male said as he stopped near her.

Her arms trembled. Though she didn't want to, she dared to
look up at him. "What—what was—who—?"

She couldn't form a coherent thought, never mind ask a
question. She wondered if she really had wrecked her vehicle and
was hallucinating. Her head hurt enough to justify the idea.

"Another contingent will be right behind this one," he said.

He reached down and encircled her waist with his large hands,
lifting her so she stood in front of him. She had to crook her neck
to look into his eyes, then wished she hadn't. His steely expression
produced a whimper in the back of her throat.

Pushing away from him, she ran towards her vehicle. Her bag
was there. She needed to get away. She needed to get in touch with
her parents.

A squeak escaped her as she was swept off her feet. She found
herself pressed against the male's chest as he scooped her up into
his arms. Even as she opened her mouth to shout at him, his eyes
flashed again. Her entire body relaxed. Every worry and concern
fled her mind. She sagged against him, forgetting about her fear
and pain and letting him carry her away from the street that
remained empty aside from her abandoned vehicle.

He smelled wonderful, she thought through the haze coating
her brain. She sensed something familiar about his scent, but didn't
know what it was. Heat radiated from beneath his drenched
clothes, soothing her. Although she had no reason to feel any safer

with this stranger than she had while facing the shadowy figures, she did.

She wasn't sure how long they moved through the rain and darkness, but when she next began to feel more like herself, she realized they were inside some kind of storage facility. They stood among rows of high shelving filled with crates and containers. Dust tickled her nose, telling her it wasn't accessed often. Thin slivers of light filtered through the shelves to their right, coming from an unseen source. She heard machinery in the distance and guessed that another part of the facility was currently in use.

The male set her on her feet. His eyes flashed again. Her fear resurfaced. When she tried to wriggle out of his grip, he tightened his hold.

"Who are you?" she asked. Her voice shook. Her knees felt just as unsteady.

He sighed. "We always go through this, Kyr. I fear we don't have enough time for the long version right now."

She frowned. How did he know her name? Why was he leaving off the "a," almost like a nickname? What did he mean by *always go through this*?

"You're just going to have to trust me for a moment," he said.

Before she could argue, he reached behind her head, cupped her neck, and bent down to kiss her. A gasp caught in her throat, but never escaped. The moment their lips touched, the sense of familiarity that she'd experienced a couple of times since he appeared blossomed into a memory. The memory of his kiss.

She closed her eyes and sank into his embrace, not having realized how much she craved it. A latent part of her mind sprang to life, reminding her of the intense attraction she shared with him. She savored the taste of him, the way his tongue felt when it

279

touched hers, the way he made her feel as he caressed her. The kiss could have gone on forever and she still would have wanted more.

When they finally parted, she stared up at him, blinking as memories shifted in her mind.

"TaeDane," she breathed.

She remembered that she called him Ty. She also remembered that the markings on his forearms glowed with ethereal light whenever they kissed, though she couldn't remember why.

The corners of his eyes wrinkled with humor. "That was definitely easier—and more enjoyable—than the way we've been going about resurfacing your memories between lessons."

She frowned. Although she remembered his name and the flavor of his kiss, and although she felt she could trust him, other important details remained cloudy. How could that be? Was he using some kind of hypnosis?

"Not hypnosis exactly," he responded. Her eyes widened. "But I am capable of reading thoughts and controlling minds."

Another word flashed though her head: *Mynder*.

He nodded. "That's correct. I am your Mynder…the *Dem-shyr.* We were born on the same day, at the same time, under the same star. The connection was inevitable."

His words made no sense. Under the same star? What did that have to do with anything?

"Fortunately for both of us, we grew to like each other," he said, running his finger along the side of her face, then tracing her bottom lip with his thumb. A shiver coursed through her. She couldn't look away from his compelling gaze. "Not that you made it easy for me. You are as stubborn as they come. It's a good thing I couldn't resist your beauty."

Embarrassment pinkened her cheeks. She looked away from him, turning her gaze downward. "I'm not beautiful," she murmured.

His strong hand lifted her chin so she had no choice but to look at him again. After a moment of studying her, one of his dark brows lifted.

"Interesting. I didn't think it was possible."

She blinked. "Didn't think what was possible?"

"For you to learn humility." He tilted his head and continued to stare at her. She once again lowered her gaze. Her face felt like it was on fire. "Your appearance is as it needs to be in order for you to learn your lesson here. Still, I never thought you'd master this one. It seems I was wrong."

Something jiggled in the back of her mind. It helped ease her embarrassment over having all of his attention on her.

"I'll bet that hurt you to admit," she said.

"We'll just say you should never expect to hear it again."

For some reason, despite her lingering fear, his response made her want to laugh. She shook her head over the reaction. There were obviously bigger things to address than his male pride.

"What did you mean by 'we always go through this?'" she asked. "And by 'between lessons?' And most importantly, what were those things that tried to hurt us?"

His brow furrowed. His gaze moved up and down the aisle, probably assessing any potential danger or eavesdroppers before he replied. She found herself looking at the wicked shape of his mouth and couldn't help but hope he'd kiss her again to stimulate her memories in answer to her questions.

When he looked back at her, he grinned. It transformed his face from handsome to sinfully sexy. Her heart galloped in her chest.

"As much as I enjoy kissing you, KyrVawn, there is danger involved in resurfacing too many memories right now."

She wanted to sink into the floor. How could she have forgotten that he could read her mind? How was she supposed to control her thoughts when he looked as magnificent as he did? What did it say about her that her attraction to him took precedence in her mind over the questions she had just asked?

"Wait a minute," she said, interrupting her thoughts before they got her into even more trouble. "My name is Kyra Vaughn. That's not what you said, though, is it?"

"Whenever you venture abroad, that's the name you take. It's a more commonly used linguistic format across the universe. But on our world, you are KyrVawn. You are the only daughter of the Guardians, ShayaVawn and BrunyrVawn. You are the Ascendant."

Her knees failed her. He reached out and helped ease her to the ground, sitting beside her. They leaned against one of the crates sitting on the shelves.

Had he said, *on our world*? Was he implying that she wasn't from this planet?

He was out of his mind.

"I have parents," she said, struggling to produce the words. "I've lived here my entire life."

"The beings living with you are Alametrians, friends of your true parents. They traveled with you from our world, and have lived with you as your parents on a number of worlds before this one. The memories you have of your life here were implanted to give you the foundation you needed to learn your lesson while on this planet."

She wanted to shake her head in denial, but he was doing something with his abilities to suppress her raging doubt. While she wanted that to anger her, she couldn't find that emotion within her, either. She sensed that this was a conversation he'd had with her before and he knew just how to control it.

"Our people are considered the most advanced, highly-evolved beings in the galaxy," Ty continued, taking hold of her hand and linking his fingers with hers. He ran his thumb over her wrist, making her pulse race. The markings on the insides of his forearms glowed again, drawing her attention. "The primary way we maintain this status is by traveling to other worlds and living among them, absorbing experience as we do. By learning to live as other beings do, we expand our minds and more fully appreciate their viewpoints on critical matters, such as intergalactic politics and manners of conduct."

It was like she had fallen into an alternate dimension. Hell, maybe she had. That made as much sense as this conversation.

"But how can we possibly blend in among beings from other planets?" she asked. Her head throbbed, making her reach up to touch the tender spot that had connected with her steering wheel. "Don't we look different than they do?"

"We resemble most beings across the galaxy. Planets that can support sentient life all contain similar molecular compositions. Thus, the life that springs from those planets is quite similar in appearance. There are, however, some planets that evolve…differently."

She shuddered. "Those creatures that tried to hurt us?"

"Yes, among others. They are the Shelvak. Their planet is the closest to Alametria."

His words made no sense, yet struck a chord within her. How could she believe any of this? Was he stimulating a suppressed memory? Was he using his abilities to implant the suggestion that she believe him? Or was she just losing her mind altogether?

After a moment, she shook her head at herself and asked, "Why did they attack us?"

"They are trying to capture you."

Her mouth dropped open. "Me? Why?"

"I told you...you're the Ascendant."

Goosebumps sprang up on her arms. She reached up to rub away the sudden chill. Although she didn't understand the title he kept giving her, she was intuitive enough to reason that it carried some significance. How had she gone from a night of humiliation at the hands of Jason Ringsted to sitting on a dirty floor listening to a hot guy telling her that her life was a sham and aliens from another planet wanted to capture her?

"I don't normally share this much with you between transitions," he said. His deep voice was softer now, prompting her to look at him. "The risk to your mental status is too great. But the Shelvak found you more quickly this time. Their reach has extended beyond its typical boundaries within the galaxy."

She just stared at him. How was she supposed to respond to something like that? Ten minutes ago, she didn't think there was any such thing as life on other planets.

"We have to get you to the correct coordinates so that we can transition you to another planet outside of this galaxy."

Her eyebrows shot up. "What? Why?"

"You still have key lessons to learn before you return to Alametria. Obviously, you can no longer do that among the worlds we—and the Shelvak—know so well."

"Why can't I learn these lessons on Alametria?" she asked.

She considered the question just after she issued it. Was she really buying all of this?

In light of the evidence she'd witnessed that night, how could she not?

Ty watched her, probably reading her thoughts. Whatever he divined seemed to meet with his approval. "Your education would not be well-rounded enough if limited only to our world." When she started to reply with another question, he got to his feet. "We don't have time for detailed explanations. I must focus on getting you out of here. I told you about the Shelvak to heighten your awareness of them from now on. Your memories of this evening will always be within your subconscious. I may be your Mynder, but I have to keep my distance during your lessons and can't always be there when you need me."

She supposed that explained why he seemed so familiar to her when she first heard him speak. She had obviously experienced scenarios like this with him in the past, then had the memories suppressed.

She started to ask exactly what a Mynder was, but he reached down and lifted her to her feet before she could. For some reason, the fact that he could so easily haul her around made her want to kick him.

"We must go," he said. "The Shelvaks managed to place a transmitter on your vehicle. I don't know whether they managed to get one on your person."

Her irritation fled. She fought the urge to strip down and abandon her clothes. Then an even worse thought occurred to her: what if they had gotten something under her skin?

"You must trust me, Kyr."

She caught his gaze and swallowed her rising panic. A deep, buried part of her believed everything he'd said. That was more distressing than the alternative. Still, her life was apparently in his hands.

"I do trust you, Ty."

He nodded. "Stay right behind me. The pickup location isn't far."

A snort escaped her. Stay right behind him? He'd have to use a crowbar to pry her from his backside when they finally reached safety.

When he moved, she moved. There were only a few inches between them as they eased along the rows of shelving and got closer to the more populated area she'd sensed earlier. Every shadow between the containers looked sinister to her. She tried to keep her gaze on the wide expanse of Ty's shoulders, but fear had her eyes darting in every direction.

Her mind raced. She still had so many unanswered questions. Exactly what did it mean to be the Ascendant? Why did the Shelvaks want to capture her? Would she ever get her real memories back?

Just how deeply did her relationship with her Mynder run?

"Try to focus," Ty grumbled. "You're distracting me."

She bit her lip and issued a mental apology. Then she did her best to clear her mind. That was easier said than done. The only way she could distract herself from her pressing questions was to focus on Ty...on how stealthily and gracefully he moved for such

286

a large guy, how strong he was and how secure he made her feel, how good he looked in his tight—

He stopped and turned to look at her. She clapped her hand over her mouth even though she hadn't said anything. His eyes rolled towards the ceiling, the silver irises gleaming as a beam of light struck them. She thought she should be embarrassed, but she found herself on the verge of hysterical laughter.

That urge died when she spotted the shadow moving behind him.

In the next instant, she was flying backwards. She landed with a bone-jarring smack on the hard ground. Pain shot through her wrists as she instinctively used her arms to break her fall. Her already thudding headache blasted through her skull with renewed vigor.

A shout of pain filled the cavernous space. She realized Ty had been wounded.

Another layer of her mental suppression eased. A memory flashed through her. Ty, years younger in appearance, knelt in a lavishly decorated room filled with people. Two of those people, an adult male and female, stood over him. Kyra watched the proceedings from a few feet away, flanked by a number of large males bearing weapons. She was used to this, having been under guard since she was born.

"TaeDane," the adult female said in a commanding voice, "according to the stars, you are fated to serve as the Mynder of the Ascendant. There is no greater honor or graver responsibility among our kind. Do you accept your fate?"

Ty's gaze moved to Kyra, then back to the male and female. "I do," he said.

The couple nodded. They each took one of Ty's hands and closed their eyes. Everyone watched in silent expectation.

Searing light slowly slid across Ty's inner forearms, creating intricate patterns. Low sounds filled the room as the spectators commented on the event. Kyra watched it all without any reaction. She knew the process of the branding was a painful one, but it wasn't as though the pain was hers. She could, however, admit to being impressed by the boy's silence throughout the ordeal. At least her Mynder wasn't a weakling.

After a long while, the light faded. The marks remained, lining Ty's tan skin with delicate white scars.

The female once again spoke, her deep purple gaze intent on Ty's. "Henceforth, *Dem-shyr* TaeDane, these markings will gift you with abilities beyond those of other Alametrians. These new abilities will grow along with you over time."

Without a flicker of expression entering his blue eyes, the male added, "*Dem-shyr* TaeDane, you have spent your formative years learning the feelings and thought processes of beings from other civilizations. It was necessary for you to complete these lessons prior to assuming your new role so that your focus will be on the Ascendant's protection during her education. You will apply those lessons henceforth."

"You will now always know how to find the Ascendant," the female said, "no matter her location. You will now always know her thoughts and feelings. Should any being ever intend her harm, you will now sense it. Your strength is henceforth enhanced beyond the ordinary."

Kyra's gaze shifted to the adult male. His expression remained placid when he next addressed Ty. "Should you ever overstep your role, *Dem-shyr*, these markings will remind you of your place."

288

The memory took less than a second to surge through Kyra's mind. Focusing on the present, she shook her head to clear it and thought of the instances in the past hour when she had seen Ty's markings glow. For the first time, she realized that kissing her and touching her in any kind of way other than for her protection caused him pain.

But he'd done it anyway.

She didn't have time to process what that meant. Right now, thanks to her inability to control her thoughts, he'd been injured. He could be killed.

She hurried to her feet. After all he had done for her, there was no way she could let that happen.

At the end of the aisle, Ty regained his feet to face four Shelvaks. A long gash ran down his right upper arm. Blood dripped from the injury to the floor. The sight of it made Kyra lightheaded. The pulse in her throat vibrated so hard that she could barely breathe.

Just what did she think she could do against these creatures? She was just a shy, unpopular girl who was probably still being laughed at by Jason and his friends.

You are the Ascendant.

The thought ran through her mind directly behind her doubts. Nodding to herself and taking a deep breath, she glanced around for something to use as a weapon. Just feet away, Ty produced the sword of light that he'd used earlier. He met the strike of one of his attackers while at the same time ducking the blow from another.

Hurrying to the closest shelf, she tried to open a crate to look for something to use as a weapon. It was nailed shut. So were the crates surrounding it. Cursing, she whirled to the other side of the aisle, where a number of metal containers were stacked.

289

Four more Shelvaks stood in her way.

They always travel in formations of eight.

Where had that thought come from? She didn't have time to ponder it. Instead, she stumbled backwards a few steps until she hit the crates. Her eyes flew wide as she fought the urge to scream. Without a weapon or any skill to use one, she'd be nuts to try and defeat these things. Turning to the right, she ran.

Her heart pounded in her ears. All she heard was her own harsh breathing and the slapping of her shoes against the floor. Ahead of her, the aisle was cloaked in darkness. Primal terror almost overtook her as she thought about being alone in the inky dark with these creatures. What if more of them were waiting for her?

A chill whispered across the back of her neck. Although the Shelvaks moved in silence, she sensed that they had reached her. A whimper escaped her.

Out of the corner of her eye, she saw a long, curved tool lying on the bottom of a shelf. Diving to the ground, she grabbed the heavy crowbar and rolled with it in her hands. Instinct had her swinging like a ballplayer on stimulants.

The tool nearly flew from her hands when she hit a solid mass. She managed to catch one of them in the side of the head. It ended up sprawled a few feet away and didn't move.

Tightening her grip, she swung again. The pronged tip caught on the fabric of a Shelvak's suit. It ripped as she pulled back, baring an unnaturally pale chest. She stopped her backwards momentum and jerked the crowbar forward again, this time hitting the Shelvak's bare flesh. It screeched loud enough to make her head feel like it was splitting in two.

A cold hand grabbed her ankle and yanked her. She skidded across the floor as though she'd been launched from a catapult. She smashed into a container and dropped the crowbar. Agony radiated through her head and arm. Her gaze went in and out of focus, but she saw the shadows of the Shelvaks as they approached.

Before they reached her, Ty landed beside her. His weapon swung in a wide arc, blazing a trail of light across the aisle. Kyra's eyes watered from its intensity. She closed them against it.

The next time she opened them, she was lying on the ground outside. The rain had stopped, but the grass beneath her was still wet. Ty knelt over her. She guessed they had escaped the storage facility, as there wasn't a Shelvak in sight. Unfortunately, she hadn't escaped unscathed. Blazing pain made her want to throw up.

"Your shoulder is dislocated," Ty said, meeting her gaze. "I had hoped to correct it before you awoke, but I had to get you away from that place first."

Tears filled her eyes. She'd never had more than a scraped knee in her life. This was what she got for trying to protect herself.

"Why did you do that?" he asked, reaching out and brushing her damp hair from her forehead. "You've never tried to fight them before."

"I don't know," she said, swallowing hard to keep from vomiting all over him. "I just felt like I should do something to protect myself."

"But that's my job."

"Well, your job sucks." Her eyes moved to his right arm. She realized that although there was blood on his bicep, the cut had all but disappeared.

"I heal quickly. Another perk of my job. Next time, leave the fighting to me."

She started to argue. He covered her mouth with one hand and shoved her shoulder back into place with the other. Her body arched as she screamed. The sound was muffled, but came from the deepest part of her.

"I'm so sorry, Kyr," he said in a hoarse voice. "There was no avoiding that."

Pride had her nodding and battling back her tears instead of sobbing like an infant. When he sat beside her and gathered her close, she didn't fight him. In truth, she welcomed it. She pressed her face against his hard chest, breathed in his scent, and felt her fear subside. His heart raced beneath her ear. She wondered if it was residual adrenaline from their close call or a result of their mutual attraction to one another.

"My heart beats for you," he murmured against the top of her head.

She leaned back to catch his gaze, wondering what he meant. That was when she noticed that his forearms were glowing. Gasping, she shoved away from him. Once they were separated, the glow subsided.

He frowned. "What's wrong?"

"Touching me like that...it hurts you."

"You've remembered more than I anticipated." He kept his gaze steady on hers. "You've never been concerned about it before."

Now it was her turn to frown. "I wouldn't ever want to cause someone pain. Am I really that selfish?"

A corner of his mouth lifted. "Not anymore, it would seem. One more lesson learned." He moved closer to her and dragged her back against him. "Kyr, you hurt me more by pulling away than you ever could by allowing me to touch you."

292

When he leaned down to kiss her, she met him halfway. Her lips parted, inviting him to deepen the kiss. He seemed more than eager to do so. His tongue danced with hers as his hands began to roam. Pleasure streaked through her. A moan escaped. The confident way he touched her told her they had done this many times before. That didn't make it any less exciting. She allowed herself to explore the hard contours of his body as he lowered them both so that she was on the grass and he was pressed against her.

This was absolutely insane. All of it. Maybe Jason had slipped something into her drink. That was a much easier explanation to believe than that she was something called the Ascendant from the planet Alametria, and that her Mynder bodyguard found her irresistible enough that he was willing to suffer just to kiss her.

He dragged himself away from her mouth, leaning over her as he caught his breath. Although she realized that his forearms glowed bright enough to hurt her eyes, she longed for him to kiss her again.

"I'd enjoy nothing more," he said. "But our time together has once again come to an end. They're ready to transition you."

Alarm made her eyes go wide. "What? Right now?"

He nodded and got to his feet, reaching down to help her up. "I've brought you to the established coordinates. We've just been summoned."

"Summoned?" She looked around, then up to the sky. "How?"

"Telepathically. As the *Dem-shyr*, I can be contacted by anyone involved in your care."

"Oh." She thought about that for a moment. "Do they also know your thoughts?"

"No." He smiled briefly. "Another one of the perks of being the *Dem-shyr*."

293

Once again, she looked up at the sky. "How does it work?"

"It doesn't matter. I'll be suppressing your awareness before anything happens."

That made her anxiety surge. "Suppress? You mean...I won't remember any of this?"

He looked away. "No."

"But—"

"Please don't do this again, Kyr. It gets harder every time."

Her lips clamped together. In her mind, there hadn't been any other times. Still, she could see that he wasn't happy. She didn't see any reason to press the issue.

Finally, she took his hand. "You'll be with me?"

"Always."

Swallowing hard, she nodded. "Okay. I trust you, Ty. I don't want to make this any harder on you than it has to be. Do whatever you have to do."

He stood for a moment and held her gaze. She sensed there was much he was trying to communicate to her without words, but she couldn't interpret it. It made her feel as though she was somehow falling short. When she heard his disappointed sigh, the feeling of failure intensified.

Before she could speak, he leaned down and brushed his lips against hers. She thought he was kissing her goodbye. Then she felt her senses dimming. He held her tight, not letting her fall when her limbs grew numb.

Where are we going? she managed to ask him through thought.

"We're going to a planet called Earth," he replied, leaning down to kiss her once more. As her eyes closed and her thoughts faded, he added, "And it is there that I hope you'll learn to love."

End

Made in the USA
Lexington, KY
01 May 2014